HELL HAS NO FURY
BY
JOHN LENNON COHEN

Foreword

Have you ever been in love or in a romantic relationship or getting engaged to be married or have you gone through all the natural process and are now married for better, for worse? Well no matter at what point you are in a relationship, the beginning, the middle, or the end, this is a must read for you.

Dave and Cath Kelly are just ordinary people that experienced every emotional sentiment that comes in a relationship between two people and for twenty years they hack-sawed every one of them off and their story is told in this titilating novel 'Hell Has No Fury'

In this epic tale of love and hate, a kind of story not unlike the movie 'The War of the Roses' with Michael Douglas and Kathleen Turner, with Dave taking the place of Oliver Rose while Cath takes the place of his partner Barbara and from beginning to end it is fraught with laughter but also with danger. This novel can be used as a relationship guide especially of what not to do as Dave and Cath do to each other for they engaged in acts of horror wounding each other with a psychological knife of a thousand cuts that always results in a slow but sure death for both parties.
The female readers will gain knowledge of how men think while the male reader will gain knowledge of how not to manage their relationships.

This novel 'Hell Has No Fury' is a black comedy that will make you laugh but it will also touch your heartstrings gently, like a feather in a light breeze as Cath and Dave Kelly go through all that life throws at them and they experience birth, marriage, and death with every intimate detail described in spellbinding fashion.

I hope you enjoy this book, my third publication after a book of verse 'Irreverent Irrelevant Rhyme' and an autobiography 'It Could Happen to You – Growing up in Ireland'. This time it is fiction that I enjoyed writing for you and watch out for more because it is most certainly on its speedy way to you.

John Lennon Cohen

Hell Has No Fury

The cold wet November morning that soaked everything to saturation did not seem to bother Dave Kelly as he climbed the short stairway of the imposing grey courthouse building. Today was to be the concluding episode in an epic marriage of twenty years, the last eight filled with the battles and conflicts that only a separating couple engage. Inside the large bland foyer solicitors and wigged barristers scurried about with large files containing the life stories of the ordinary people that were also present. There were nervous looks on the faces of the many and an aura, a stench of fear filled the entire concourse and this also engulfed Dave for no apparent reason. He looked out for his legal team of solicitor Tom and barrister Justin finally spotting them engaged in conversation in a corner and as he waited he looked around at the newly vamped building. It was rectangular in shape with consulting rooms on the right hand side and this is where the deals were made and the futures of every man, woman, and child involved were decided. If no agreement can be reached here then a judge decided; and rightly or wrongly, this is the system in Ireland for the break up of marriage. In the centre of the room is a large imposing stairway that led to courtrooms on either side, just like the ground floor; stairway to heaven but in most cases it's a stairway into hell.

Dave's thoughts drifted back to when, in this very place, they tried, sentenced, and executed murderers by hanging and imagined the condemned man being led up the stairway for his final drop through a trap door that took him into the next world and with this very thought a cold shiver shot throughout Dave's body.

His solicitor Tom approached in a dither and Dave knew he did not even see him.

"Tom I need a word with you"

"Yes ok, I will be with you in a moment"

"This is very important to me and it won't wait"

Tom stopped in his tracks and glared at Dave.

"Ok what is it?"

"I have a very bad feeling about this today and I have no confidence about our case"

"What in hell brought this on"?

"I just have a bad feeling that everything will go wrong for me and I want you to negotiate the settlement that they were offering at the previous July sitting"

"I cannot remember what went on last week never mind four months ago". "Remind me again"?

"They were offering a lump sum of seventy five thousand as my share of the house and I would maintain the children until they were eighteen"

"Right I will see what they say"

Tom went off with Justin to negotiate with the opposition as Dave reminisced about his married life to Cath.

They met twenty five years previously by chance at a house party on a Saturday night when Dave wanted to be elsewhere but his long time friend persuaded him to go. Dave is the chatty type who would talk to everyone there, especially Cath, who was the only potential conquest but he wasn't really bothered one way or the other as she was not his type because she was plump with white freckled skin, short stumpy muscular legs and red hair dyed blonde. She also had a massive gap between her two front teeth that reminded Dave of a claw hammer so she was definitely not on his menu as he preferred petite dark haired women. However he did make a date with her for the following evening in the Planet Bar, a place that he never frequented.

That Sunday night Cath went into the Planet with her friends Dara and Hattie but there was no sign of Dave. Dara looked at Cath with sympathetic eyes before inquiring.

"Are you sure he said the Planet Bar"?

"Yes it was the Planet ok".

"I don't understand this as he always goes next door to the Venus".

"Well he definitely said the Planet".

Cath was upset and went to the toilet and her friends quietly stared after her before Dara began to whisper to Hattie.

"This does not look good and maybe he gave her a bum steer".

"What do you mean"?

"Well Dave or the boys never come in here so perhaps he is trying to avoid Cath but we will give him the benefit of the doubt and go next door to the Venus when she comes back".
"I thought you would never say that". "I don't like this place either".

When Cath rejoined the girls they persuaded her to go next door although she wanted to stay just in case Dave did show up.

They climbed the stairs to the Venus Bar and sat down in their usual seats beside their other friends. Dave was with them and greeted the new arrivals to the company with his usual friendly banter.

Dara broke the ice,

"Hey, were you not supposed to be in the Planet"?
"Me? No. What would I be doing in that place"?
"Ah it doesn't matter".

Dave covered his tracks well as he forgot his date with Cath and the girls put it down to her mistaking the venue. Dave did get with Cath at the end of the night much to the amazement of their friends as they would never put them together because they were the complete opposite. Dave's friend Enda was most amazed of all and cornered him in the toilet.

"Are you really going to go with that thing"?
"Sure any kind of a ride is better than walking"

Dave answered back half joking.

"You are a crazy man".

Enda then stuck some black chewing gum between his front teeth, put two toilet rolls up his trouser legs to represent Cath's rather big calf muscles and the gap between her teeth. He them mimicked her unusual walk strutting around the toilet like a wounded chicken as they both fell about in hysterics.

"How can I look her straight in the face after that"?
"Just don't make her smile".

They were both still in fits of laughter when they rejoined their friends and every now and again Dave would explode in laughter when he would think of Enda's antics.

Cath, never thinking that the cause of their behaviour was about her, asked,

"What are you two laughing about"?
"Ah it just a joke Enda told in the toilet".
"Well are you going to share it"?
"God no". "It's a mans joke and much too rude for ladies".

Cath was satisfied with his explanation and was happy that Dave considered her a lady. But Enda would every so often smile down at Dave behind Cath's back with the black gum between his teeth causing Dave to go into fits of laughter.

Then at the end of the night Dave and his new date left together. Cath had a car that she drove home even though she had many drinks. She drove to her mother's house and invited Dave in and he willingly accepted. They snogged passionately even before they reached the sitting room and when they finally reached the couch both had their coats off. Cath responded to every move Dave made and he soon had her braless where he gently caressed and kneaded her rather large nipples. Cath moaned and groaned as Dave nibbled her earlobes but he wanted to see what he was feeling between his fingers. He sneaked a peep down and with the dim light coming from the kitchen he saw the biggest nipples ever and they reminded him of Jew-Jew sweets (sugar coated jellies) or cigar butt ends. They were dark which was in much contrast to her otherwise milk white body peppered with freckles. Dave moved down and kissed them softly while Cath responded with more groans as he moved from one to the other. He lifted her loose fitting skirt expecting Brigid Jones knickers but they were just ordinary much to his relief as he regarded such items as passion killers. Now on his knees he ran both hands up the insides of her now wide open thighs with the lightest of touches stopping just short of her vagina. This drove her crazy and she adjusted her hips so that she was closer to her tormentor. Dave teased a little more and as if accidentally, brushing up against Cath's pussy that made her squirm and shiver till finally he massaged her pubic area. Quickly he removed her pants and opened the red folds of her vulva that were glistening and very wet. He moved his finger up to gently knead her clitoris and with a finger of his other hand placed it inside her pussy to find her G-spot and Cath had to bite on a cushion to muffles her cries. Dave then put his tongue deep inside her pussy before he started licking and sucking her clitoris but had to hold her hips as she writhed in ecstasy while at the same time undoing his jeans. When he went to enter her with his now pulsating penis she pushed him away in a nonchalant manner that took him by surprise but he respected her wishes even though she had all the pleasure while he had none. He supposed that flicking her bean was alright for a first date but expected more to come at a later stage.

They made a date for the following week and a casual relationship began, much to everyone's surprise as they would never put Dave and Cath together in a romance because they were complete opposites. Dave was a hopeless romantic whereas Cath could or would not show her feelings to anyone. She was twenty eight while he was twenty three and they both had previous relationships that ended in heartbreak so they were perhaps a little cautious. Dave didn't feel that special magic he had with other girls and it was more of a fun friendship and he felt safe that his heart could not be broken with her. On the other hand Cath's philosophy was 'treat them mean to keep them keen' and she was expert at this whether by design or by her natural personality. They met every Friday, Saturday, and Sunday nights in the same bar and Dave's set routine for the weekend never changed except that Cath would never go to the RC Disco Club that Dave always frequented every Saturday night.

He with his friends would walk up to the 'strip' where all the favourite local bars were situated in town, while she drove up collecting her friends as she went. Dave spent all his money on Cath, plying her with drinks and taking her to nightclubs so that during the week he would have to borrow from his sister to keep him supplied with cigarettes but he didn't mind this as he was a generous man. Cath was of the mind set that the man in a relationship should have to pay for everything and she stood rigidly to this rule.

The first time he met her family her sister Freda and husband Dan were visiting from Dublin for the weekend so there was a big get-together. Cath's mother Mary was regarded as the queen of her castle as she had seven children consisting of five girls and two boys where Cath was in the middle. Mary was a nice widowed lady who demanded respect from her offspring and never took sides or interfered in their relationships. There were three left at home: Paula and Noel, who were still single but in serious relationships with partners John and Nicola, and then came Cath. Dave noticed a green air of uneasiness within this family circle where all seemed to be jealous of each other and snide remarks of contempt about status, attire, and even hair-dos were the order of the day, especially from Paula who seemed to have a giant chip on her shoulder. She had the evil habit that if she knew something sordid about a person in her company she would spitefully embarrass them by mentioning it aloud. Her partner John was a giant of a man, over three hundred pounds in weight, but he agreed and complied with everything conjured up by Paula either because he loved her or was scared that he would not get anyone else; however no matter what the reason, he stuck by her although at times she treated him very badly. Noel was a better person who had social skills that were lacking in Paula and he had a strong woman in Nicola, who kept him in check with a tight rein and she needed to do this as otherwise he would run riot.

Mostly it was Paula in this family who displayed an air of conceited self importance, arrogance, and she was self centred to the core which made Dave feel very uncomfortable and he was so thankful that he was not like her. However he thought her lofty attitude was laughable because they were all living on a local authority housing estate especially built for the poor, which possessed all the usual trappings of crime by the underprivileged because of destitution. This family saw it all, with the father doing all the things that men did at that time, worked hard for bad pay, drank and gambled sometimes all his wages and that is why Dave had the greatest of respect for the queen of the castle mother who kept the family unit going despite the transgressions of her husband.

The floor of the courthouse foyer gleamed and Dave noticed for the first time a faint aroma of polish as he sat there alone. He looked up and caught a glimpse of Cath who had the support of her brother and sister who seemed to be arguing with her legal counsel as they made gestures with their hands towards them. Dave thought - this is typical, with Cath sitting back and letting others engage in the frontline of battle for her, while she looked on with her appropriate smug expression, an expression that was unique to her. He was often caught in this position with her and had to rescue the situation on many occasions.

He remembered once when just going out with her, there was a party in a bar on the 'strip' and Dave was invited with his partner. They arrived as the bash got into full swing and while he could mingle quite well, Cath on the other hand could not. This seemed to make her jealous of his outgoing personality and she was likely to throw a verbal spanner into the works for her own satisfaction.

Knucksie, a long time friend of Dave's, who had migrated to England many years previously came over to say hello. Knucksie was a hard man and perhaps left home to get away from his reputation of fighting and causing trouble everywhere he went. However Dave liked him and felt comfortable in his presence.

"Well mate, how is it going over here for you"?

"Ah Knucksie, it's been years since I saw you. Where are you living?"

"I'm in London mate and it's great! Do you ever see any of the geezers?"

"What?"

"Ah sorry, mate! I mean the guys we used to hang with".

"No not for a long time. It's hard to get used to you with an English accent, with all their jargon".

"Well mate it's like this, I had to make myself understood as the Brits hadn't a clue what I was saying to them at first so I had to adapt to their ways and sayings".

"Sure when in Rome! Oh by the way this is Cath".

"Hello. Nice to meet you".

Cath just nodded to acknowledge his greeting and Dave thought this was a peculiar reaction. He was unsure if she had too much to drink, or instantly took a dislike to his friend so he just passed it over and continued to talk to Knucksie. Dave had to go to the toilet and excused himself and left Cath with his friend. When he returned there was a big row brewing and now a butch looking lady who happened to be Knucksie's sister had joined the company.

"What the hell is going on?" Dave hurriedly interrupted.

"This woman is insulting me saying I was 'putting on' an English accent".

"Yes you are, you went over in a boat and came back in a booat!" Cath retorted.

"Dave, you know that I'm in London this past fifteen years and I can't help the way I speak".

Cath mocked his every sentence and the butch female interrupted.

"If you don't shut your ugly mouth I will shut it for you".

"At least I do not look like a man, ya dike!"

The butch lady made a lunge at Cath and had to be restrained by Knucksie who took her away to the opposite end of the bar near the exit. Dave followed them.

"Listen I am so sorry this has happened but she is drunk and doesn't mean a word".

"Well it didn't sound that way to us". "She upset us both with her insults and we didn't do anything to cause it".

"I can't apologise enough".

Dave was getting more embarrassed by the moment and recognising this, Knucksie put his arm around his shoulder.

> "You are a good man Dave but that person will give you plenty of problems, believe me".
> "Yes what are you doing with that ugly bitch"? "She's an evil cunt and only for my brother I would have boxed the ugly head of her".
> "Calm down sis, enough, it's over". "Dave we are going to go home now". "It was good seeing you again, I think"?
> "Ah I really am so sorry".

They left in silence and Dave knew that if this had to be fifteen years ago Knucksie would have pole-axed Cath without a second thought thus his reputation and it was strange for Dave to see him behave so completely different, acting as a peace maker. His sister seems to have taken over his mantle and Dave knew by the angry look on her face that she would have carried out her threat on Cath but fortunately for her, Knucksie had mellowed in his fifteen years away.

Dave returned to Cath who was happy with herself as she sat swaying with a smug expression on her face. He did not mention the incident as he knew it was pointless speaking to a drunken Cath so he got her coat, took her outside, and put her in a taxi while he walked home alone. He thought about his relationship and wondered if he had seen the real Cath that she had carefully hidden from him? He definitely saw a different side of her; a dark evil side that saw her snidely mock his unsuspecting friend. This was calmly executed with scalpel like precision that cut to the bone without obvious reason and without fear of reproach. Dave mulled over the events of the evening but could not just pinpoint what it was that sparked off the incident. They were having a fun night together and it all changed when a friend came over to say hello. Dave suspected that Cath felt that she was not the centre of attention so took it out on his friend Knucksie in a most undignified manner. This certainly shocked him completely as he would never want to be associated with such a vindictive cruel person.

However he didn't mention it again and neither did she but he had a mental record that would stay with him. Dave was learning more and more about Cath and discovered that she had this built-in defence mechanism that if you don't talk about her misbehaviours they didn't happen and so she was of the mind set that she never did anything wrong at any time in her life. Although she did often brag about one incident that happened when she was only a little girl of ten years old, when one of her friends got a new white dress and admitted that she was jealous. So when out playing on the road with her and another friend, they lured white dress girl down a laneway and when they got her down there they threw mud at the poor girl who went home crying. But the jealous Cath just laughed and remains laughing to this day, while Dave thought this to be serious and not funny as she had a core of rooted jealousy, an envy that caused her to do awful things but worse still, these awful things made her happy.

The memories came flooding back as Dave sat in silence in the courthouse foyer and thought of happier times before he met Cath. His mind wandered to a time when he was alone, not having a steady girlfriend and at this time the thoughts of how his future would turn out came swamping in, filling his mind with glee and he was happy back then.

This particular night was calm with a sense of mystery as Dave walked along one of the main thoroughfares in his hometown. Everyone was in party mood as this was Saturday night in the hub of entertainment that was called 'The Strip' where Images, The Venus and The Planet were the hip bars in this Mecca of entertainment where everyone sought out the holiday atmosphere, sought out love and perhaps a lifetime partner and Dave was of the same mind. This was early 1980's Ireland, when the economy was fairly stable with no major political upheavals on the horizon but this was a false sense of security and the calm before the tempest. Dave was approaching his mid-twenties, gaining plenty of experiences but still had not got a titter of wit and without any doubt he could be bought and sold quite easily. But this was his personality and he liked it because it never caused him any problems and he got on well with most people. However he had a few disasters with relationships and had his heart broken without understanding why because when he falls in love it is for the long term, and for keeps.

The employment front did not look any better for him either and he never seemed to secure a good job that he liked doing but he remained happy enough and optimistic. But there were questions deep in his mind of what was this life all about, what are we humans and why are we here? He would often ponder that if human beings were destined to live life alone without a partner and never to have a good job was this destiny or just bad luck? He thought about this because every time he met a girl, fell in love, thought she felt the same way and everything seemed to be going great when all of a sudden the girl would change her mind and leave him without cause or explanation. He found this to be the same case with employment, a job would be advertised in the local newspapers, and knowing that he would excel in the position, he was always passed over and never got the job. So it can be understood the reason for his deep thoughts but he was lucky in another way for he had a great family.

Dave had a very close – knit, loving family with his mother and sister living at home and they loved him dearly, warts and all, and always gave him the feeling of belonging to a very special unit.

Dave walked up the steps of Images Bar on the 'strip' and on entering the atmosphere was electric with loud music; disco lights and a fashion show all rolled into one. Images Bar would not be out of place on the Costa del Sol in Spain for it was full of single women who looked absolutely fabulous in the latest fashion and Dave often felt like a little boy in a sweet shop not knowing which one to go for. This was paradise for him as he just loved women, the way they looked, their company, their aroma and their personality but most of all he loved if a girl fancied him and when in a slow danced she would snuggle into his neck gently kissing it. The closeness of another human being in his arms made him feel so good, so cosy inside, that he longed for it for the long term.

He joined his friends at the bar where they always took up the same position. This was because the ladies would come up near to them to buy their drink. There was Enda and Jack, both single and looking for that elusive special female, that is if she did exist for real. The banter would start when they were all present and the usual chat up lines would be tried on the unsuspecting women within earshot. Enda would be first to remark.

       "Wow lady, you're looking real good tonight"
       "Oh thank you very much".

This would open up the conversation and when the girl responded, she would receive all the compliments of the day. But if she ignored the friendly gestures, well, heaven look out, for she then would receive all the insults. Dave hardly ever engaged in this but did enjoy the banter as his friends came up with some funny but very uncomplimentary phrases.

"Did you just get out of Drumcar for the night?"
Drumcar is a special school for the mentally challenged.
"Hey, your dress is lovely, where did you buy it, Oxfam?"
Another time when Jack was chatting up a female police officer, that is titled a 'Ban Garda' in Ireland, he asked her
"What do you work at"?
"I'm a Ban Garda"
"Ah you're right, Ban all the fucking Garda".
Dave was very unsure what the lads enjoyed most, giving compliments or giving insults but it was a great laugh either way. Sometimes he would get the distinct impression that Enda didn't like women's company at all because he often used the expressions,
> "Women are only good for two things, riding and making your dinner and sure your mother always makes your dinner". He would even point out a girl and say,
> "Do you see that one over there?"
> "Yes".
> "Well, I wouldn't ride her with somebody else's dick". "In fact I wouldn't ride her into battle". "Sure look at the state of her". "A sniper wouldn't take her out", nor the tide".

Perhaps the reason for this is that he had seven sisters and first hand knowledge of the female species, especially when all their friends came around to his house at the same time. However this is the way Enda was and the ladies loved him despite his crudeness whereas Dave and Jack were more quiet and gentlemanly. If they fancied a lady she never knew about it because when she came into their company they got tongue-tied and couldn't speak and the lady always thought that they were unfriendly. So there you have it, the women they fancied and wanted to be with were never asked out, and the ones they fell in love with were never touched or made love to, what plonkers, and idiots as Enda would say?

Dave's mother drilled it into him from a very young age to always respect girls and don't engage in what she called 'dirty tricks', that is, anything to do with sex, as she was a devout Roman Catholic who's rule was that you can have sex but you have to be married and even then it is a sin to enjoy it. Well, she passed this catholic chaste paranoia and guilt firmly on to Dave with the result that he developed into an oddball in the company of women he fancied and grew to love.

He started to become acutely aware of what and whom he fancied, as they say, 'what floats your boat' and there were many that just sailed on by without a word from him. At the time, in looks, he liked small, petite girls but not too thin with long, straight, shiny, dark hair. Unlike most men, he didn't like big breasts which he thought to be deformities and like balloons that had too much air inflated into them and were ready to burst. Yes, Dave liked small tits and as a friend used to state 'anything that you can't get into your mouth is a waste' and perhaps he was correct on that score, Dave thought. He loved shapely waists and hips with an exaggerated bottom and slim slightly bow-shaped legs but fat legs with 'cankles', that is a calf and ankle all in one, were definitely out. He didn't like big wide feet or hands on women as they always reminded him of men's extremities and in fact he didn't like anything big about girls at all.

Dave loved them to wear figure hugging jeans for casual wear but for dressing up loved two types of attire that he felt were the most exotic and erotic ever and sure to turn heads every time. The first is a tight fitting dress hugging every curve of the body and as low cut as a lady would dare with the dress going right to the floor but with a split from the bottom up the side ending at the hip and when the lady walks her leg is revealed in a most alluring fashion. The second is a short mini dress just covering the crotch tantalisingly and with a long coat or cardigan reaching the ground behind. No pantyhose, but pure unclad legs and when they sit down, so what if a person gets a flash, a glimpse of their underwear, sure, this is another thing men just love. He believed that the primary colours are always best as they stand out stunningly; not forgetting black and white, where underwear should always be white.

Dave knew exactly the secrets of what attracted men to the opposite sex but what could he do to attract females to him? He was never sure. What he did know for sure is that if ladies dressed in this way they would most certainly turn heads, be belle of the ball, and if that special man does not come near them, well, he does not deserve them. On the other hand he could be like Dave, a little shy and awkward with the lady he fancied, and he wished they would just go up to him, just to give him the benefit of the doubt. One definite turn off for Dave and a complete no-no were tracksuits and trainers at any time so if they are wearing them he would rather not see. This is the mind of men and Dave was no different.

Dave and his pals moved on from Images bar to The Venus Bar because the top floor was also a restaurant and could serve alcohol later than normal bars. The Venus was run by a very astute businessman and it boasted three floors catering for three different types of clientele. The ground floor had disco music, the middle was a sports bar, and the top was a romantic restaurant so everything and everybody was catered for under one roof but late in the evening they always decided to grace the top bar. This was dimly lit with candlelight on every table and had soft romantic music piped subtly to encourage the mood. The clientele were mainly starry-eyed couples that were totally engrossed in each other; and in Ireland at the time, if a man asked a lady out for a meal, he was definitely serious about the relationship. There were also groups of ladies - wannabes that longed for a relationship and also the 'has-beens', married couples who were there in an attempt to recapture their younger days or just to be nosy about who was going out with whom. Then there were Dave and his friends, there for the late drink and the craic and sure they entertained everyone no matter what their station, especially the unattached single ladies.

At that time Dave was quieter in personality than usual having just come out of a two-year serious relationship and he missed the girl, the love, the closeness not forgetting the great sex. She hailed from a seaside village close to his hometown and she ticked almost all of his boxes in what he fancied in a woman. He often wondered as to what is this place that people are transported to when their partner decides that they are not the one? Their world is turned upside down like suffering bereavement with emptiness inside that is void of all comprehension. All of the plans, the joy in life goes out the window and never once did they ever think this would happen knowing the person so much, well, thinking that they know the person, that a plan B was never even considered. Dave did realise that it is everybody's prerogative to change their mind but without any telltale signs, taking another down the road of life to suddenly and without warning, change direction and go down another road alone or worse still with somebody else.

Since time immemorial, the greatest thinkers on this planet, men and women, have tried to figure out the enigma, what is love? The non-tangible entity that affects every living being bringing great joy but alas sometimes great misery, and everybody is susceptible, from the greatest of kings and queens to the lowest of the low on this planet.

Dave and his friends thoughts were on holidays and they had some great adventures on their two week annual vacation, some would say their entire life was a vacation, but as they always said "to hell with the be-grudgers because we are not here for a long time, we are here for a good time". Their first holiday away with the lads was to the Irish holiday resort of Tramore, County Waterford in the south of the island. This is a beautiful beach resort with miles of golden sand and amusements to cater for the tourist but in a small way, by world standards. This was in 1973 and a four-berth caravan, mobile home, was booked but the only trouble with this was that ten people were intending to go there. The day for departure arrived and with the fervour of schoolboys their exhilaration was very evident as they excitedly made their way up to the train station with rucksacks firmly attached to their backs. There was Dave, Boo, Daweser, Macca, Bowler, Enda, and Jack to name but a few and their age at the time was sixteen but going on twelve. Bowler was the leader because he had the most sense of the troupe and he did all the arrangements of booking. However when they arrived in the Tramore campsite, six of the gang had to hide outside while the attendant took the other four to their home for the week. Well, they were never in a caravan before but it was so small they wondered if the four persons had to be dwarfs or Leprechauns. Nonetheless they all placed their rucksacks therein and went for something to eat before going to the pub. The O'Shea's bar had a big cabaret lounge that catered for maybe a couple of hundred people and the intrepid tourists were made very welcome even though they were attired like the English pop group Slade, donning denims that were worn short on the leg above the ankle with the hem rolled back exposing the white on the inside of the jeans with black socks and of course the figuring hugging jean jacket and all this topped off with platform shoes. Also, each and every one of them had long hair, as per the fashion of the era, and they felt really hip with this garb. Sure, they thought they were 'the bee's knees', as older people looked on in amazement.

They were seated around a large table when the cabaret began and the band replicated the actual record sound of all the contemporary pop groups as they swayed and sang to their favourite tunes. The gang felt very privileged to experience such talent in abundance for there were not only the usual three guitars and drums but also the band contained a brass section with trumpets, trombones, and saxophones.

The noise reached a crescendo as the lounge filled to capacity and people attempted to be heard above the music but this only added to their enjoyment. One of the mates Daweser did not smoke or drink alcohol but he was crazier than any of them and he really knew how to enjoy life without putting any external substances into his body. His stimulus was beat music, especially that of 'Noddy Holder' and the band Slade; that seemed to push all his excitement buttons and he took on a life of his own when any of their music sounded. Now not contented with dancing in the aisle beside their table, he proceeded to mount it and dance erotically to the deafening drones of the Slade song 'Mama, we're all crazy now'. The rest looked on and thought: how appropriate and how crazy is this as they viewed a swaying sea of souls dancing in a frenzy, listening to the band but all definitely focused on Daweser as he gyrated. The next person of the gang that went to the bar to buy a round of drinks just couldn't believe what the barman said to him as he pointed in the direction of our table.

"I will give you all a pint but I am not serving that guy with you."

"Which one"

"That blonde guy, that crazy bastard dancing on the table, I think he has had enough to drink".

Well he just hadn't the nerve to tell him that the lemonade was for him and when he came back and told us what had happened, sure the lads all fell about laughing.

When the band were finished and the bar closed it was time to go dancing for real so they headed next door to the ballroom but the doormen wouldn't let them in, much to their disappointment. At that time denims were considered inappropriate attire for dancing but seeing that they were not trouble makers and only wanted to dance, he suggested that they go to the car park alongside the ballroom and they could hear the music and this they did, all twenty of them. Their numbers had swollen that evening as more friends arrived from home and they danced with delight in the half-lit car park. The doormen kept an eye on them but as they were just dancing and having fun, they proceeded to direct everyone with denims to the car park, their very own ballroom. Well, seventy percent were female much to their delight and as a slow set of music began, they paired off with whom they fancied. Then it was 'every man for himself' as they in unison had the bright idea to sneak off back to the caravan with their new girlfriends. Dave arrived back in fourth place as three others with girls beat him to it and if it was uncomfortable with eight people, it was certainly painfully cramped with forty vying for a space. Well there was no kissing or cuddling as even a contortionist could not manage this in a small four-berth caravan with forty people present. People were everywhere and anywhere they could find, all the seats were filled as were the worktops, the fridge, cooker everything so the door was left open as their number spilled outside. They sang for about an hour as one by one the females went home and the rest grabbed what space there was left to get their much-needed forty winks.

Dave thought back on this time and knowing that it was so great to be young and carefree where nothing seem to be a problem and life just rolled on as with time and tide.

However their night of fun did have its consequences, as bright and early the next morning the campsite supervisor arrived to their temporary home with a list of complaints but even he raised a smile when he opened the door and one of the company fell out on top of him. He, Daweser had slept standing up against the door and he got the nickname 'Horse' after that.

Don't Cry Over Spilt Curry!

Oh, but how times had changed for Dave, as he was now in a relationship with a woman who was completely different from anyone he met before and he wondered if she could be the one he would spend the rest of his life with, to love him, to support him, and to be his best friend. He was very unsure because he had been in love before and this new relationship with Cath certainly didn't feel anything like love as he knew it. He never felt with her that great, cosy, happy feeling inside that he experienced with other girls that he certainly loved. Nothing matched up in this relationship as she was not his type at all and in fact was the complete opposite in looks and personality. The dark hair, the dark eyes, the quiet type personality that he felt was mysterious and would never let you down, especially in company. Alas these were all missing with Cath. He pondered as to why he was remaining in a relationship with her but came to the conclusion that he really enjoyed her company as she was good fun most of the time, that is, when she wasn't in the envy mode. However she kept this close to her chest and didn't show it often except when her guard was down with too much alcohol. He had heartbreak before with other girls but felt safe with Cath because he felt that she could not break his heart as others did, as he didn't feel that intensity of love for her. He thought that maybe this is the way relationships are supposed to be: successful when a person just likes their partner without the intense, crazy feelings of love, because he was in love before and it always ended in disaster and heartbreak. Now if Cath were to walk away from him he felt that it would not affect him like what he had experienced before. Was this the way all married people felt, Dave wondered?

They continued on with their stormy weekend relationship, more often than not having a row on a Sunday Night, never seeing each other during the week but then meeting up again on the 'strip' on the following Friday night. On one such Sunday night Cath was in a very bad mood and there was nothing that Dave could do to cheer her up. On their way home she decided that she wanted a curry and Dave knew he was running very low on cash so he checked his pockets to discover he had £3.50, just enough for one curry. He had no problem spending the last of his money on Cath and she stopped at the Chinese take-away and he went in for her order. On their drive home Cath became so much more argumentative that when she stopped at her house Dave had enough and as he went to get out of the car said:

"What the fuck is wrong with you?"

"Well if you don't know, I'm not going to tell you" Cath replied without even looking at him.

"Ah, I've had enough of you and your moods."

He opened the door and as he went to rise felt something hitting the left sleeve of his white jacket. He stood up and looked, it was the curry he had bought with his last few pounds and now it was splattered on his jacket and lay on the road. Casually he bent down and scraped all the curry off the road and from his jacket and when he had finished he stooped into the car where Cath was sitting with that smug smile like the cat that got the cream. Dave then carefully poured the curry over her head before he slapped the now half empty carton on her head. The thick yellow fluid seeped slowly down, covering her hair while discarding chicken pieces which seemed to stick to the top of her head as it made its way down her front and her back. Not a word was spoken during this process and Dave just closed the door and walked away leaving Cath sitting motionless in the car. On the one mile walk home Dave smiled to himself as he thought about the incident and wondered if Cath enjoyed her curry!

The Road of Tralee

The days were getting shorter as September announced its arrival with a splattering of rust on the foliage around town. Most people had gone abroad on holiday, mainly to Spain, so they all sported great tanned skin that seemed to become luminous at night, perhaps artificially enhanced, and even if it was freezing outside they remained scantily clad.
Cath didn't take a summer vacation as she worked as a hairdresser in Jane's Salon; well salon is too fancy a word to use in this case as it was a little, damp, upstairs room with four sinks for washing hair and when Dave first saw it he remarked:
"I didn't know that Jane was into gardening?"
"What do you mean?" Cath replied.
"Well there are mushrooms growing on the walls of this place".
The top of the walls and part of the ceiling were black with mildew growing wild and Dave thought this was a serious health hazard but no one complained because the boss was a bully and not to be crossed. Cath, now aged thirty, worked here since she left school at fourteen with little education but remained a subordinate tending to the slightest whims of her boss Jane. One of these was holiday time and Cath would never dare to ask for holidays when all her friends were going because Jane had already booked at this time so Cath was always left with off season vacations. Traditionally hairdressers had Mondays off but Cath didn't as she babysat Jane's children while she went shopping in the city but of course never got paid for this extra duty and never asked. However this was life for Cath and she bitterly resented it but always secretly. She felt very hard done by from her family having to leave education at fourteen years of age and having to go to work although she was in the middle of six siblings with the older and the younger remaining at school. Perhaps her parents thought she didn't have the capacity to meet the education demands or they needed extra income at the time and they felt that Cath's education was expendable and was sacrificed. Then there was her younger sister Paula who was even more resentful and twisted, who was envious of almost everyone, who bullied Cath to no end, always keeping her in check and under her thumb. When she escaped the clutches of her family and went to work for Jane in the hairdressers she experienced the exact same treatment and all of this had a detrimental affect on her mind that made it twisted and

warped, languishing in her very subordinate, downtrodden life of scapegoat and ultimate servant. She resented all of this and the people she blamed for her predicament but didn't know how to fight back. She wanted to fly but if her wings were not clipped they were certainly tied back!

Jane's shop was never registered as a business but Jane had the blatant audacity to operate under the shadow of the Revenue Commissioner's office either through ignorance or sheer hard neck and even some of her clients were unsuspecting revenue employees. All of this caused problems for Cath as she was never a registered worker in government records; if she was to become ill and couldn't work she didn't get any payment and ultimately had no employment rights. Of course the business was illegal as it did not exist in records but Jane made a fortune with a very sizable clientele.

The end of August was the only time slot that Cath had for holidays and as all of her friends had already been away abroad the previous month, she was left with a long weekend away at the Kerry Festival, The Rose of Tralee. Dara and Hattie, Cath's boozing buddies, were going, as were Jack and Enda, Dave's mates and the five decided to travel together in Jack's car. Dave could not go as his work was in short supply. He had only three days a week so was short on cash and anyway could not afford to take the time off without pay.

Thursday announced itself with thunderous rain and Dave awoke with the bashing against the window of his bedroom. His mam always had tea and toast ready which was great, if not always appreciated, especially with a Monday morning hangover that only added to the fact that Dave was not a 'morning person'. However today was different and he felt a certain air of excitement as if something special was about to happen.

After the dawn duties of showering, dining, and dressing he made his way out to work where he met Enda who was emerging from his house just twelve doors from Dave's.

     "It's a pity you cannot come with us."
     "What?"
     "You forget?" "Today is Tralee Day and we are off."
     "Oh yes, ah don't mind me, I'm still half asleep". "Listen, have a great time, and don't do anything I would".

They both laughed as they parted company. Dave went through the day like any other and the next day was no different but now the weekend had arrived and it was normal for him to go out with his friends but they were away, so he decided to stay in, causing great surprise to his Mam and sister. They decided to get munchies and watch the late film on television. The following day, Saturday, was a day of leisure in his household with everyone having a long lie in. The evening came quickly and Dave notice that the cloak of darkness crept in earlier at eight o'clock, declaring that autumn had definitely arrived and the first signs were the greens of the earth were beginning to turn into a red colour.

Saturday night was party night but Dave felt at a loose end with his buddies and girlfriend away so he wondered for the first time how they were getting on. He was going to stay in again but come nine thirty the party clock alarm sounded in his head and he just had to go out and head for the 'strip'. He walked up alone and was soon in the bright lights of the town centre which was always buzzing, however a little of its magic was lost on Dave now that he was alone.

He climbed the stairs to Images Disco Bar and ordered a drink from his usual place in the corner. The fashion show continued as usual but now he felt awkward and even viewing this spectacle made him uncomfortable. He was just about to leave when two ladies from his neighbourhood joined him which swayed him not to move on. They were of an older generation but still looking for romance that had evaded them either by design or fate. They worked together in the local cigarette factory but didn't smoke which Dave thought strange. They were dressed to perfection both wearing white dresses of different design which highlighted their tanned skin. Maria had dark hair, dark eyes and looked Italian or Spanish; Dave couldn't decide which but he knew it was definitely a Latin look. Her friend Lisa was the complete opposite with fair hair but both had the same gentle, friendly personality that made him feel comfortable.

    "How come you are here on your own?" The dark haired lady inquired.

    "Ah, all me mates are away in Tralee for the weekend along with my girlfriend".

    "So when the cat's away the mouse will play?"

    "No, it's not like that at all. I just feel a bit lost, at a loose end with all me buddies away".

    "Will you go clubbing tonight?"

"No, in fact I was just going to leave when you came in but I decided to stay and have another drink with you, just to be sociable".

"Ah, that's very nice of you, there are not many gentlemen left around here". "I will tell you what, we are going to Tralee tomorrow and we can give you a lift there if you would like?"

"Wow that would be fantastic, thank you so much".

Dave made the decision to go to Tralee without any thought at all but this was his personality, the way he lived life, and his motto was never look a gift horse in the mouth, in other words 'never miss an opportunity'! He was so excited with the thought of the trip as he just loved travelling, whether it is car, coach, train, boat, or plane and once he ventured as pillion passenger around Ireland on a motorbike. He bade his farewells to the girls after making arrangements to be collected at lunchtime the following day. He skipped home thrilled with the very thought of his new adventure and when he got home his sister was still up and he borrowed twenty pounds off her for the trip and went to bed in a very happy mood.

At twelve noon the girls arrived to Dave's house as arranged and he jumped into the back seat attired in only a t-shirt and jeans. The girls look surprised that he had no bag with him.

"Do you not have any luggage?" Maria asked.

"Eh no, sure I am only going for the day's craic".

The two look at each other and laughed gleefully.

"What's so funny?"

"Well we have two large, full suitcases so if you get stuck we can loan you a t-shirt!"

They all laughed out loud as Maria drove out of Dave's street.

"Here, I couldn't wear a t-shirt with sequins dotted all over it and anyway I don't have the equipment to fill your t-shirts".

"What do you mean by that?" Lisa, looking back, asked Dave.

"Well I haven't got the boobies."

Dave said pulling the chest of his t-shirt out with two fingers imitating and exaggerating a ladies chest. The all exploded in happy laughter. They continued with their banter and told jokes and sang songs from the nineteen sixties and seventies which suited Dave because he knew them all. This was because his sister Mary was big into pop music, having a boyfriend who played drums in a band. So without fail, a book of lyrics with all the latest songs in the hit parade was purchased every second week thus the words were firmly fixed in Dave's mind. The six hour journey didn't seem so long as the car made its way through the midlands heading for the southwest coast of Ireland with every town and village being entertained from the car with the strains of Elvis Presley and the Beatles songs.

They finally arrived in Tralee and the place was thronged with people walking about and the girls ask Dave where he wanted to get out.

"Here will be fine".

Dave said, not wanting to say that he really needed to use the bathroom. He got out of the car and the girls looked slightly concerned and asked.

"Will you be ok here?"

"I will be grand, sure why wouldn't I be after a lovely trip down with two gorgeous ladies accompanying me?"

"Ah, that's a lovely thing to say" said Lisa and Maria nodded in agreement.

They were concerned for his well-being, leaving him alone in this strange place with a multitude lining the streets and sad because they were losing his company as he entertained them for most of the journey. He bent into the open car window and kissed the two ladies, thanking them sincerely for their kindness.

Maria thumped the steering wheel with both hands before saying,

"You know what Dave? It is lucky for the girl who gets you and I hope this lady you are coming down to see appreciates you".

Dave laughed as he bade farewell to his lady friends; as they drove off he looked around to see where he could use a bathroom but all the doors of the bars were closed so he decided to go down an empty alleyway where he would be unseen. Just as he was about to enter the alley he met some giggling girls from back home who shouted at him.

"Hey Dave, Cath is down the street in Trendy's disco bar and she is having a ball!"

"Good for her but did you see Enda and Jack?"

"Yes, they are there too but you won't get in because it is jammers and they have closed all the fecking doors".

"Ok thanks".

Dave rushed down the alley and was looking about when this door opened and a man stood there staring at him before saying.

"Are you wanting in boyo?"

"Yes please" Dave replied in an exasperated tone.

The man opened the door wide so Dave happily entered and quickly made his way to the bathroom. Washing his hands he thought about the trip down and what Maria said when they were parting kept repeating over in his mind. Did Cath appreciate him was just one of the things that now bothered him? They had far from an ideal relationship, just meeting up at weekends and consuming vast amounts of alcohol, thus not really getting to know each other at all but Cath seemed to be quite happy to do this all the time. Their friendship was certainly casual as they would just meet, drink until the bars closed and then have a grope at the end of the night, heavy petting is where it ended, period. Dave did not feel fulfilled with this at all; sure he enjoyed the craic of the evenings out, but there was emptiness, a lonely vacuum in the whole thing. There was no romance, no passion, no sex in the proper sense of the word and certainly no love. Dave missed all these things and wondered why he continued in this relationship as it was? He was on the rebound from a good romance when he met up with Cath so was she just filling the void of a female companion? Sure that's all it was as she was just like one of the lads in her manner and association with him. But she was not fulfilling his needs as his former partner Jan did.

They would talk for hours on end, being alone together during the week and even if when apart they would telephone each other and talk endlessly. Sure they had their time of going out at the weekends to bars and discos where they really enjoyed each others company. The love-making with Jan was second to none, filled with romance, passion, and adventure as they tried all sort of things in different places. One time when he called for her on a date night he entered her house being greeted excitedly by Jan's siblings who let him into their living room, where he engaged in banter. He could hear Jan's mother giving instructions as she was giving her the car for the evening.

"No alcohol at all madam, do you hear me?"

"Yes mother". "I will only have six pints of Guinness then".

"I won't give you the keys if you're irresponsible".

"Don't be silly mother, I was only joking".

They entered the living room and Dave could not take his eyes off Jan for she wore a very short mini skirt and he just loved this. His attention to Jan's attire was noticed by her mother who said to her.

"Now you be careful tonight" and turning around to Dave and giving a stern look continued "and you too".

Dave knew exactly what she meant but Jan was oblivious to her mother's warning.

"Mother, leave Dave out of this!" "It's me who's driving, not him".

They got into the car and the mother watched as they drove out of their driveway but before they reached the end of the street Dave had his hand up Jan's skirt, gently massaging her pert vagina and she quickly drove to a car park where they made mad passionate love for an hour. Then later in the evening while slow dancing Jan got horny and they went out and made love again but this time on the pitch and putt golf course and Jan went into hysterics when Dave said

"Honey, I think I got a hole in one there!"

At the end of the night they went back to Jan's parents house where it was arranged for Dave to sleep on the living room couch but Jan had other ideas and sneaked him into her bedroom blocked the door with a heavy table that both of them had to lift into place and they giggled when one of the legs hit Dave on the thigh. They made love again but very much constrained as they didn't want to waken anyone. The next morning Dave arose early and went for a shower; he was about to go under the refreshing water when there was a gentle knock on the door. Dave stopped in his tracks and listened, then coughed out loud to give notice that the bathroom was engaged; however there came another knock so he opened the door and Jan pushed in. They giggled again as they showered together, gently foaming up each others private little places and when they were drying each other off, Jan clasped her legs around Dave's waist which caused him to unbalance and he staggered back against the door. She began to writhe up and down on his erect penis, her knees banging against the door. Five minutes into this there came a loud knock on the door causing them to freeze in their tracks.

"Who is there"? Jan breathlessly shouted.

"It me, will you let me in, I am dying to pee!"

It was Jan's older sister.

"Use the other bathroom, I am busy here and don't go into the living room as Dave is sleeping over".

With that statement they both started the giggles again but continued with their love making and when it was over Dave sneaked back into the sitting room unnoticed by the rest of the family.

His partner Jan was almost Dave's ideal woman, small and petite with dark hair, dark eyes, and sallow skin. But she also possessed an intelligence that he appreciated and they could converse about almost anything, which satisfied Dave. However he was concerned with her age as she was seven years his junior and being just in her teens he knew that very often with teenagers the hormones are flying about erratically causing them to change their mind about relationships and who they want to be with. Dave's fears were justified as their relationship ended when Jan decided to move abroad for adventure; although wanting him to go with her she was going anyway, with or without him. This devastated him as he had unspoken plans for their future together and this was certainly not on his radar at all but he had to accept and let her go from him.

Dave was made feel very welcome in the bar which was filled with locals and not a foreigner or stranger in sight. This was certainly a bar geared up for its regular customers who engaged in small talk after watching a Gaelic Football Match on TV so it was definitely not suited to Festival goers; however he felt comfortable here.
He ordered a pint of Harp Lager which was brewed in his home town and when he did so caused the entire clientele to stop and stare at him, even the bartender. Dave looked around at these people, some with weather beaten red faces, perhaps from the farming community, attired in Aran sweaters with flat caps and he was amazed by their crystal clear steel blue eyes. He turned his gaze back to the barman and said "Ah I will have a pint of your best stout" and the customers returned to their conversation. He didn't know for sure if the bar didn't stock Harp Lager or if it was a thing like 'if you want to be accepted as one of us, you will drink what we are all drinking'. Dave didn't mind this at all thinking of the old adage of 'when in Rome, do as the Romans do'! He engaged in banter with the clientele who seemed to be ancient years old and relics of Ireland from the distant past as most wore tweed trousers, jackets and flat caps, rounded off with brown brogue shoes. They would not be out of place one hundred years before now and they were 'talking antiques'. Dave smiled as this thought flashed across

his mind. These were distinctly Kerry men who had their own culture, their rules and outlook about life and their own language and as Spock would say to Captain Kirk in Star Trek "It's English Jim, but not as we know it".

The conversation moved from the price of turnips to sport and finally swung to singing with an impromptu song being belted out from an old man farther down the bar. Dave loved this but didn't know the song as it was a very old ballad sang in the Irish Gaelic Language. The singer stared at Dave as if he was singing this just for him, telling him a story that he could only understand in part. His eyes told more than his voice and Dave understood that it was a sad song about the famine, hunger, lost of life, and the bleak story of the many 'Coffin Ships' of emigrants who left Ireland bound for a better life in America. Many of these emigrants didn't make it as they died in their thousands on these long voyages across the Atlantic Ocean hence the eerie title for these ships. The old man finished to cheers as he donned his flat cap firmly back on his head and drank down his stout in one go. Dave, not to be outdone, gave a rendition of the old ballad 'Banna Strand', a beach in Kerry that shot to fame with the story of Sir Roger Casement who attempted to land arms for the Irish Revolution. He got the same treatment when finished and downed his stout in one as there was another waiting, free gratis.

Dave decided to move on in an attempt to find his friends which was the reason for his visit in the first place but when he went outside all the other bars still had their door closed. However many people now thronged the streets, all in happy mood, singing and dancing so he decided to mingle with the crowds in his quest. Eventually he met up with his friends who were merry and in great mood, that is, all except for Cath who skulked in behind her two female companions. He was greeted with great gusto by Enda and Jack who cheered and embraced him but the girls were not as enthusiastic by the expressions as they closely huddled together and whispered to each other. They firmly closed ranks and their secret would remain a secret and what Dave didn't know was that Cath had met up with an old boyfriend the previous night and she was on her way to his hotel to spend the night with him! Now with his presence her plans for the next part of her evening would definitely have to change as Dave had ruined it for her.

"You mad bastard! Where the fuck did you come from"? Enda enthused.

"Er Dundalk! you know the wee place six hours north-east of here"!

"No I mean when did you arrive and where did you go"?

"Well I'm here since six bells and I was bundled into a bar full of Kerry men and there was great craic".

"Ah we were in that big hotel and you couldn't move with all the pussy there".

"I see you all were successful in shifting them as usual, so did you miss me"?

The three of them exploded in laughter but the girls remained noticeably quiet rigidly sticking to their plan of being tight lipped being afraid to give any hint of what was really on their minds.

"Well stranger"

Dave directed his stare at Cath who reacted with just a nervous smile and little eye contact. He knew for sure now that something had happened and was curious as he could read her like a book but knew when to push it or not.

"Aren't you happy to see me?" he enquired.

"Well yes, but I am just surprised".

"I will have to remember not to surprise you again then."

Still she could not look him in the eye and stared at the ground or away into the distance.

"So where are we going now?" Dave asked.

"Feck, we are going to bed as we are knackered being here from Thursday till now drinking!"

"Ah OK and the camp site is located where?"

"Just down at the end of this road!"

Nothing more was said as they made their way and got into the tent. It was a tight squeeze but they were snug and before long they were all sleeping.

The dewy dawn gave way to drizzle then heavy rain that woke Dave as he lay prostrate between Cath's and Hattie's sleeping bags. He turned to face the top of the now saturated tent and contemplated the events of the day before, the car journey, the night's craic in the Tralee bar filled with locals and then finally meeting Cath who was not pleased to see him. He could tell this from her friend Dara's expression and also from her when she eyed him but all the time he thought that she would be pleased to see him as they hadn't seen each other from Thursday to Sunday but he was mistaken. That old Led Zeppelin song began resounding in his mind 'Lying, cheating, hurting that's all you seem to do. Running around with every guy in town putting me down for taking someone new!' Eventually they all woke, interrupting Dave's thoughts and Jack and Enda began to slag him off.

"Wow you crazy mad bastard coming all the way down here just to see your beloved"

Enda stated with a big grin. Jack agreed with him and added,

"Yes you are totally crazy, totally mad in the head, ya header ya".

"Would you two shut it and have you anything to eat I am starving"?

Dave had not eaten since the day before!

"No we have not a thing as we ate out all the time" was the nonchalant reply.

The rain eased off and they decided to pack up the tent and make ready for home. Enda asked Dave

"How are you going to get home? Jack has no room in the car".

"What?"

Dave was both shocked and annoyed by the question but as always tried to save face.

"The same way as I got here, no thanks to you lot".

Cath and her friends just busied themselves putting on make-up and grooming their hair, not noticing Dave's conversation and when they had finished they packed their little bags and got into the back seat of the car. The lads packed the tent away and got into the car and were just about to drive off when Enda opened the door and gave Dave a six pack of lager, closed the door and Jack drove off. Dave stood there gaping in disbelief, thinking that this was only a prank being played by his friends pretending to leave him six hours drive away from home with no money, a T-Shirt, a pair of jeans and a six pack. But reality soon sank in as the car drove out of the campsite with Cath waving out the rear window. Well fuck you shower of snaky bastards Dave thought to himself as the rain came thundering down again with more force than ever. He put the six pack under his T-shirt so as not to get the cardboard wet and disintegrate causing the bottles to fall out. There was no shelter either so he just made his way out of the campsite muttering obscenities to himself. He found his way out of Tralee on the road to Dublin with the rain pelting down but at least it was on his back. He was thankful for small mercies as he trudged along and began to hum that old song 'I'm singing in the Rain' and at one stage was going to dance to the music in his head. He walked and walked but not one car passed him and he began to think that he was the only person left on this planet of Kerry. He came to a hamlet and the rain suddenly stopped and the sun came out. It was warm and steam began to rise from his drenched T-shirt and jeans when he spotted a man operating a digger about one hundred yards further down at the side of the road. He walked towards him and the driver then spotted him and staring with eyes firmly fixed like he was a sniper. Dave continued to approach and when he was about ten yards away the driver stopped the engine and alighted from the digger. This man was huge, giant; maybe six feet three tall, broad and about eighteen stone (250 pounds) with hands like shovels and a head one and a half times the size of normal. He was dressed in clean overalls.

"Well boyo what takes you here to this part of the world"?

Dave had to listen carefully to his question as his dialect was completely different from what he was used to. So Dave, now exhausted sat down on the kerbside and related his story. The man sat down beside him.

> "Ah Jesus, Mary, and Joseph, sure weren't they locked out of everywhere as well. They are great friends you have indeed, so feck them".

Dave agreed and asked his new friend with all this wisdom if he would like a beer.

> "I most certainly would indeed; sure I'm dying with the drought".

Dave gave over a bottle but had no opener so the guy put it between his teeth and pulled the two bottles open, much to Dave's astonishment. They sat there drinking, in the now beaming sun that dried Dave's shirt and talked about everything, even solving world crises with one sentence. It wasn't long before the six pack was gone and pointing to a bar across the road the man asked

> "Will you have another drink?" Dave replied "Yes but I have no money!" "Did I ask you that?" The man retorted. "I have no money either but this is my local so come on before they run out of the fecking stuff".

They entered the bar which was packed, with hardly any standing room but the man knew his way around and guys just moved aside and let them in beside the bar. Dave was unsure if this was being polite or respect or fear but he didn't care as he knew he was in good company.

"Two pints of your best stout, me good fellow please" came the order and the barman duly obliged but with stout it had to be poured properly: filled three quarters of the way, left to settle for 3 minutes or more and then filled to the brim. When the drinks arrived on the counter the man proclaimed to all there,

> "Ah be the Lord God would you look at that, sure isn't this the best invention Ireland gave to the world"?

Everyone there seemed to agree and echoed "Aye you're right there"! The man then turned to Dave and toasted

> "Here's to you me good fellow". "Now drink up before they run out of the fecking thing".

The continued their conversation of everything under the sun and although the man was merely a construction worker, he possessed a fantastic knowledge and a philosophical wisdom that suited Dave's outlook to perfection. However this wisdom was all related in a strange dialect that was very comical and whereas he understood the meaning he couldn't but go into hysterics of laughter. The stout was flowing with ease and Dave was the worse for wear as his head began to spin into alcohol oblivion when all of a sudden the man proclaimed

> "Well now it is time for the spuds and time you resumed your journey" and with that swallowed an almost full pint of stout.

He then took the now staggering Dave by the arm and ushered him out into the middle of the busy road. He then proceeded to walk in front of an oncoming car, held both of his gigantic arms aloft with a certain authority and the car screeched to a halt. He stuck his head inside the opened window and said

> "Where are you going?"

> "Limerick" was the curt reply.

> "Well here take this fellow with you" and with that he opened the back door and shoved Dave inside.

Now, three bottles of lager and almost eight pints of stout on an empty stomach before midday had the effect of putting Dave into a drunken deep sleep so the hour long journey to Limerick City was unrecorded in his mind.

Dave awoke to shouting and when he gathered his faculties thanked the lads for the lift and got out of the car. They left him on the road to Dublin City where he began hitch-hiking and before long he was travelling at speed towards his next stop in a large van. He exchanged pleasantries with the kindly driver and time passed quickly soon to arrive in the midland of Ireland. They bids their farewells as the driver turned down a side road leaving Dave in the wilderness of the countryside which seemed far from civilisation, with no houses in sight. Being isolated and alone he began to ponder the entire events that occurred over the weekend; Cath going away without him which didn't bother him at the time but it did now and worse still it didn't bother her in the slightest. His mind rambled with posing more questions than answers, was she only passing her time with him till she met someone better because they didn't have dates as such but just met up in the local bar at the weekend and he saw his friends more than her. Another thing that bugged him now was that they hadn't full sex but just heavy petting sessions where he did all the action and she just lay back taking it all, whereas he had been in relationships before and the sex was always a two way thing. Now that Cath had left Dave high and dry, 'up shit creek without a paddle', he wondered was this a sign of what their future may be like, if they were to have a future, so he noted this in his mind about how self-centred and heartless she could be. He was also disappointed with his friends for leaving him behind as he would never do this on anyone, ever.

The autumnal evening began to close in as the sun set on the beautiful Irish countryside and Dave noticed the birds singing lullabies to their young and this brought a good feeling to his otherwise troubled mind. Sure if the birds can survive in this no-man's-land then so could he, an intelligent but sometimes irrational human being, he thought to himself. No traffic passed in what seemed like ages and just when Dave was about to give up hope of another lift that night, headlights appeared in the distance, raising his diminished expectations. A big truck pulled up beside him and he gratefully accepted the driver's offer of a lift to Dublin. The driver was a great chatty man and Dave was in the mood for such banter where they shortened their four hour journey by telling jokes and everything was pleasant. They arrived in Dublin just after midnight but it was on the western outskirts of the city and Dave had to negotiate his way through the city to the airport in the northern area that was on the way to home town. This foot trek took two hours to complete and he was rather happy, if exhausted, to find himself in the Drumcondra area of the city with just an hour's drive to Dundalk. He almost immediately got another lift with a young married couple and he accepted with delight, not even bothering to ask where they were going. He again felt happy and began to relate his adventures of the past two days which the couple found to be extremely funny. Then with a lull in the conversation the couple had a private confab and when finished the female turned around to Dave and said

> "Listen, you are never going to get another lift at this time of night so we have decided to trust you and give you a bed for the night". "Of course, only if you would like"?

Dave was bowled over by this most generous of offers and it certainly restored his faith in humanity. He accepted with great humility and was even more surprised when they showed him his bed, the top bunk in their children's bedroom. However he was so tired he took off his shoes and clambered up the steps and was asleep before he hit the pillow. He awoke to the wonderful aroma of cooking and six eyes staring fixedly at him. The three children with age range from six to two years old were bemused by this giant in their presence and it reminded Dave of the Jonathan Swift children's storybook of Gulliver's Travels when he was shipwrecked in the land of Lilliput where all the inhabitants were tiny.

He amused the children with stories before investigating the now very alluring aroma and the children followed while he sang the song from the Disney Movie Snow White, 'Hi ho hi ho its off to work we go'! The children mimicked Dave's every movement as they marched towards the kitchen. The lady of the house greeted him and her offspring with equal enthusiasm and after a welcomed breakfast she drove Dave down to the main Dublin to Belfast road for the last leg of his journey. He bade his farewell as her car drove away and the children waved until they were out of sight.

Dave used this time for reflecting on the past days and his intrepid journey finding it amazing and mysterious all in one. He went through it hour by hour, the trip down with the two girls and how they passed their time singing, the evening in the Tralee bar alone but meeting new friends. But then the reason for doing this trip, meeting up with his girlfriend Cath, and the cool reception he received from her, laboured his thoughts to a high degree. She was none too happy to see him and this was obvious by the expression on her face and the faces of her girl friends. Did he spoil their party? Or was it something else? But sure, he was her boyfriend and they were an item, so why behave like this? Did she have second thoughts about their relationship? He concluded that she was away with her friends but also his friends and now he wasn't quite sure if he missed her or them most! Then being left behind by this gang, these people that he called his best friends and worse still his girlfriend, really baffled him because he knew in his heart of hearts that he would never leave anyone stranded, let alone a friend. Now as he walked along the busy Dublin to Belfast road another thought struck him that he didn't know where exactly he was the previous day and he did not know a single name of anyone who came to his aide. He pondered his journey out of Tralee attired in only a t-shirt and jeans while the rain pelted saturating his entire body leaving his situation more miserable but just when he thought he couldn't take any more, he remembered how the unique characters he encountered just seemed to appear at the correct place and time.

Especially the crazy road digger and his philosophy, and the loving couple who sheltered him for the night. Dave felt that in a way these people were all angels sent to uplift him, to guide him, and to protect him from all the elements of life. There were seven of them in total, the 'man mountain' road digger in the Kerry village, the two rough looking characters driving to Limerick while he slept in the back of their car, the van driver who took him to the midlands, the truck driver who ferried him into Dublin, and of course the couple, all helped along the way.

Before long he was speeding towards his home town with another driver who decided to assist in the last leg of his intrepid journey and unknown to him a rebuke was being bestowed on his girlfriend and mates from their larger circle of friends for leaving him stranded so far away from home. However after his initial anger and a little self indulgence with all this sympathy, Dave just got on with life, not being a man to seek retribution. His philosophy was always to forgive even if it took longer to forget.

Love on the Rocks

Dave and Cath continued their rather stormy liaison, meeting just at the weekend in Images Bar on the strip. There was no intensity, no passion whatsoever attached to their relationship and it could be said that they were only friends through alcohol. This suited Cath who was far from being romantic, which is unusual for a woman. She also had no ambition to better her status in life but was prepared to work for Jane for the rest of her life although she was being used, not even being a registered employee and had no welfare entitlements. Taking a day off, even if ill, was not an option because if she didn't work she didn't get paid and it was a difficult life that Cath resented and which caused a deep festering ulcer within but she would never do anything to upset Jane. Cath had no confidence in herself, no self worth and the cause of this was being treated as a subordinate, first at home then in her work place. This was her station and she accepted it because she lacked the courage to change. On the other hand Dave was a happy-go-lucky guy with ambition but never landed a good job and had to opt for menial tasks. He continuously attempted to better his status, often re-educating himself and always on the lookout for the elusive, well paid job, however it never came. Dave left school early to seek an apprenticeship to become professional in a trade but this never happened for him. So he opted to seek employment in the best paying jobs around, the two large breweries, the cigarette factory, and the multiple shoe factories in his home town but this didn't happen either. He was frustrated at first with his lack of success after attending several interviews with each of the businesses, having his hopes dashed even though he would be selected in the last five for the job.

He loved Cath but not in a romantic way and he thought that maybe this is what partnerships in the long term needed to be like to survive. He was in love before when his heart would skip a beat when meeting his girlfriend but this was different, because with Cath, well, it was like meeting one of his buddies. He enjoyed her company and even being alone with her but never wanted to rip her clothes off and make mad, passionate love. No, she didn't affect him in this way like other females did and this was a problem but he didn't recognise it.

The courthouse foyer got busier now as the wigged barristers scurried about frantically endeavouring to do last minute deals with their client's futures. Dave wondered why or how they didn't slip on the gleaming polished floor but sure if they did they would be in for a big financial windfall with compensation with the right legal advice and representation. He smiled to himself as he caught Cath glaring at him from the background of her legal team, her brother, and sister. They seemed to be constantly engaged in legal wrangling, debating while Cath just posed in the back as if she was an observer and not the accused.

Dave remembered this well, going back to their stormy relationship, when after three years of drinking together he decided to make it a permanent arrangement. He took the courage and asked her to get engaged to be married and set out a plan for this to happen but he knew quite well that he would have to take the reins as Cath would just sit back and let things happen. This was because she was used to people doing things for her in her life, deciding what is best, and in fact taking control of almost everything. Now Dave was not like this as he felt that it was like caging an animal and not allowing it to be free, to be as its purpose, but in this case he had to act or else they still would be meeting up in twenty years time just for their weekends of drinking.

He did all the romantic things though; asked her mother for her daughter's hand and she said yes but cautioned him that he could not leave her back. Dave laughed at the idea but thought, did she knew something he didn't? Why would he want to leave her back? However he dismissed the very thought and when he and Cath were alone, popped the question. Her living room was dark, lit only by the light emanating from a dim lamp in the kitchen and there was soft romantic music in the background: Foreigner's 'I want to know what love is'. The scene was perfectly set and Dave got down on one knee, looked into her eyes and took hold of her hands.

"Honey, we have being going out for three years now and I think it is time!" He paused momentarily as she looked uncomfortable.

"I think it's time we made this permanent and if you would do me the honour and marry me?"

Cath took a deep gulp of air before finally smiling and nodding her head.

"Yes I will"

They embraced and kissed passionately!

He could see tears in her eyes and gently brushed them away as he again stared into her eyes.

Engagement

The day finally arrived for Dave and Cath to go to Dublin to get engaged to be married as was the tradition in their hometown, fifty miles north of the capital city.

Dave awoke early and the greyness of the sky couldn't dampen his enthusiasm for what lay ahead. His mother and sister were up before him and made him breakfast but he preferred just to have tea and toast. They were more than excited for him but he missed a big brother or fathers chat of reassurance that he was indeed doing the right thing but unfortunately he never had this and went blindly ahead with all plans in his life without a male mentor or point of view.

Cath was late arriving, as usual, which made Dave fidget and feel anxious that they would miss their train. Cath's arrival was announced by the hooting of her car horn and Dave went to the front door accompanied by his mother and sister. The embraced each other and Dave noticed tears in his mother's eyes.

"Well the best of luck to you Dave"
Mary said as she embraced him.
"I hope everything goes well for you today son".
"Thank you so much mother, you are not losing a son but gaining a daughter".

Dave then went down the short pathway to join Cath in her car but he noticed that she was in bad mood.

"Hey what is the matter? Are you having second thoughts"?
"No it's not that; I just had words with our Paula".
"What the fuck was she on about now?"
"Oh it doesn't matter, I will be fine".

Cath brushed a tear from her eye and began to drive to the train station and what Dave didn't know was that Paula, who was immersed in the thick, green slime of envy from an early age, had upset Cath greatly, on what was supposed to be one of the happiest days of her life.

Dave just couldn't understand jealousy in any form and cringed with its exposure, especially between siblings. Paula wanted and needed to be first in everything to do with her older sister. She needed to be first to have a boyfriend, first to get engaged, first to get married and first to have a baby and if this didn't happen then the green eyed

monster would appear. So with Cath being first to get engaged, Paula's green claws struck Cath in the cruellest way possible.
They didn't speak much on the journey and arrived in Dublin's Amiens Street Station one hour later. They walked hand-in-hand through the city and arrived in Angier Street where the recommended jewellers were situated. They looked in the shop window and Dave wondered what kind of ring Cath would choose before clumsily entering. Dave had a word with the assistant not to show any rings costing more than five hundred pounds and this was strictly adhered to. Cath browsed through many trays before choosing a single solitaire diamond ring that was fifty pounds under Dave's budget and both were extremely happy with the choice. Dave had a discount voucher given to him by Cath's brother which made the purchase less severe on his pocket and he could have some extra cash for the celebrations.
Dave then took Cath for a sumptuous lunch before meeting up with her sister Freda and her husband Dan who were both bartenders and lived in the city. They were great fun and Dave liked them and their attitude towards life. They were married many years but had no children although trying and this made their married life incomplete. The drinks started to flow, beginning with the customary champagne for celebrations and both Cath and Dave enjoyed their company so much that they missed their scheduled train to return home and also missed two later ones.
Finally they said goodbye to Freda and Dan and made their way to the train station four hours later than planned but they were happy. Then on the journey home they threw coins into the Boyne River at Drogheda as the train passed over the viaduct because it is tradition for good luck. When they reached home Cath drove into town and Dave only then realised how inebriated she was as she navigated the roundabout at the police station the wrong way round.

"Honey you went the wrong way round the roundabout"
"Oh did I?"

She proceeded to do it again so Dave decided to say no more for fear of what she may do next. He thought to himself that a journey with her may not be overly exciting but it will always be eventful.
They entered their local bar on the strip where their families and friends had gathered for the celebrations and this continued until the small hours.

The following week, when the revelries were over, they opened a joint bank account to save for their wedding. However only one lodgement was ever paid into the account much to Dave's dismay and this was because Cath expected that he pay for everything and just couldn't understand her approach to this very important element of their future together. He knew that Cath was very miserly with money and would let him spend everything he had on her although she had money in her purse but now she was not willing to save in a joint venture. This disappointed Dave very much and a row ensued over the issue but Cath just laughed it off leaving him to wonder if she was serious about spending their life together as partners in all things but she seemed not to want to share and Dave realised that this was a major problem for their future together as a couple. Sure he had to go and collect her from work to open the account which she did reluctantly but now she just wasn't prepared to continue paying. He eventually figured out that she was of the mindset that 'what's yours is mine and what's mine is my own'; this is an old adage.

A very old couple who were married over sixty years came over to Cath's house one evening to congratulate the newly engaged couple and when asked.

"What is the secret of a lasting marriage?"

The frail, grey haired lady with sparkling blue eyes turned to Cath and said

"Remember this, my dear"; "A well fed dog doesn't stray!"

Dave thought what wise words but would Cath remember them?

Noel's Big Day

Dave's mind was in turmoil as he waited patiently in the foyer of the courthouse; this most non aesthetic of rooms where evil begets evil and the innocent can be victims for a second occasion. He thought how sad is this, that society, and in this case partners, have to throw themselves down at the mercy of the law of the land allowing complete and utter strangers to decide their future with one stroke of a pen.

There was no crime committed here, so why do people have to engage a legal team and let a judge decide on their married life, who is right and who is wrong, and then the future of both parties? The judge only listens to the testimony of both parties for maybe half an hour; half an hour to view a marriage, half an hour to decide the future of everyone concerned but his decision can destroy lives of one or both parties, their families, and their children.

Dave pondered the power that this one man had and wondered how he could sleep at night without nightmarish visits from the innocent victims who come before him cap in hand expecting a fair judgement, the women, the men, the children, and their families. What if he gets it wrong? If this happens, he is responsible for unseen hardship and suffering by one stroke of his pen.

Dave shuddered at the very thought but now was joined on the bench by two ladies from another town who were attending for the same reason as he. Both were nervous but determined to gain justice and a legal resolution to the defunct marriage. He could see that the lady was very angry with her partner as he didn't even bother to show up for the hearing.

> "Hi there, I take it you are here for a marriage break-up; what happened with you?"
>
> "Ah don't even mention it! I was married to this bastard for five years and he was screwing around with every girl he could get his hands on". "Our marriage was like a big joke to him and he even tried it on with my friend here."
>
> "Oh feck, that is hard to take."
>
> "Well I am going to take him to the cleaners for sure."
>
> "Ah OK I wish you luck".

Dave thought, well at least there is no one else involved in his marriage break-up, on his behalf anyway. But he wondered if Cath felt the same anger as this lady sitting beside him? He glanced over to see that her brother Noel and sister Paula were still engaged in debate with her legal team while she looked on. The realisation then struck him that he was very alone with no support from him family or friends while everyone else there had someone to lean on at this very traumatic time in their lives.

Dave remembered one Christmas when he bought presents for all of Cathy's family at home. He worked in a shoe factory at the time so he bought them shoes that he made there and while her mother and brother Noel were delighted, her sister Paula opened the shoe box, peered in and said.

> "They are awful and old fashioned and I wouldn't wear them"

She threw the box aside as the last syllable left her bluish evil lips but Dave paid no heed to her insults. However he did notice that he seldom or never got a present in return from her family. Now these very same people were here in this courthouse determined to bring him down no matter what.

Dave's mind then roamed back to the time when Cath's brother Noel was getting married to his beloved partner Nicola and everyone was agog with excitement. The ceremony was performed in a beautiful little seaside village, an ideal romantic location just outside town. The church was high up on a hill overlooking the sea with breath taking splendid vistas of the Cooley and Mourne Mountains. The day went off smoothly without any major incident much to Dave's surprise and a great time was had by all.

Noel and Nicola moved into the home house with his mother and sisters while his own house was being build and this would save the couple vast amounts on renting an apartment although both had high paying jobs in the civil service.

Dave like both of them equally and could tolerate their unique idiosyncrasies much of which he admired. Both were clever and level headed and complimented each other just like partners should. Nicola kept a close eye on Noel because if left unleashed he could become wild and go mad on the drink but she was always there to reel him in.

One time when Dave was on only three days work, he offered to decorate Cath's mother's house. He began on a Monday, Cath's day off work, and he began stripping the wallpaper in the entrance hall and the living room. Then when he began to hang the wallpaper Cath says

"Here that is not straight"

So he took it down and redone it but still she was not happy so after five attempts he got the strip of pasted paper and wrapped it around Cath's body including her head. They both laughed hysterically with this action but Cath decided to leave Dave alone to finish the work. He papered the hallway, the living room, and he even tiled the kitchen in part.

Noel arrived home from work as Dave was up a ladder fitting the wallpaper and says

"Wow that's a great job you are doing there"

"Ah thanks Noel". "Glad to be of service".

"But you're a fool because you will get no reward or thanks for it".

Dave was shocked by the statement and put it down to maybe he is just in bad mood after perhaps having a row with someone in the house; or could it be that he was giving him some insight into the real core of the family? Dave was unsure and just dismissed it as a rash statement but Noel was correct for he was never offered any reward of any kind.

Broken Arrow

Dave and Cath continued with their stormy relationship and nothing changed at all even though now they were engaged to be married. They didn't save money and had no date set for the wedding and Cath seemed so complacent about the whole thing. Dave wondered if she just got engaged to brag to her friends because she refused to save and talk about their future, preferring to sit back and let him do all the saving, planning and she would just go along with it. But Dave figured partnerships should not be like this and that both must be involved in everything together. So with her being so hoity-toity and her devil-may-care attitude, he began to act the same way and carried on meeting her only at the weekends for drinking sessions. He realised that he was getting nowhere with her and felt he shouldn't have to coax her into action as it was like pissing against the wind. He remembered the old adage of 'You should never try to teach a pig how to sing; you are only wasting your time and upsetting the pig' and so true especially in this case.

They had many fights, all because of drink and one time she even snogged a friend of Dave's behind the couch in her friends Dara and Hattie's house with Dara encouraging it. Dave went into a fit of rage and left but he never liked Dara after this. Cath always portrayed a person who was a push over but she was far from this.

Then one sunny summer's day on a Sunday afternoon, when Dave had Cath's car as she was too intoxicated to drive home the night before, he was to collect her from her house at three o'clock but he didn't arrive out until nearly ten after three. He tooted the car horn and waited as he planned to take her out to the beautiful Cooley Peninsula where mountains and forest sweep down to the azure blue waters of the majestic Carlingford Lough but by the look on her face he wondered if this would happen. She opened the door and slammed it shut.

"You're late"

"Well that's some greeting". "So what the heck is wrong with you"?

"If you don't know I am not going to tell you"

"So I am supposed to be a mind reader now, am I?" "What did I do wrong on you?"

"Ah just feck off and leave me alone".

Cath continued to rant and rave and Dave did not know what it was all about and wondered if it was just a bad hangover or a row with her lovely sister but he decided to say nothing as there was no point. She was angry and he was not the cause of it but was getting all her frustrations offloaded and on to him. Then while driving he caught her with the corner of his eye pulling her engagement ring off in her rage and throwing it at him. He slammed on the brakes and the car shuddered to a halt about half a mile from her house. He stuck his hand out the opened window in an attempt to catch the ring but failed miserably.

"You know what?" "You are a fucking bastard and a conceited, mean, selfish fucking bastard at that". "Now look what you have done".

"Oh my ring, my ring" Cath shouted out as she opened the car door and got down into the gutter to find her precious ring.

While she was down on her knees at the side of the road Dave drove away looking in the rear view at this pathetic sight while smiling to himself.

The ring had hit the inside of his right arm which was resting on the opened window sill and fortunately rebounded into his lap but Cath didn't know this and he was not telling. He did not do this in an attempt to teach her a lesson but rather wanted to finish with her for good and she gave him an ideal opportunity.

Dave drove to his home house, left the keys inside, and walked up town to meet his friends. He felt relieved and unburdened and relatively happy that he didn't have to please anyone now but himself.

Cath on the other hand had to eat humble pie and walk into his house to collect the car keys to drive home. The thoughts of being dumped provoked her now and filled her mind with such anguish as she didn't want to be left on the shelf. She agonised over being the eldest left in the family with now having no boyfriend while her younger brother Noel was due to be married that year and her sister Paula was getting married the following year. How could she face life alone? Left alone with her aging mother, tending to her needs as she got older; no, she was determined not to let this happen and cringed at the very thought of being an old maid.

Cath had relationships before which all ended in heartache not unlike Dave's but now she was in her early thirties, her body clock was moving on and she began to brood for her own offspring.

She, along with Paula, lived the high life of the storied profane ugly sisters, trampling on people's emotions without a second thought of consequences just to please their own desires. But she slipped up badly before because she fell in love with a man from the North of the country and held him firmly with talons of steel. Letting her guard down she eventually got pregnant and when the guy didn't want to know she secretly went to England to have an abortion. This was a most traumatic time for her as she didn't want to be known as a loose woman and it would spoil her chances of getting a new boyfriend who would have to accept her child as well as her. So with the help of Jane who sponsored the trip to England, she went off, accompanied by her sister Paula. They made up a bull yarn that they were going on a Fun Trek Holiday across Europe as they had done before so that no one ever expected what their trip was really all about. They even invented stories of events from the trip but these were all events that occurred previously. One of these was an adaptation of the famous song 'Singing in the Rain' that had new words as well as a dance routine so deceit came easy to them and no one ever knew. The song 'Nine to Five' (Titles Morning Rain in the USA) by Sheena Easton was blaring out on every radio station as Cath with Paula went on their mission and she detested the singer and song as it reminded her of a dark time in her life.

Now that Dave was free he could spread his wings and return to a happier way of life but he avoided places where Cath may go as he certainly did not want to meet her. He avoided the uptown strip that he always frequented, preferring to go to a back street bar, McManus's Pub and it was here that he met up with his long time pal Pat but Dave called him by a nickname 'Barney Bluffer'. They were so delighted to meet and like long lost brothers, greeted each with a 'high five' and a man hug.
This was a very old, quaint bar where nothing had changed from the 1940's and evidence of this was that there remained a sign on the glass panel door leading into the bar in bright red writing 'Men only'. Seemingly women were not permitted into bars in olden days but could have a drink in a little room called 'The Snug' and McManus's Pub possessed one of these although women were now welcome unlike the day of yore.
Dave settled into life as a single person with ease and going to the RC Club on Saturday Nights accompanied by Barney, was a must

and it was here that he met up with many ladies and casually going off with them for the night. He felt safe in the knowledge that Cath would never go there although he had often asked her to go. Both he and Barney had great times together, meeting up in McManus's Pub playing darts, engaging in all types of banter with the clientele, and going to the RC Club for the ladies, sure life was sweet for Dave with no pressure what so ever. He had a new job with a company car, sure he couldn't ask for more but one night when he was in the pub his tyres were slashed in an act of vandalism and he just couldn't understand the mentality of people who carry out such deeds. However it was suggested to him that Cath might have something to do with it but he dismissed this as being untrue.
Then one night while at the Club they spotted two beautiful girls who were new on the scene and Dave said to Barney.

"I will take the dark haired lady and you take her friend".

"Right on". Barney replied not taking his eyes of his quarry.
They made their way across the crowded dance floor to where the ladies were standing but in the confusion of the many people there, it was Barney who took the dark haired lady while Dave took her friend. He didn't care at all and chatted to this lady with ease. She was tall, slim and elegant; she had real natural blond hair and sparkling sea blue eyes but most of all she had a great personality and Dave liked her plenty. Then at the end of the evening after buying her drinks, dancing, kissing passionately on the dance floor, it was time to leave her home.

"Wow I never met a real true blond, is it really natural?"

"Of course it is"

His mind wondered with curiosity.

"Are you blond all over?"

Then with a twinkle in her eye she gazed into his eyes and said;

"Well that's for me to know and for you to find out".

Dave was so excited with the prospect that he took her by the hand and went over to Barney where he and his girl were still dancing.

"What's the story buddy?" "Me and Hannah are ready to go now"

"Ah Cynthia has got her own car so there is no problem!"

"OK when you are ready I will follow you both in the car"

"That's great and we are just going to head off now".

They lived about twenty miles away in a beautiful seaside village and Dave followed Cynthia to a secluded car park on the back beach. Here he snogged Hannah, kissing her passionately for an age but they talked for hours on end about everything under the sun. He felt really comfortable with Hannah but didn't want to start a relationship having just finished one, so he kept it casual although he was in two minds.

Cynthia tooted her car horn and Barney came over to Dave's car while Hannah paused for a time before getting out.

"Ah would you look at the two love birds all cosy in the nest", said Barney while looking into the car and with that Hannah gave Dave a final kiss goodnight and got out of his car. Barney got in.

"Here, I thought that I was supposed to ask the dark haired lady?"

"Well with the crowd pushing I was directed straight to Cynthia and sure what could I do?"

"You lying fucker".

They both went in hysterics with laughter but as they drove this soon ceased as Dave ran out of gas fifteen miles from their home.

"Now who is a stupid fucker?"

"Shut the fuck up and think of what we can do"

"Well its pitch black out there and we are miles from anywhere so we will just have to sleep it out till the morning and see if there is a filling station anywhere in this God forsaken place!"

"Good idea Batman".

With those final words they reclined their seats and fell asleep. The morning announced itself in easy fashion with a thin veil covering the early sun and thick dew lingered in the fields surrounding Dave's car as they both awoke.

"Oh fuck I don't like the look of this place".

"What are you on about?"

"Look at the fog coming out of the fields. You would expect Count Dracula to appear at any moment!"

"Will you fucking stop being so silly and come on till we get some petrol or we will be here for the day".

They made their way down to a village about a mile away where they found a filling station open and borrowing a can they got some gas for their journey home.

They both had dates with Cynthia and Hannah and went out together several times. Dave's relationship with his girl got intense and they began to make mad passionate love almost every time they met and they just couldn't get enough of one another. He liked everything about her, slim body, long shapely legs, long straight natural blond hair that he thought looked and felt like silk but most of all she had a personality that gelled with his, like a hand with a glove. He did eventually find out if she was blond all over but had to use his cigarette lighter to do so as the interior light in his car was not working. She had the most beautiful vagina he ever saw and her blond pubic hair was just as silky as the hair on her head so much so that he couldn't stop playing with it. Her labia folds were tight and were a light pink not like the crimson one he was used to seeing. Yes, Hannah had everything that Dave desired and it was decision time for him.

Meanwhile Cath in her effort to win Dave back would go to his house almost every evening and talk with his sister Mary and his mother and whereas they admired her determination not to lose Dave, they were more than surprised with her audacity as she had portrayed a rather shy, unimposing lady.
When Dave would see her car parked outside his house he would go into his neighbours and sneak in the back door until she had gone, never wanting to meet her face to face, not even on his own safe territory.
Mary's friends were bemused with Cath's actions, especially one of them, Stella, and when she would call she would always enquire
"Well, is the stalker not here?"
Of course her announcement was referring to Cath.
In reply to this his mother Margaret said
"Ah that is one determined lady and she will get him by hook or by crook!"
However, Dave wanted to stay well away from her because he reckoned when it's over, it's over and there is no more to be said or done.

The court house began to become more frantic now at the first cases were called and judging by the smirk on Cath's face she was confident of a perfect outcome in her favour. Dave, whose mouth was as dry as unbuttered toast, swallowed hard which distorted his face as he dreaded the thoughts of going before a judge to air all the discrepancies within their marriage. A marriage that he felt was a loveless sham that existed on paper only and as he pondered these thoughts he spotted an old friend Kevin who was a musician in a band that he was involved with. He wondered why he was here but didn't get a chance to talk with him in the frenzy that was happening all around.

However he remembered back to better times, when he met up with Kevin's friend Jordi for the first time as an eleven year old when he was forced to live with his aunt Kate in another part of town. This happened because Dave's father, who lived in England, decided to return home and throw his estranged family out on the street, which had a very traumatic effect on the whole family, especially Dave because he was entering puberty and about to go to secondary school. They had to leave their home with just three bags of clothing, one for each person, his mother Margaret, his sister Mary and him. Whereas all else was left behind but firmly ensconced in their memory. He had to leave behind all his lifelong neighbourhood friends, causing him to feel very lonely as he didn't venture outside his aunt's house because of the trauma and shame that he felt deep inside. Being just an eleven year old child he didn't know how to deal with such feelings and the others in his family were all adult and seemed to just get on with their lives.

When eventually he did venture out after months being cooped up he met this gaunt looking boy who was tall and slim with long curly dark hair and dark eyes. He wore a crimson red sweater with blue cord jeans and sure Dave thought he looked hip. His name was John but he liked to be called Jordi and he lived just two streets away from Dave. They struck up a friendship immediately and he soon discovered that Jordi was big time into music and about to start his own band. They had common taste in music and loved 'The Beatles', especially singer/song writer John Lennon and would sit for hours on end at Jordi's piano singing all their songs.

Jordi went on to form a band called 'Altered Images' with Dave being involved as a roadie. He also composed and staged two musical plays that were smash hits locally but was never really happy with his musical status because he wanted his work to be known by the masses, on the world stage so to speak. He became manic depressive, a trait associated with all men of genius, and Dave would often call to try to cheer him as he sat alone in a darkened room pondering world recognition while he listened to 'Stand by Me'. Now although Dave was his best friend he knew he could not give him what he needed but just tried to bolster up his confidence, for nobody really saw this private side of his great friend and in company he would show a happy-go-lucky type of individual but Dave knew different.

Jordi eventually went to South Africa where he found his niche, composed 'jingles' for television and radio advertisements, performed in concerts where he topped the bill with his own brand of music.

He also found love, got married, and had one child but unfortunately Jordi passed away at the tender age of forty. Dave couldn't believe this and got it hard to take in and mourned his death with heartfelt sorrow but he also celebrated his life because he achieved what he wanted and what he needed to fulfil his dreams, even though it only lasted such a short time.

Dave's thoughts were intruded upon by his solicitor who startled him by announcing

"There are two cases in front of us and then it's our turn"

"Oh Tom is there no chance of a deal with them?"

"No, out of the question, they won't even talk to us".

With that he scurried away to talk with other clients who seemed just as worried as Dave but he tried to relax by thinking of good times but this interruption by Tom disturbed him deeply and thoughts of death at the hands of the legal executioner lingered.

Death be not Proud

The evenings were becoming dark and the trees had lost all their autumnal leaves giving a bare look to the landscape in town. Dave didn't care much for this time of year as it always reminded him of death, death of the summer, death of the year, and made him sad with its passing. He was extremely conservative and didn't like change in any form and now dreaded the thoughts of the dreary dark days of winter, being alone with no steady girlfriend. Cath still came to his house and he still avoided her but her visits became less frequent much to Dave's relief.

November proclaimed itself by spreading a flu epidemic; this was not good for Dave's mother Margaret who suffered from bronchitis that affected her breathing and almost every year of late she would have to go into hospital for rest and for much needed oxygen. This year was no different and as usual she was taken into hospital but it didn't cause much concern as it was normal practice. Dave and his three sisters, Mary who lived at home, Margaret who lived in town, and Brigid who lives in the next town twenty miles away, all visited her each evening.

Dave for the first time began to notice how frail his mother had become because normally she was a sprightly seventy two year old lady who went about her daily household chores with ease. She was always slim but now she looked scrawny and was totally incapacitated, unable to move her tiny frame while just lying there helpless, depending on oxygen to breathe. The thought never entered his mind that she would not recover, although her time in hospital seemed longer, but she did say to him "I think I am bucked this time". He reassured her by interjecting "Mam don't be silly sure you always come into hospital at this time of year and you will be home in no time".

Then one evening they were all gathered around the bedside when a nurse came up and asked for a Mr Kelly and Dave being the only man there said "That's me!" She continued "Doctor would like to see you now". Dave went along with the nurse who showed him into an office where a man with his back turned, draped in a long white coat, was writing at a desk. The nurse announced "Doctor, here is Mr Kelly" But he kept on writing. Then all of a sudden he dropped the pen and swivelled around and proclaimed in a nonchalant fashion "You know your mother is not well. She has terminal lung cancer".

Dave got weak at the knees and didn't know where to look or what to say and inside he was screaming in disbelief. Eventually he gathered his faculties and muttered under his breath "Oh my God" before asking "How long does she have?" The doctor replied "Well we just don't know with these things, it could be three days, three weeks or three months." "I'm sorry" were his final words before he turned around and continued writing.

A disturbing thought hit Dave now as to how he was going to tell his sisters who remained at the bedside. He walked about aimlessly, his mind in turmoil with shock and disbelief at this horrible news but he was determined not to spring it on them as the doctor did on him. He composed himself and went to the door of the ward and motioned for them to come out and go to the waiting room. They did so and when he had them all sitting down he began "I had a chat with the doctor about mam and the news is not good". "He doesn't expect her to get better, she is very ill with lung cancer so assume the worse". The four huddled together and wept uncontrollably.

The whole scene was surreal, like a dream, an unreality because this man in a white coat had told them that their mother, the person they lived with all their lives who loved them unconditionally, was going to die very soon. This was the very time they all dreaded within their minds and hearts because losing your mother is the most difficult part in the life of any child no matter what age they are.

They gathered their composure and returned to their mother's bedside and she did not notice their red eyes or the girl's running mascara as she was sleeping. They took turns to hold her hand and remembered when she took their hand as a young child shielding them with a protection that only a mother can give her child and would feel safe in her strong but gentle hands.

They now tried to return the favour although she may not have known.

The following days and weeks laboured slowly to pass for Dave and he went to visit his mam both in the afternoon and evening without fail. She got no better or worse but remained just lying down and sleeping mostly. Then one afternoon Dave was surprised to see his mother sitting up in bed with no oxygen tubes and she was as bright as a button, talking away as if she had a miraculous recovery. Sure he couldn't wait to get home to tell his sister Mary who was delighted with this great news. But when they went back up that evening she was back gasping for breath, back on oxygen and lying down in a semi comatose state. This sight disturbed the family to a great extent and again sadness filled their hearts.

Margaret's condition did not deteriorate or get any better and she wanted to go home as it was nearing Christmas. Dave went in and asked the doctor would it be possible to take his mother home and curtly he responded "Yes, we can do no more for her here". These words resounded in his mind, breaking his heart as the medical profession were admitting defeat being unable to cure his mother but he also had a feeling of delight that his mother was coming home where she belonged, especially for Christmas. The hospital staff ensured that she was snugly wrapped up against the winter chill while they placed her in a wheelchair and took her to the front entrance where Dave then took her in his arms and placed her into his car. He tried to make light conversation on the journey home but she was not fit, gasping for air, but he knew she was happy to be going into her own bed and surrounded by familiar things and of course the people she loved.

Mary and Dave tended to her every need while family and friends came to visit but the woman was not able for much although she tried. Christmas day came and as much as they tried they just couldn't get into the spirit and the glittering baubles that twinkled seemed to add to their sorrow as the angel looked down on them from the tree top. In the early evening Margaret wanted to get up from her bed so Dave carried her up to their small cosy living room where she sat up on the couch. But, so unlike her, she was disinterested in everything and just stared vacantly while labouring to breathe. Mary put her new dressing gown on, a Christmas present, but the rest remained unopened as she wasn't even fit to remove the wrapping paper, being so weak. She remained there for just half an hour before requesting to go back to bed and both Mary and Dave ensured that she was comfortable but when they came back to the living room they hugged each other and wept in silence for their mother.

There was no Christmas in their house that year.

New year's came and went just like any other day and in the month of January, Mary, assisted by her other sister Margaret, tended to their mother, changing bed clothes and applying salve to prevent bed sores. She told them about strange thoughts she was having that one moment she was surrounded in a hard shell and couldn't move but the next moment she was as free as air and looking down at herself from above. Dave knew that this was the transition period between life and death as he had read about it with people having near death experiences.

He had a new job as a company sales representative which took him away out of town, much to his dismay as he wanted to be on hand and near to his mother should he be needed. Then one day in early February while travelling in heavy snow his car slid back down a steep hill and ended up in a ditch. The crash did not harm Dave but he had to get the assistance of a farmer with a tractor to retrieve his car. When he got back to town he attended the family doctor who signed him off work which suited him as he could stay at home.

Now at this time Mary was staying up all night, every night, with her mother as her condition deteriorated somewhat, leaving her exhausted. So Dave suggested that he stay up as he didn't have to go to work and it would give Mary a much needed break. He prepared for the night ahead sitting on a chair beside his mother's bed in the dark as the light seemed to disturb her and hurt her eyes. She hadn't even got the strength to move onto her side and Dave asked her did she want to shift and when she weakly said yes he gently moved her onto her side. He returned to his seat but every second of that night he breathed with her in unison and if there was a pause he would take a sharp intake of breath willing her to continue.

Margaret stirred in the early morning at seven and her breathing was shallower and Dave recognised this change so he woke Mary who immediately came into the room. "Are you OK mam can we do anything for you?" But there was no reply, only the sound of gargling in her throat as she stared upwards. "Dave, I think this is it"! "What shall I do"? "Go and get Margaret first."

Dave drove out to fetch his sister with his mind blank, like in a trance, but he remained calm and in control. He took Margaret to his house and then went to ring a Catholic Priest and doctor from a call box, as they had no telephone in the house, before fetching his uncle. But when he arrived back his mother had departed this world as peacefully as could be.

Mary and Margaret were at her side when she turned to them and looked, a single tear ran down her face as if she was sad to say her final farewell before entering into the realms of mystery and of the spirit world.

Dave remained calm throughout and busied himself with actions and anything that needed to be done he volunteered immediately. This was the way he coped with his grief but inside he was screaming with the agony of heartache as he loved his mother dearly and would miss her because she was like a mother and father to him as his father lived in England and only on occasion came home for short periods.

The family waked her in the house for two nights and neighbours, friends, and family came to pay their respects with some taking sandwiches, cakes, and biscuits for the visitors which were a great help to them as very many people came.

The day finally came for her removal to the church and for Dave this was the most heart-rending moment as he knew his mother would never come in the door of the house ever again. He wept profusely with this thought as they carried her coffin out the front door where many people had gathered to escort the cortège. Grief and mourning affects everyone in different ways and for the Kelly Family it was a surreal feeling like being in a trance where you just go through the motions without being fully aware as to what is happening in reality. The church was filled to capacity as the coffin was led up the middle isle by the priest who prayed over the remains and informed the congregation of the time of the requiem mass the following day. People queued up to offer their sympathies with the family who braved the heartache inside to be courteous and to thank them. Then when everyone had done their duty the family went home in silence and Dave and Mary went straight to bed as they were exhausted having stayed up for many nights. However they didn't get much sleep as they tossed and turned all night with their minds perturbed with anguish.

Dave and Mary awoke from the little slumber they had managed to take and they were shattered with tiredness and with grief but they had to face another day of sorrow when they would take their beloved mother's body to her final resting place. The events of the past days, weeks, and months had taken their toll as neither of them had eaten or slept properly in all of that time and now it was the final day.

"I am completely wasted" Dave said to Mary in a low hoarse voice.
"Me too and I am all cried out" she agreed with his sentiments.
"How are we going to get through today?" she asked, not expecting an answer as it was more of a statement than a question.

"Ah we will get there; we always do!" he replied, lifting his tone. The church was again filled to capacity for the requiem mass which passed without incident until the final hymn when they were leaving. It was Margaret's favourite 'Nearer My God to Thee' which pulled at their heartstrings and they could almost imagine her singing it along with the choir.

They then walked behind the hearse for the mile or so to the cemetery and when they reached the opened grave Dave and his sisters shuddered at the thought of their mother lying in the cold ground. The priest performed the eulogy and prayers before the cemetery staff lowered the coffin into the ground and a deafening silence enveloped the entire scene for what seemed like an eternity. The hush was only broken by the stifled sobs from the sisters and Dave supported them by putting his arms around their waists ensuring they did not collapse. Again people came up and offered their condolences and shook their hands but there was an emptiness that seemed to take over in Dave's mind. The comforting hands and the gentle embraces: whereas all of these helped, there was nothing that could replace the empty favourite chair where his mother always sat with her loving smile that made his life so worth living but now all this was gone and gone forever. Remembering an old saying that his mother frequently used 'you never miss the water 'til the well runs dry' brought a smile to his face and he figured how right she was. But he now thought about life and death, especially his own mortality, and concluded that surely this could not be the end of a person, or could it?

In the following weeks he pondered this, looking to science as well as religion for the answers but none came easily. He was aware that both were flawed as they were from the minds of men where both relied on theory although science attempted to prove although inconclusive and incomplete. So he had to formulate his own thoughts about God and the hereafter.

His entire concept of God was not one that he learned about in the Catholic school he attended or the church he was required to participate, it was much greater than that. Because he knew the whole conception of God was puzzling, enigmatic and the one thing that has occupied the minds of mankind since they began to think and reason; who and/or what is God? Dave studied and observed the human consciousness and perception of God as creator, manager, keeper and controller of the vast cosmic machine, the entity that is called the universe.

From time immemorial Homo sapiens, thinking man, contemplated life and death and laboured with the question – Why?

What is the logic, the reasoning for birth, life, and ultimate death? Mankind needed to have an answer, therefore even if there wasn't a God it would be necessary to invent one to conclude and to satisfy the human thinking process; of course this was attributed to the great French writer and philosopher Voltaire.

Worldwide all the human tribes had the same concepts and this perception came with the medium of mass communication.

The peoples of the orient had Buddhism; the middle earth had the Bible and the Koran while the peoples of the Americas had the Great Spirit. They all conjured up the same concepts regarding birth, life, death, the hereafter and an entity God that was creator, manager, keeper, and controller of it all.

Then as humankind became more civilised and organised, religious groups were formed with each one claiming to be the true religion and the one correct one to have. Some even took it a step further, stating that all other religions were wrong and worshipping a false God while at the same time branding them pagans and heretics. They set themselves up as the elite religion, going to war with other religious groups, slaughtering each other because they were different. Some groups even killed their own followers because they disobeyed the rules, dared to question the validity of teachings or even had ideas or thoughts contrary to the teachings of the particular group. Being human the groups divided in sub-groups and splinter groups and again all claimed to be correct. But logic and reason contends that they cannot all be right, if any at all. But each has the correct basics that are mainly passed over, never adhered to in full, except by the rare few who have got it right. These people are called mystics!

Dave observed all the religious groups worldwide since the beginning and if all their own particular set of rules are stripped away, there remains just one, one vitally essential rule – to Love. Love God with all your heart, mind, soul, spirit and being; and Love all others as yourself but you must learn to love yourself first.

This is humankind's ultimate target achievement! It should be its only target achievement for the individual, for the group of individuals, for all religious groups and for all the countries on this planet. When this is achieved everything else will fall into place and the only important essence of life will be known, hungered for and everything else will be seen in its true light and what they really are: trivial and insignificant. Dave realised this and with the observance of organised religious groups; none of them preach this as the most important thing in life but prefer to highlight their own religion with their rules as the only true religion and that the others are wrong. Why? Perhaps if they did proclaim Love to be the ultimate thing in life and people learned to achieve and live it then there would be no need for any organised religious groups. Control would be lost and peace would reign worldwide.

In their struggle and quest for comprehending and understanding life and God humankind equated God with all human traits, characteristics and idiosyncrasies, even placing a gender on the entity that of a man, and Dave thought this to be ludicrous.

The supreme creator that manages, keeps and controls the entire universe and everything therein could not possibly be a human being and therefore could not possess human characteristics. But this was their only means to endeavour to comprehend and identify with a supreme being into their thought process. Human attributes in any shape or form are not divine but are entirely human. Thus anger, vengeance, revenge and punishment cannot be attributed to God as these traits are entirely human. God is Love, the supreme entity, perfect and pure in a perfect dimension incomprehensible to the human mind and thought where everything exists in perfect harmony.

The physical world, earth, planet was never perfect but works the way it is supposed to work. God does not wreak havoc on the inhabitants as thought because of some misdemeanour, some sin! No the planet itself spews up molten lava from volcanoes; earthquakes and tsunamis are caused by natural movements of tectonic plates that the land and water sit upon. Hurricanes, tornadoes, typhoons, floods, droughts, heat waves and cold snaps are all caused by the natural cycle of climatic weather. These are all normal, natural physical events of this planet that have been in existence from the beginnings of the earth and not as thought in some religious quarters, punishments from God. Some attributes of human beings and their resulting actions can cause the planet not to function as it should which in turn can be harmful to the inhabitants. Power, greed and selfishness can cause famines, droughts and climate change with the depletion of the ozone layer allowing harmful cosmic and solar rays to enter and go beyond the planet's atmosphere.

How is evil explained by humankind? Again Dave pondered this question and concluded that it is defined in human terms! Evil is the exact opposite of Love! He was aware from science that the law of the universe states that if one thing exists it must have its complete and exact opposite thus if there is light there has to be dark, if there is a plus there has to be a minus, if there is Love there has to be evil. How else could anything be distinguished, measured or derived? Thus if a great good exists, a great evil must also exist. Again humankind attempted to explain this in very human terms which are flawed and contradictory.

They state that the supreme perfect pure entity in the place which is the same – God in Heaven – had a close assistant, an angel who became envious of God's power and being a subordinate revolted, causing God to cast the angel and his followers out of heaven and into a place called hell. This is humankind's explanation of what happened but it is completely contradictory in the following: God is perfect in the perfect place therefore everyone therein is perfect so there could never be an envy, revolution or punishment as these are all human attributes. No, the answer lies in the law of the universe of opposites must exist so if we have God Love we must have Devil Evil as one cannot exist without the other thus if heaven exists then so does hell. But humankind endeavoured to comprehend and explain to satisfy to their logical way of thinking. Human physical beings can only imagine what the spirit world is like and then put it into context with the physical world but the same law of opposites govern both worlds. Hence there is only one God who is perfection, purity, Love who is in the place, Heaven which has the same qualities. Therefore there is only one devil that is in the place of hell and the complete opposite of God and heaven.

The many different groups of organised religion who all claim to be the only one true religion are all following the one and the same God no matter what the call the entity – God, Jesus, Allah, Buddha or any other name devised by mankind and no matter what rites, ceremonies and rules that these religious groups devised which are human, there remains only one rule, one law that is vital to life in both worlds and that is Love.

Without Love nothing exists and that was Dave's final conclusion and he was sticking by it until proven otherwise which he thought most unlikely.

Cath meanwhile was always present although remained in the background but Dave did notice her and behind it all appreciated her support at a very bad time for him.
He couldn't understand her persistence in pursuing this defunct relationship because he felt that love should come easily and if you love somebody you should love all about them: the way they do things, their personality, the way they talk, walk, smell, and of course the way they look, their chosen friends, and the places they frequented; all these things should attract or at the very least be most acceptable to the other person. However Cath wanted to change Dave, especially his outgoing personality, the friends he chose and the places he went. He didn't understand this about her; perhaps she felt threatened by all of these things and wanted him all to herself so she could mould him into a person she really desired. But if she only had knowledge of and understood the old adage 'you can take the horse to the water but you cannot make him drink'!
He for the most part stayed away from places that he could possible meet her, preferring to go out with his old buddy Barney especially to the RC Club just outside their town of Dealgan. They had a fantastic time together engaging in bar games of darts and shooting pool while attracting females by the score. However Barney and Cynthia became more serious and began to date on a regular basis while Dave and Hannah only met up occasionally.
Then one evening Dave went to the RC Club alone and was standing at the bar when Cath, her brother Noel and his partner Nicola came in and got a seat near the dance floor. Dave acknowledge their presence by waving over but then turned away not to be too familiar. However during the course of the evening Nicola came up to Dave and began a conversation with just small talk at first but then she began talking about Cath and how much she missed him. Dave politely tried to change the conversation but Nicola persisted and asked him to go and talk to her but he refused. Then she said " well at least take her out to dance, just for old time sake" and again he refused as he didn't want to give false hope and he certainly didn't want to go back into a relationship with her. However, with all Nicola's persuasion and against his better judgement he went over

and took Cath out to dance and it being a slow dance she held him very close and snuggled into his neck.

Now at this time Dave was very vulnerable with his mother just after passing so he was still in mourning and with his buddy Barney off with his new girlfriend and he being alone there, he let his guard slip and went home with Cath much to everyone's delight, everyone that is except Dave.

However she behaved ideally and never picked a row as she didn't want to lose him again and even went on a three day severe penitential retreat to the island of Lough Derg to pray that they would get back together.

All of this was done not because she loved him but because she didn't want to be left on the shelf, so to speak, as she was thirty four years of age and all of her siblings especially the younger ones and most of her friends were in serious relationships, married or about to get married, so she was not going to be left out. Anyway if she didn't get Dave and was alone she would be left in her house to single handed look after her aging mother and she was determined not to let this happen.

Make Me an Island

The court house became less frantic now as cases were being heard by the sitting judge on the circuit court. It is called the circuit court because it rotates around different towns of a certain district with different judges also being rotated.
Dave wondered did Cath's legal team have one up on his because they wouldn't entertain any kind of debate for settlement this time but on the other hand they were determined not to let it go before the judge at the July sitting. Did they know something that made them so confident of winning her case but it wasn't as if new evidence came to light because it was a civil case where nobody was being accused of anything, so why the change of tactics now? His legal team didn't seem concerned either way and he wondered if they were confident of victory or were they just being complacent? He began to fidget more now, indicating that he had a bad feeling about going before a judge and a familiar sickening sensation churned his stomach into knots as to him, the worse case scenario began unfolding.
Dave remembered another time like this when he went back to Cath after their broken engagement and her stalking him relentlessly. They continued on where they left off but for him it was just passing the time and his romantic interest in her was null and void although she had changed her attitude about their relationship to a degree. Cath was determined to keep him attached by doing things that she never did before and became more romantically passionate without having to be out of her mind with drink. Being a hairdresser she would offer to wash and blow dries his hair in the kitchen of her house while her mother watched TV in the sitting room. The kitchen was an extension built on to the house and access from the sitting room was through an opening the size of two French Doors but it was open plan. Cath would wash Dave's hair in the bathroom and then take him into the kitchen for the blow dry where she would seat him on a dining chair facing the entrance but out of sight of her mother. Standing provocatively with her legs opened and each side of Dave's knees she would begin by massaging his head which he loved and in turn he would seek the opening on her wrap around skirt and tease her by running his hand up and down her bare legs. She would have never allowed this before while sober but now she had a change of heart and was willing to try almost anything for to

please him. The blow drying got really intense when Dave would cup her vulva with his hand causing her to part her legs even more and let out little whimpers of pleasure. He would pull her panties to one side exposing her now saturated vagina and play with her pert clitoris making her squirm and writhe with delight.

This went on continuously but always stopped short of full intercourse leaving Dave frustrated to a degree and he began to think that this was as good as it gets.

The Catholic Church which they all belonged to and were brought up in: their traditions taught that sex was taboo even between married couples. Their belief stance was adamant that sex was for procreation of children only and nothing else, therefore it was never to be enjoyed in any sense of the word because in their eyes in was a sin. So in a nutshell they said yes you can have sex but you cannot enjoy it even if you are married. Men also ruled the roost here and a woman was duty bound to have sex with her husband whenever he wanted and a wife would be admonished by a priest if she failed to allow this and the husband informed him of the fact. This is their rule of conjugal rights but Dave thought that this was a crackpot society driven by a male orientated church that treated females as second class members with no say. Thus according to the Catholic Church, sex before marriage was a heinous crime, a mortal sin especially if you enjoyed it.

But to Dave sex was more important than the church's view and felt it was a celebration of love between two people. It is the culmination of time spent together where intimacy is at its peak after getting to know each other by talking for hours on end about everything under the sun; walking hand in hand where crowds are unkind or alone on a moonlit beach on a balmy evening: the sand tickling your feet but both of you walking on air. Then having a nice candlelit meal with a glass of wine where you do not really notice the other diners because you are focused on the person sitting across the table from you. Their eyes sparkling in the flickering flame of the candle lit room, their pupils dilated, exaggerating their size but never the depth of these jewels, these windows of the soul and mirrors of beauty. Then alone in a quiet darkened room where the only light is emanating from an open fire casting a veil of intimacy and shadows of love where nothing is hidden. Outside the world keeps on turning but you would not notice if it stopped because your mind is so fixed so focused on that special person beside you whose heart is pounding just like yours and your mind is in a swirl of delight. You both undress and get naked but you realise you have been naked all the time with this special person beside you, for you have told them your innermost secrets exposing your heart and soul's most intimate stories but in a sanctified trust that can only be had with your soul mate. This is the ultimate nirvana for two people together in love that musicians sang about, that poets wrote about since the beginning of time and suddenly you both understand what they were talking about, but you, like them, cannot explain it. Then as you lie there quietly gazing into each other's eyes, something else is going on now, the spiritual connection is revealed and each and every cell of both bodies are mingling and tingling with excitement, you can feel it like electricity but you cannot explain. Then that most sacred of acts between two people when their body are united culminating in the ultimate moment of orgasm, the highest pleasurable point known to human beings when the body and mind behave independently of the person. The whole essence of your being is transformed into a quivering mass of uncontrollable enchantment and momentarily, the being is transported beyond the galaxies. For each, the other person came through time and space to this very moment to connect in mind, in soul and in body where two become one as this special time becomes truly eternalised.

These experiences blew Dave away but unfortunately they never happened with Cath as intercourse didn't occur but just a fumble or grope in the dark. Perhaps she was too steeped in Catholicism and felt that it was immoral to have pleasure in sex but for whatever reason she didn't allow it with Dave. He nonetheless thought that the church was nearly advocating a stance of 'wham bam thank you mam'! He also felt that if God created anything better than sex or chocolate, He kept it to himself!

That year the summer peaked in August and Cath and Dave decided to go on a camping holiday to the west coast where they could bathe in the majestic beauty of Keem Bay which was lapped by the waves of the Atlantic Ocean. Dave knew this place well as he came here on one of his first vacations with his youthful friends and now he was here with a lady friend but would she appreciate it? Keem Bay is situated on the western end of a beautiful picturesque mountainous island that is dotted with scattered quaint villages and even quainter people. This is the place where at times the rich and famous visit to get away from it all and where they will not be pestered by fans and in fact their stature will just be ignored by the islanders.

Dave and Cath set up their canvas home on the edge of a sandy beach and freshened up in the bathroom of a nearby bar. It was eight thirty in the evening and the sun was beginning to set in the clear blue sky as they drove to a restaurant near the access road bridge to the mainland. They parked their car outside and while they got out they heard a man call to them. He had an English accent and Dave squinted to see who it was but with the sun setting directly behind them he could only see the silhouettes of a tall slim man with dark hair and a fair haired lady who were waving down at them. Dave didn't recognise them but thought they looked familiar so he just waved back to be friendly and to acknowledge their greetings but as he turned away to walk towards the restaurant door Cath said

> "For feck sake, is there anyone who doesn't know you even in this secluded place?"
>
> "Sure I don't know who they are and they were just being friendly so what's the problem"?

Cath was not too impressed and envied Dave's outgoing personality because she always wanted to possess this quality but remained shy and bashful; however Dave didn't pay much heed at this point in time. They were shown into the restaurant's ante room by a pleasant smiling waitress where the menu was surveyed but just before choosing Dave noticed some photographs of famous celebrities on the walls and asked the waitress were all of these patrons. When she nodded in the affirmative, he asked excitedly

> "Was that who I think it was who are just after leaving?"
>
> "Yes, they are regular visitors", was the nonchalant reply.
>
> "Oh my God" Dave exclaimed, and immediately rose to his feet and quickly made his way to the door, leaving a bewildered Cath alone at the table. When outside he scanned the horizon but they were nowhere to be seen and he disappointedly came back inside to the gaping Cath who immediately enquired:

"What the feck was that all about?"

"Oh God do you not know who that was?"

"No"

"That was Paul McCarthy and his wife Linda, you know The Beatles"!

"Oh right" was Cath's reply and she went on reading the menu as if it was an everyday occurrence. She was not into popular music and was not excited even with the most famous band on the planet. She preferring the Country and Western stuff that Dave didn't appreciate at all.

They enjoyed a beautiful culinary feast with a shellfish platter of lobster, crab and shrimp that were landed that day by local fishermen. Afterwards they drove back to Keem Bay and walked barefoot on the sandy moonlit beach where Dave stared in awe at the beauty of the star studded sky. The only sound was that of the waves falling gently onto the beach. He pondered his own destiny and was Cath part of it as he did not feel true romance with her but wondered if things would change and he could fall in love with her, the kind of love he experienced before with other partners. Of course he ensured that all the all the right settings were in place, the island, the meal, the moonlit beach, but that vital ingredient that his heart longed for was missing.

They returned to their canvas home, kissed each other goodnight but slept in separate sleeping bags. Dave stayed awake listening to the motion of the ocean and wondered what Cath's thoughts about their relationship were. She seemed to be quite content despite her cruel self righteous indignations especially after a few drinks but surely she could not be happy just to go along for the ride just like a barnacle on the bottom of a ship?

The morning was greeted by crimson sky that was highlighted by a pale hazy sunlight and as they walked along the narrow road, they met a local man who proclaimed "Storm coming in". They both smiled and nodded just to be polite but didn't pay much attention and went about their day as normal. So after their morning rituals they drove all over the island to discover many storied places like the lake where a 'Loch Ness' type monster was sighted. They had lunch indoors at a small hotel as the weather closed in and the island became dark, wet and windy. Dave noticed while out on a headland that the ocean began dropping about five metres below the rocks and he knew this was not a good sign. In the afternoon the wind became stronger and what they didn't know was that the island was in direct line for the tail end of a hurricane that had brushed against the eastern seaboard of the United States and was now racing across the Atlantic towards them. They hurried back through the driving wind and rain that rocked their car persistently to their canvas home which was just off the beach. Dave half expected the tent to be gone with the wind as debris was flying everywhere but to his amazement it was still there. The sea facing upright poles had bent in half flattening one side but it remained firmly anchored to the ground. He struggled to get out of the car as the gale pushed against the door but managed to do so and he fought against the force of the gale and the rain that was now mixed with grit from the beach. He told Cath to remain in the car as it was too dangerous as he struggled for almost an hour to dismantle the tent and to gather all their belongings and put them into the car. Tired, exhausted, and totally wet through to the skin, they booked into the nearby hotel who welcomed them with hot soup and they were glad to be in comfort and relative safety as the eerie dusk fell.

After tucking into a hearty meal of Irish stew they retired to their room which was small and quaint but comfortable with single and double beds. Cath hopped into the double after undressing in the en suite bathroom and Dave did likewise but chose the single. They sat up and laughed about their adventure in the midst of a hurricane and were in awe of the tremendous power of nature. Cath then asked
"Are you not coming over to sleep beside me?"
"Ah Cath I am so exhausted, I am ready for sleep" he answered drowsily!
"Well then, will you put the light out?"
"No, I can sleep with the light on or on a bed of nails at this minute so if you want the light off, switch it off yourself."
Now with that answer Cath jumped out of bed, much to Dave's surprise as she was completely naked and exposing her half inch nipples and her ginger minge. She teasingly bent down in front of him as if she had dropped something and with that he says
"Ah hold on a minute, maybe I will come over to your bed"
Dave had a quick change of mind and always remembered the old adage of 'never look a gift horse in the mouth' so he unceremoniously jumped from his bed and into Cath's. He never saw her like this as she was so horny that he felt that she could have shagged one of the local donkeys but he was happy to say the least. Why did she have a change of heart about full sex? Was it being away from home, away from friends and staying on the island that made her more romantic? Was it Dave's intimate company both day and night that changed her mind or was it something else? Dave

didn't care because if he was being offered full sex on a plate he was going to take it and enjoy it.

He didn't have to engage in much foreplay as her vagina was swimming and the little man in the boat (her clitoris) was almost drowning as he placed his index finger inside to massage her g-spot. She moaned and groaned like she never did before and he mounted her like a rodeo star on an eager filly. The intercourse was so intense that the hurricane outside could have come into the room but they would not have noticed as he lunged with all his might plunging his stiff erect penis deep into her pussy. He was so strong that the headboard keep crashing against the wall, forcing Cath to put her hands up to hold it but then with a mighty scream of ecstasy she heralded a tidal tsunami wave of sperm filling her up as Dave's penis throbbed relentlessly making both of them quiver uncontrollably as they climaxed together.

"Wow that was great!" "Now why can't we do this all the time?" Dave asked excitedly.

"What's seldom is wonderful" Cath retorted, going back to her usual self.

"But did you not enjoy it"?

"Yes it was OK"

Dave was disappointed but did ask her for a repeat performance right away thinking that this may have been a one off never to happen again. However she answered in the negative but also said "I promise I will do everything for you once we get married!"

He was shocked with this as marriage was the last thing on his mind as he wanted to feel real love inside and be happy in the company of his partner. He wanted to feel real love coming from his partner not just in words but in actions but alas for him Cath was not doing so.

Do you take this Woman?

Dave looked over, across the now almost deserted courthouse foyer, at the smirking Cath, smiling like the proverbial 'Cheshire Cat' who got the cream. She liked what she was hearing, that everything was going to be alright and would work out in her favour and for her this was mission accomplished. He recognised this smirk from before as everybody was panicking and doing everything for her while she lay back and just let them get on with it.

Dave remembered back to the time when they came back from their island holiday where they had found closeness alone together but this all changed now and their normal relationship of weekend drinking buddies resumed. It was if the holiday never happened and there was no intimacies save for gropes in the dark after a night on the booze where Cath would just lie there and be pleasured by Dave but she always stopped short of full intercourse.

Then six weeks after coming home Cath asked Dave to meet her at lunch time on a Friday and this was a new thing to Dave. He felt excited as he thought that Cath wanted to spend more time with him and not just to drink.

They met in the darkened entrance hallway to Cath salon and she looked paler than normal but Dave put this down to her having a black coat buttoned up to the collar and the absence of make up. They greeted each other with the usual profanities before moving across the road to the hotel to have lunch. Dave noticed that Cath was pensive and only quietly answering him if at all so he asked

"Is there something wrong?"

He just had the words out when he thought that maybe she wanted to break up with him and this is why she asked him to meet at lunchtime. He was prepared but would have to act sad so as to not let her see his true feelings and whereas he cared for her but felt he did not love her in the proper sense of the word. She then quietly uttered

"I am late"!

"Late for what? The last bus home? The Train to Dublin? Late for what?" Dave was puzzled.

"It's not funny, my period is late!"

"Wow so is mine, it must be the bad weather."

"I am serious."

Cath looked directly into Dave's eyes and he could see that she was indeed serious as she began to fill up so he immediately moved closer to comfort her and to reassure her that everything would be alright. He went into automation and asked her to go to her doctor to confirm the pregnancy and she agreed but she wanted to attend a different doctor as she felt ashamed and uncomfortable to even broach the question with her long term family doctor. Dave again didn't find this to be a problem and said that afterwards they should decide what to do next. Cath now brightened up a little knowing that she was not alone but had the genuine support of Dave who she knew would look after her. He left her back to work not even touching his sandwich as food was far from his mind. He kissed her on the cheek reassuring her again that everything was going to be alright as he walked off. Cath was delighted with his reaction to her news and felt that she would be married to Dave sooner than she could have ever have imagined. Now she did not have to face the prospect of being left on the shelf as a thirty something single person that lived with her mother for the rest of her life and this was something that she was determined not to let happen. She knew Dave better than he knew himself and if she was pregnant he would marry her and look after their baby out of duty if for nothing else. Dave walked in a trance like state oblivious to the people he encountered and to his surroundings as he contemplated the predicament and what his next move should be. He found himself at the back of a church and whereas he was not overly religious, he always turned to God in a crisis and he needed him now more than ever before. He prayed for guidance to do the right thing but if he was going to be blessed to be a father, so be it and he would try to be the best father ever. His mind wondered back to two months previous when in Keem Bay where one single act of union between him and Cath resulted in the miraculous; for he felt that the creation of a baby was indeed a miracle and he was ecstatic to be part of it. He remembered the ultimate point of climax when every fibre of his being shuddered as if he could feel every one of his twenty three chromosomes leave his body in the seminal fluid, entering into Cath's body where they swam relentlessly until they found the ova containing her twenty three chromosomes and the strongest sperm, the most microscopic of entities was allowed to enter. Then the twenty three unite to become forty six and miraculously a human being is created. Wow these thoughts blew him away and he thanked the good Lord for allowing him to experience it. The joy overwhelmed him now and he wanted to shout out as if he had scored the winning goal in a cup final but restrained himself in the company of God but was elated with the prospect of being a father. He then ran over to his office where he looked up the telephone number of a doctor and made an appointment for Cath; it was to be later that evening and he just couldn't wait to tell Cath who agreed to leave work early.

Dave looked around the packed waiting room wondering if any of these patients had the same joy that was bubbling up inside him and allowed himself a pleasant smile. Cath was more nervous, flicking through a magazine not taking in any of it content and the wait seemed like hours to her, leaving her more agitated. Finally she was called into the doctor and Dave held he hand, gave her a kiss on the cheek, and wished her good luck. She was only gone in moments when she had to go to the bathroom to provide a urine sample and when she eventually came out didn't give anything away from her expression. He arose and they went into the hallway and he said excitedly

"Well, well, what's the news?"

"It's positive and I am pregnant."

"Wow, I am going to be a daddy, and you are going to be a mammy whoopee"

With that he held her in his arms and swung her around in a joyous dance that from on high as he felt that in heaven too they were rejoicing. Dave vowed from this moment on that he would be a good husband and father no matter what although he was not prepared for this eventuality. He had no savings and no assets except for himself but he had a new job that he could earn a good income and this was vital for their future together. Being ever the gentleman he formally asked her to marry him and she accepted excitedly as if this came out of the blue. He was determined to make a go of this marriage despite his reservations about Cath's true personality and her outlook on life but he was willing to put these issues aside to concentrate on the more important concerns facing him now.

Cath was delighted to have landed Dave and never for once thought that he was only marrying her because she was pregnant. She was also delighted to be in the family way as she was in her mid-thirties and her body clock was ticking fast so action was needed and her mission was accomplished. However her being in love with the idea of a wedding for which she was able to boast to her friends, being a wife and mother, she never really put much thought into the realities of the status. These were the furthest things from her mind, she was getting married, she was going to be a mother, and that was it, period so her very own reality cocoon was firmly intact and would remain so no matter what.

Dave went to see Cath's mother privately to formally ask for her daughter's hand in marriage and despite him being nervous she immediately put him at ease and made it a most pleasant experience. She made tea and they chatted for ages and when he was about to leave she said

"Now remember Dave what I said when you two got engaged?"

"There is no leaving her back."

They both laughed out loud and he hugged and kissed her as he had great respect and love for this woman and he knew in his heart that she would never be a problem inside or outside his marriage to her daughter. However on the other hand Cath's dominant sister was a different kettle of fish altogether and she would have major input, influence and interference that would be a challenge to Dave in his married life and he would have to face this constantly.

Cath decided to pick an ideal time and tell Paula her news when they were alone together in their house.

>"Well sis I have something to tell you when you have a moment!"
>
>"Yes and what would that be?"
>
>Cath sort of pretended that she was asking for Paula's permission and blessing.
>
>"I wanted you to be the first to know that I am getting married."

Paula's face turned from a smile to a pale grotesque expression which was fuelled by the ugly green monster of envy that would turn milk sour with just one look. She then proceeded to viciously attack her older sibling.

>"Feck you anyway, this is my year, my wedding, and you are ruining it. Noel got married last year and nobody ruined it for him but now you take it away from me to marry that thing you are going out with! You had this planned all the time."
>
>"Well actually, no. I'm pregnant!"
>
>"Feck you again, I wanted to be the first to have a baby, you are just an old slut."

Cath ran out of the room and went upstairs to the bedroom she shared with Paula. She just couldn't face the barrage of insults being blasted at her, however no matter how much venom that emanated from Paula's mouth, Cath was more than happy to be getting married and for more than one reason. She would be saving face in not being left on the shelf as an unwanted item while her younger siblings got picked and ultimately married as she watched on; but now she could smugly brag to her friends and hairdressing clients. She would now not face the prospect of having to stay at home to look after her aging mother and all that would entail. She was very determined not to let that happen. She sacrificed the indignity of being single and pregnant; taking a daredevil chance that Dave would marry her, and sacrificed the chance of being the recipient of the wrath of her envious sister to achieve her ambition. Now, laying on the bed, a smile of contentment flitted across her face as she thought about how she had played Dave who reacted just as she thought he would and then some. Of course he was oblivious to her whole scheming and in fact everyone was. He also didn't know that he was to be the sacrificial lamb in the wrong place at the wrong time because if it was not him, it would have been someone else for he was merely a component, although a vital one in the bigger picture that Cath envisaged for her future. Cath lay there with a contented smug smile as she listened to Paula ranting and raving talking to herself in the kitchen downstairs. Yes for Cath it was mission accomplished and nothing or no one was going to upset her objectives.

Meanwhile Dave's family greeted the news with joy and excitement knowing that their baby in the family was finally going to settle down in life even though they had very little time to prepare but this would not be a problem. They crossed each bridge as they came to it and this was a time of celebration that created a real buzz in the entire family.

Now with everyone informed of their impending wedding it was time for preparation and organising the church and priest, bridesmaids and best man, guests, and function room for their wedding reception. Everything was happening so fast because they had only six weeks to sort out all the arrangements that Dave didn't get time to think of the enormity of the situation and his future. One vital item was where they were going to live so he sorted out a mobile home and Cath's boss Jane allowed them to site it on a piece of unused ground near her home.

When the dust settled, Dave began to worry about his sister and her child as he was leaving them alone in their house without a man present. He knew she was strong but she felt more secure with Dave being there and they supported and relied on each other especially after the death of their mother. He pondered this new life as a husband and as a father with wonderment but never for one moment thought it would be with Cath because after the broken engagement he was not going back to her. However he was resigned to the fact that he was going to be a father, the best kind that a child could have no matter what.

The day and weeks trickled by with his priority being wedding success so he threw himself headlong into the effort but snags began to appear and definite cracks became obvious in his plans. Cath was insistent than no children would attend the wedding and Dave had to fight hard with her to agree to let his sister Mary's child Terry come. Cath could be so stern at times but always unseen by others.

  "No children are coming and that's it."
  "Well Terry has to come; sure he is like a kid brother to me"
  "No! If we let Terry come, all my sisters will want their kids to come."
  "For feck sake Cath he lives with me and I want him there."
  "We will see."
  "Listen madam he is going and that's it. You can sort out your sisters."

Dave didn't understand this family at all as he never experienced such rivalry, such jealously among siblings but it was true that Cath's sisters would object strongly that their children could not attend. They used them as a showcase and bragged about them, boring the unsuspecting listener until they were nearing suicide. Dave was delighted he hadn't to deal with them as he had enough troubles of his own. Cath also decided to scrutinise the guest list, especially Dave's, and objected to many of his intending invitees. One in particular was a close family relative who was a dear who didn't attend functions as such but was always thrilled to be asked. However, she was a definite 'no' from Cath for whatever reason which left Dave very troubled as he felt that Cath was being unreasonable and rejecting his family and friends. He sat in his sister's house almost in tears after she questioned almost every single one of his guests, belittling them in no uncertain manner. Not one of his work colleagues were invited although all of hers were, along with some of her clients. He was so embarrassed about this because his supervisor was being used to take Cath to the church in his car. Dave thought to himself 'what the hell am I getting into with this woman that I do not love in the fashion of an intending groom and bride?' But he promised that he would stand by her, marry her and be the legitimate father to their child that he was so looking forward to but Cath was not making things easy for him. He was not happy at a time of what should have been a joyous occasion planning for their future life together and he pondered that if they were at odds with their marriage arrangements so what would it be like for other more important decisions? His challenge about his guests was met with equal hostility and whereas he never backed down, Cath got her own way and if Dave had thirty invitees Cath had ninety. Of course this was unknown to him at the time! She held all the trump cards, all the wedding invitations, so every guest had to go through her.

He decided to just concentrate on his own part of this sordid affair and happily arranged his stag party which was a night in his local, McManus's Bar, that was just off the main thoroughfare in town. Everyone was invited, all males in his family as well as all his friends, to this evening of singing, frivolities and of high jinks where almost anything was acceptable. One of his friends had a guitar and he belted out songs from Billy Joel: Uptown Girl, Just the way You Are, Always a Woman and Vietnam among the many other renditions. Then at the end of the night in the bar they descended upon a late opening Chinese restaurant where they had more alcohol along with their meal. Dave, who was shoeless as they got mislaid in a stunt striptease, was in his glory and so happy to be among friends who were celebrating just for him. When they had finished their meal John, Paula's fiancé who liked to organise things when Paula wasn't around, went up and was speaking to the Chinese owner and for some reason Dave thought that he had paid for all, so he went up and thanked the owner for his hospitality and the lovely meal and left with his entourage. However, the meals were not paid for and the owner didn't speak good English so no one ever knew what really went on in this man's mind.

The six weeks went by so quickly that Dave couldn't believe it and when he awoke that morning of his wedding, sat for what seemed like an eternity on the side of his bed. This was actually his mother's bed, the one in which she passed away so his thoughts were deep, would she be happy for him? Would she smile with pride that her only boy and youngest was getting married, starting a new life with a new wife and a child on the way?

The best man Jack called for Dave to go to the barbers for a hair trim and shave and they both felt special being fussed over which was an unusual treat for them. They then got suited up and drove to the church outside town for the ceremony but stopped short to visit a pub as Dave tummy was churning with anxiety. Dave had a brandy with port as suggested by the bartender to settle his stomach and had two more before he began to relax and his abdomen began to loosen.

"Here's a crazy thought buddy."

Dave said without fear of any impunity

"Let's go to the airport now and have a holiday, just me and you like ordinary times."

Jack looked at his not knowing what to say or do and thinking that it was just cold feet and pre-marriage nerves, blurted out

"Go away you header, you are crazy."

But Dave was not crazy, he was serious and felt strongly now that he was making a big mistake, the biggest mistake of his life.

After one last cigarette outside the small church they both went inside taking the top pew on the top right hand side where they chatted. The church was relatively empty and Dave noted that they were early, a rarity on his behalf because he detested waiting around. His mind began to wander as to how and why he got here to this very moment in time and now he felt trapped, frozen like a bunny rabbit in the headlight of an oncoming car waiting for the inevitable to happen. Noticing the altar boys lighting the candles he thought about how he and Cath went out to her parish priest to make arrangements for the wedding and how grumpy and unpleasant he was to them. However he put it down to him being an old man but respected his years and office but when on the second visit he was rude Dave lost it.

"Have ye done a marriage guidance course?"

"Em no father"

"You know you are supposed to do this course or I cannot marry you?"

"Em no father"

"So when do you propose to get married?"

"In ten weeks time, father"

"Oh that's completely out of the question as you have to give at least six months notice and have completed a marriage course"

"But father…"

"No buts and that's it. You know that these 'shotgun' marriages never work."

"What? Do you know what? You are a nasty grumpy old bastard not fit to be wearing holy cloth. Man of God me arse! We could have gone elsewhere, where we would be respected and treated with kindness but we are Catholics and you are rejecting us."

"Well go elsewhere."

"Don't worry we will! Cath, don't mind that grumpy old bastard."

They both got up and stormed out of the parochial house as these final words left Dave's lips. Cath was very upset and crying but Dave was in a rage.

His thoughts were interrupted as he sat there relaxed, legs crossed and arms folded, by the music starting up with everyone standing up. He did likewise and looked around to view what was happening as if awakening from a dream. Cath was presented to him by her brother Noel and she did look good in her cream wedding dress. She could always put on a show for occasions and kitted out just fine and this was no different as her pregnancy bump was well disguised in the folds of her dress! Dave looked at her and she gave a nervous smile revealing the large gap in her two front teeth and Dave thought 'oh why did she have to smile?' As it always reminded him of a claw hammer! However he just took her hand and looked at the ground as she led him to the altar to take their special pews.

This for Cath was a day that she thought would never happen for her, expecting to be left on the shelf like an old jar of stale sweets that nobody wanted and this was despite the fact that she was only in her thirty fifth year. However it was happening now for real and she had a man who was not perfect, not a great catch, but beggars cannot be choosers so she would work on him to mould him into what she wanted. Anyway she had put up with worse things in life: being subjugated at home by her sister, at work by her boss, so she felt she could handle anything. She was determined not to be an old maid left to care for her mother because this for her this would be most shameful while her siblings and friend were all married and having lives of their own. Her thoughts were interrupted only by the priest beginning the wedding ceremony with the announcement 'we are gathered here today..'

The wedding ceremony seemed to go on and on for Dave, and Cath caught him a few times looking at his watch while giving him disapproving stares. His mind wandered more in the boredom of an hour that felt like four, *'gee I wish he would get on with it'! 'I wonder what is for munchies'. I hope I ordered turkey and ham, my favourite!*

Dave was then startled by the resounding question that made him realise he was away in a different place "Do you take this woman?" His mind flipped over again momentarily *'Well no, would you fecking take her?'* "Yes" Dave blurted out. "I do" says the priest. *'Well you said it and fair play to you'*. "What" Dave answered not paying much attention? "You answer with, I do" the priest retorted. "Oh yes, I mean I do" Dave replied with much effort as his mouth was now dry. The next thing Dave remembers was signing the marriage register and he was tempted to write 'Mickey Mouse' but decided not to as his movements were being scrutinised and he would not be officially married if he did so. He recalled one man who was married for years when he discovered that officially he was not married at all because the ceremony was never recorded in writing or was lost somewhere in transit, therefore he and his wife had to make it legitimate by re-doing their vows. Dave decided not to wear a wedding ring for two reasons and one was because his mother would often point to her gold band and say 'Ah the hoop of hardship' so he did want a repeat of her life to fall upon him and secondly he felt that the whole thing was a sham although he would adhere to the vows made and strive to be happy with this situation. After the church ceremony they all drove the short distance to the reception which was held in a bar/restaurant function room and Dave thought about how Cath's old aunts refused to attend saying that they would not lower themselves by going for 'pub grub' and he laughed at the very idea. Photographs were taken outside and with it being so cold not everyone stood for the snapshots preferring to go inside to the warmth of the bar and Dave felt likewise. Cath's clan grumbled and the green eyed monster was evident as Paula and another sister had words which were not kind to say the least and Dave thought *'what the fuck am I getting into'*?

They were all called in for their meal with Dave and Cath as guests of honour being the last to enter to music of 'Congratulations', a song by Cliff Richard and they were ushered to their seats on the top table. However when they were seated Dave noticed the two tables running down adjacent to theirs were occupied by Cath's family on one and her friends on the other. He just couldn't believe it that not one of his family were seated in front of him and didn't know if this was done on purpose, through pig-headedness, or by sheer ignorance. Jane, Cath's boss, and her husband 'numb-nuts' with all their friends occupied the table where Dave's family should have been so they had to go sit away to the side where they could not even see the bridal party's table as there was a large pillar in the way. Dave was in shock and soon began to realise that this day was all about Cath, her family, and her friends and he was just there as a composite part because for a wedding you have to have both a bride and a groom. The top table was occupied by Cath, Dave, bridesmaid Paula, bestman Jack, Cath's mother, and Mary, Dave's sister who was representing their mother. Noel, Cath's brother was also there and who was representing their father but there was no one representing Dave's father. So it was left to his brother-in-law to make his way up from the side table to welcome Cath into the family and Dave was horrified by all of this. He remembered a friend saying about marriage with the Happy Couple 'The Bride and Her Mother' well he thought now that this is so true in his situation with Cath who was just delighted to be married to anyone in fact and her mother who was delighted to be getting rid of her. There was little conversation between Dave and Cath save for words in the form of orders, of disapproval and, of chastisement.

"Make sure Jack reads out all the well wishing cards especially from Jane and Paula."
"Yes OK but there are so many and everyone will be bored silly."
"Listen just do as I say"
"OK OK"
"And go handy on the drink, that's the third pint you've had already"
"Would you ever fuck off and not be annoying me"

Dave was so angry with Cath for her persistent disrespect of him and his family and for telling him what and what not to do. He felt like just walking out, getting into his car and driving away but he stuck it out and looking back he often wonders why! After all he was willing to comply with all the rules of matrimony even though he felt that true love was not in existence with them but he needed help from Cath who would never reciprocate in any manner or form. The words of her parish priest rang out clearly in his mind now 'These shotgun marriages never work' and although the deed was just done an hour before he wondered if by any chance he could be correct? However he put all these negative thoughts aside for he was determined to enjoy this day and decided to party well despite Cath's objections. So when the meal was over and the restaurant staff needed to clear the rooms for dancing he retired to the bar where he caught up with his friends. Barney Bluffer, his two brothers and their lovely partners were his best buddies at this time and he enjoyed the banter with them. It was a great respite for him to be rescued and away from the hostilities of Cath and her family especially her sister Paula who he was sure was turning green with envy and this was something he could not understand. She was raging that Cath was married in the same year as her and what made her rage more was the fact that Cath was pregnant. This gnawed away at her insides making her body and face contort with depravity so now she was determined to get pregnant by any means. Dave tried to imagine the sexual act between her frail one hundred pound body and her three hundred plus husband's bulk and reckoned that she would have to go on top otherwise she would be flattened completely in the unholy ritual. Whatever way the act was achieved she was now using a technique that she heard about to ensure pregnancy to assist it on its way and this was to lie on the bed with the bottom of her torso raised into an ninety degree angle so that none of the sperm would seep out of her vagina thus reversing the forces of gravity.

Dave's cousin attended the wedding with his relatively new wife and new baby who was only weeks old, intending just to stay a little while to show their respect for Dave and his family. But when Cath and her family saw him with the baby the green eyed monster raised his head again and angry grumbling began to spurt out of the mouths of the uncouth especially Paula who approached Cath.

"I though we agreed that no children would attend"
"Yes that's right"
"Then why is there a child here?"
"Where?"

"Over there with some relation of his"
"OK I will deal with it."
Cath called Dave over to remonstrate.
"Here I told you there were no kids allowed at this wedding so tell them to leave now."
"What are you talking about? There are no children here."
"Your cousin is over there and his wife is holding a baby so get rid of them now."
"Ah for feck sake it is only a week old baby sure what harm could it possibly do?"
"I don't care what age it is!" My family have plenty of children and they were not invited so neither is this one"
"But you and your family made these rules for their own sake not for anyone else"
"Just get rid of them"
"Wow you are such a cold hearted person and you pregnant yourself"
"Hush up or somebody will hear you"
"So what if someone hears me, sure it's no secret and nothing to be ashamed of now that you are married and it would be more shameful if they heard what you are asking me to do"
"Well just do it for me, please"
"OK I will have a word"
Dave approached the young couple but had no intention whatsoever to do as Cath asked but rather to thank them for coming to his wedding despite having a young baby to care for.
"Well cousin are you enjoying the craic?"
"Yes it is great and it's a pity we can't stay as the baby won't settle. We would have got the mother-in-law to baby sit but as you can see he won't relax at all. We are so sorry for taking him here but we wanted to show our faces."
"Ah for feck sake you and the baby are welcome here"
Dave took the wriggling baby in his arms and immediately it settled down and began to sleep much to the amazement of his company.
"Well feck me, you are a natural with babies, honey do you see this?"
"I do and I think we will hire him to baby sit in future"
"I have to get used to this as I will be doing it constantly next year"

"Gee are you going to be a daddy as well?"

"Yes it was bound to happen some day sure aren't we great wee beatlers"

The three of them busted out laughing causing everyone to stare and wonder what was going on. Dave handed back the baby and walked them to the door. This caused Cath to smirk with satisfaction but she did not know that Dave had not asked them to leave.

However the wedding reception was a great success despite the annoyance caused to Dave by Cath and her lovely family. They had a band, a cabaret act and a disco and well over a hundred people attended the after meal party.

When Cath and Dave were leaving it was a very emotional time for both of them but for different reasons. Cath smiled with that infamous smirk of satisfaction while Dave wept with feeling knowing that he would struggle with this new situation that he found himself in: married and with a new baby on the way. He didn't feel confident in Cath as a partner, a companion, a wife and mother, or as a lover. He struggled to find solace in this the deepest of anguish as he pondered the future with forlorn. The guests all gathered around them before they said their individual goodbyes and on the way out Dave met his best friend Barney who was also weeping because thinking of the great time they had together from youth until now but this was all going to change, life was about to change for both of them and they realised that nothing would ever be the same again. They hugged each other in a man hug slapping each other's backs for what seemed like ages and neither wanted to let go.

The newly wed couple had booked into a hotel for the night and to then begin their honeymoon the following day. However, when the wedding was over and they arrived at their hotel, Cath's family and friends were there and another party was promptly organised. Dave didn't mind this but he just wished that some of his friends were also told about this as he now felt isolated like a gladiator of Roman times in a den with all the lions.

Then after a few hours of singing and drinking Dave decided he was just too tired to go on and he and Cath retired to bed in the very early hours. There was never a thought that staying up late, drinking, and smoking would be damaging for the baby's health or the health of the mother in fact because this was the mid-eighties and whereas these things were known by the medical profession but were not broadly advertised thus the ignorance of the people in general.

The Aftermath

Dave and Cath spent their honeymoon in the capital city of Dublin and it was a quiet affair compared to the weeks leading up to their wedding. The dust had firmly settled now and the realisation set in that they were husband and wife beginning a new life together and with a baby on the way. Despite this they had no savings and nowhere to live except for a one bedroom mobile caravan home that had to be made habitable, however Dave did not worry and was confident that things would come right as he would now plan their future while Cath had a laid back attitude knowing that Dave would do all the right things.
They moved into the caravan which was located on the edge of waste ground in a field that was owned by Cath's boss Jane. He had it plumbed for water and connected to the electricity supply. It was comfortable and had everything for short term living and the only problem was the entire walls and windows got saturated with condensation when the heater was on.
They both continued with their lifestyles, Dave went to work as a salesman working long hours into the evening while Cath continued with her hairdressing job. She still continued with her nights out with the girls but objected when Dave wanted to do the same, so begun their first married disagreement.

> "What is your problem with me going out with the lads for a night? I don't have any objections with you going out with the girls!"
> "We always did this since before I met you and all we do is sit together and chat"
> "Yes you go out to gossip and drink. Sure how would my night out be any different?"
> "Because I know you and when you go out with the lads you get carried away and don't know when to come home"
> "Ah that was before, but I am married now with responsibilities so that won't happen"
> "I don't believe you but if I agree to let you go out you have to come home at eleven"
> "What! Here, I am not a schoolboy with a curfew and I never will accept that"

Dave didn't understand Cath's attitude towards this and whereas he really didn't want a night out with the lads he was going to have one because of her attitude. He would rather be in the company of his new bride but for some reason she was stubborn and wanted things her own way without any reasonable compromise. Dave was learning fast that Cath set the rules and it was perfectly OK for her to go out, get drunk when she pleased but it was not OK for Dave and being a rebel by nature he would do the complete opposite but he wished that things were not like this. He wished that Cath was not like this and everything would be fine and dandy, but unfortunately it was and this was reality.

There we no intimate relations between them at all what with Cath heavily pregnant and with Dave working long hours he just never thought about it. Then one night Cath went out with her girl friends and came home late and very drunk, she woke Dave and demanded that he have sex with her. His weary eyes opened in fright as he attempted to gather his thoughts of what was happening, Was it a dream he was in he thought but reality struck as the smell of alcohol filled his nostrils as Cath, now naked, put her face close to his. He pulled away as he couldn't bear anyone that close especially with a breath that reeked of garlic, onion and alcohol and one of these alone was repugnant never mind the three mixed together.

"Ah Cath I am so tired, can you please go to bed and we will talk about it in the morning?"

"No! I want a ride now, I am horny"

Cath staggered as her slurred speech left her lips and she fell so Dave rose immediately and put her to bed and wrapped the duvet around her to keep her snug. He was very concerned for her health especially now being pregnant while smoking and drinking to a degree that could affect the baby's well being. He was also afraid to have sex with her as she was now eight months pregnant and just four weeks away from delivery time. The next morning Dave made tea and asked Cath if she would like some as she had just awakened with her eyes bloodshot and mascara daubed in streaks on her paled freckled face. She nodded in agreement and got up to sit opposite him on the table.

"You were in great order last night"

"Why what happened?"

"Don't tell me you don't remember?"

"Well, em no"

"You came home about one o'clock drunk as a lord, stripped totally naked, woke me and demanded sex!"

"I did not! You must have been dreaming"
"Oh I am afraid you did"
"And did we"
"No, I put you to bed as best as I could and slept up here on the bench"
"Ah OK"

Cath was in denial or really didn't remember as she had mixed her drinks of wine and vodka, a lethal combination at the best of times on any occasion but even worse for anyone who is pregnant.

"Honey, do you think you should be drinking so much in your state?"
"Ah I just had a few"
"Maybe a few too many as you could barely walk and you fell down in between the bed and the wall. I had a hard job trying to lift you up from that narrow space as all you would do is laugh and demand sex. I didn't want to hurt you or the baby in any way but you didn't help with the state you got yourself into"
"Well I am perfectly OK"
"Yes, you are now"!

Dave was disgusted with her attitudes and actions as if she couldn't care less about the new life growing inside and this upset him to a great degree because for the first time he was going to be a father and he relished the thought. He would often when Cath was asleep beside him in bed put his arm around her tummy and whisper to the baby growing inside. He would say things like 'I do not care if you are a girl or a boy, we will do things together and I can't wait to hold you in my arms and watch you grow into a man or a woman. I will always be there to love you, comfort you, and protect you from anything in life We will have great times together, you and me, oh I cannot wait'.

He was so looking forward to the big event but wondered did Cath feel the same even though she didn't show it as she maintained a lifestyle that was contrary to a healthy pregnancy. They lived life as best they could in their little shelter away from everyone but both stayed away as much as possible using it only as a sleeping arrangement. This was because the caravan would have been cosy in summer but absolutely freezing in winter and now this is what they faced, cold dark freezing nights coming up to Christmas and if even a slight breeze was blowing the whole place swayed in harmony.

Dave worried about bringing a baby into this environment and realised now how much he missed his parents who could advise on such matters especially his mother with regards to the baby's needs and comfort. He missed the father figure who would advise on setting up home but alas these were all missing and he and his new bride were very much isolated and no one seemed to care as they got on with their own lives. Cath's mother had a three bedroom house and lived alone as did Dave's sister Mary but no offer of help even in the short term was forthcoming although Dave did have co-ownership of his home house but the agreement was that if one got married they moved out and he adhered to this.

The festive season of Christmas with New Year came and went without much fuss and the newly weds went to a hotel for Christmas dinner arranged as usual by Cath's sister Paula but Dave didn't mind this time as it was something new and unusual for him.

February announced its presence with a sprinkling of sparkling white frost that covered the land in a fairytale setting and this heralded the coming of their baby, and for Dave a very special baby. He pondered the miracle of life with the how's and why's; they did not seem to matter now as this new life that he was responsible for was growing inside of his partner Cath. Sometimes when she was sleeping he would put his arm around her and place his hand on her tummy and feel his creation kicking as if to say 'I am here daddy', Then putting his ear in the same place to hear the heartbeat as if to verify this miracle. The feeling of the power of greatness and creativity overwhelmed him now and for the first time in his life he felt connected to the mighty universe and he was surely an integral part of everything that existed. He thanked God for all of this.

Cath felt comfortable in her pregnancy and was able to do the usual things like work until the very final stages. The baby was comfortable also so Cath went a week overdue and the medical staff who were looking after her were showing some concern over this but as the saying goes 'when the apple is ripe it will drop'. However they decided to take her into the maternity unit of the hospital the next week and both Dave and Cath were excited at the prospect of being a mam and dad really soon.

He felt like he wanted to celebrate and Cath agreed so they went out on the Saturday night and had a great night ending with a chicken curry on the way home.

Then on the following Monday they packed a bag for her stay in hospital and Cath said
> "I am really nervous about this"
> "It is only fear of the unknown and just imagine when you come back here you will be a proud mother with a beautiful little baby. Now try to focus on this"

Dave tried to reassure her with his words of comfort and support.
> "But what if…?"
> "Listen Cath, nothing will go wrong and I will be with you all the time so you are not alone in this. We are together as one".

Dave felt powerful and assured because he recognised that Cath depended on him alone and despite her lethargic apathy to romance he thought that maybe their relationship had taken a turn for the better and it had a chance of progressing. Cath did depend on Dave now as she knew that no one, not even her sister Paula, or her friends would be there when she would go through the unknown mysteries and the pangs of childbirth. But everything went through her mind now with the Old Catholic preaching's of punishment and revenge of God lay heavily on her thoughts that she imagined that God would punish her for terminating an earlier pregnancy just before she met Dave. He reassured her in expressing his views that God does not operate like this because He is pure unconditional love not the vengeful one proclaimed by the church. Cath knew in her heart that Dave was a good man and believed all his words of wisdom.

They hugged and embraced for what seemed like an eternity in the middle of their little caravan home, tears welling in both their eyes. Dave then led her to the door and took her hand to ease her down the high step to the little pathway that led to the road. He opened the back door of the car and helped her in and with that Jane, Cath's boss, came running up to the car to wish her luck. This momentarily interrupted their togetherness a feeling that they didn't experience often and both wanted to keep it now more that ever.

Jane had a 'mother of sorrows' expression as she stuck her head into the car bypassing Dave as she did so and uttered profanities about pain and agony and Cath just nodded and smiled to be polite. Dave drove slowly to the maternity unit of the hospital wanting to savour these special moments of togetherness where Cath depended upon his strength that he was so willing to give without condition and whereas she knew that he could not experience her child birthing pains, he would be right there with her to comfort her in distress. They were greeted at reception by a young nurse who was pleasant but professional in her manner and this made them both feel at ease. Cath underwent a general medical examination and sure everything was fine and dandy save for there was no sign whatsoever of the baby making a move to be born. The day passed uneventfully and after consultation with Cath's gynaecologist, the maternity staff decided to induce her labour by inserting a saline drip while encouraged her to walk up and down the small corridor. This was standard procedure and two other expectant mothers moved about slowly with their mobile drips. Dave couldn't help but smile as he thought they looked very funny as they ambled about like the way zombies would walk. He walked along with Cath though and joked to take her mind off her fears in this beautiful little maternity unit that welcomed the very new citizens of the world. It had just seven wards, four of which were private that could be booked in advance under the special care of the gynaecologist who was on call for every patient. Cath decided to go private as it was her first child and she wanted special attention just in case of any complications. There were two delivery rooms and this is where all the action took place, the culmination of nine months of morning sickness, heartburn, cravings, and the awkwardness of extreme changes to the female body with a large progressive swelling in the abdomen that stretched the skin and tested its elasticity. Dave pondered the greatness of women who willingly undertook such a sacrifice that can be filled with discomfort and severe pain to ensure that the human race remains in existence and now realised that this is what makes mothers so special. He thought about his own mother having gone through these events five times but not in a hospital with all the modern technology at her disposal but in her home with the help of a midwife. This brought about joy four times with the birth of Dave and his three siblings but it also brought sadness with the loss of a baby boy who miscarried and he just could not even begin to imagine the heartache of this. However he would have welcomed a bigger brother in his life as he would be someone to emulate and look up to but alas this was not to be.

Cath began to feel uncomfortable in the early afternoon as the early pangs of labour took hold and she decided to lie down. The nurse in charge placed another monitor around Cath's tummy and this acted like a speaker for all that was happening inside, the sound of fluid gurgling and rushing around but above all the miraculous sound of the baby's heart. They both listened in awe while looking into each other's eye in silence and this special moment was only interrupted by another sharp overwhelming pain that caused Cath to turn her gaze to heaven for relief. She put her hand out for Dave to hold and she gripped it so tight that their fingers turned white with the tension. The nurse came in again to check for dilation and decided it was time to move Cath into the delivery room and Dave's mind raced with joyous excitement that caused his own tummy to tighten in knots but he remained calm never showing the turmoil within. He remained focused on Cath, trying to imagine her excruciating pain and he remembered a grandmother telling her young pregnant grandchild when she asked if it was painful having a baby and she, rather crudely, replied that it was like shitting a rather large turnip. This caused a smile to flit across his face momentarily as he waited outside the delivery room. Cath was in a panic inside and insisted that she wanted her husband to be there with her so the nurse came out and asked him if he felt strong enough to come in as she couldn't cope with two patients at the same time where priority would be with the mother. He nodded in agreement and said he would be fine and followed her inside. The delivery room was a strange place for Dave and he noticed all types of surgical instruments in glass cases whereas Cath didn't see any of these as she was stressing and in pain. There were large chrome coloured thongs not unlike the ones used for lifting food of a barbecue but stranger still was a large clear bottle type contraption not unlike what cowboys used to drink whisky from in the old wild west movies. This bottle had two rubber tubes protruding from the top and at the end of one was a suction cup while the other one had a soft oval ball that could be depressed by hand. Dave thought these to be rather crude instruments for this modern day with all the technology at the disposal of the medical profession but seemingly natural child birth remains the same from away back in history.

The indignity of what society frowned upon, a woman naked from the waist down, her legs opened wide, exposing the female secret of secrets, was far from the minds of the beholders. This was much greater than society, their rules and regulations, for this was where time, space, and the universe converged as one entity in the creation of a human being.

Dave looked on in amazement and his logical mind wondered how the contents of the rather large bump on Cath's tummy could possibly come through the rather small orifice of her vagina in comparison? Cath's contractions continued more severely now with the pain almost unbearable but she managed to control her wants to scream the place down. She moaned deeply her head moving from side to side and the young nurse in trying to help said

"Now Cath take control and do not push until I tell you. Use the breathing technique you learned at the ante natal classes" Cath took offence at this remark and for once in her life she hit out in retaliation.

"Are you married?"
"No"!
"Did you ever have a baby?"
"No"!
"Well how would you know what I am going through or what I should do? And where is my gynaecologist? I am paying him enough to be here!"
"He is on his way here, probably stuck in traffic"!

The nurse cowered away and offered no more advice not wanting to exasperate the situation any more than it was developing into as she felt her patient was stressed enough. Cath was in a panic as she had no confidence in the young nurse and relied on her gynaecologist who always put her at ease on visits to his clinic during the previous nine months but now he was missing at this most crucial time when she needed him most. Dave said nothing but just reassured her by holding her hand because they both knew that there was nothing in the world that he could do to remedy her situation and she had to go through this alone even though he was there beside her.

They then heard a whistling sound coming from the corridor outside the delivery room and then entered this man, sauntering in with his hands in his pockets in a brazenly unconcerned fashion. Dressed casually in tweed trousers, brown shoes, and a mustard coloured shirt, he was not very tall with thinning hair and could be mistaken for an oriental gentleman with slanting eyes. He greeted Cath with a smile and acknowledged Dave's presence with a nod and a wink. At first Dave didn't know who this person was and thought that he was just some orderly doing his rounds and was in the process to protest for this blatant invasion of privacy when Cath spoke up.

"Ah doctor you are here at last, I don't think I can do this"!

Dave was more than relieved as he didn't want to have a fight in the middle of this entire strange, surreal situation and even more so when the doctor turned to him and with another wink before turning back to Cath and saying

"Now Cath just relax and we will get this show on the road"
Cath did relax and her anxiety quelled somewhat although her pain didn't but she felt safe in the knowledge that she was in professional hands.

He then got the glass bottle type contraption down from the glass cabinet and still whistling tested that it was in working order before placing it at the opening of Cath's pelvic cavity. He depressed the oval shaped ball at the end of one of the two tubes creating a vacuum and the plunger began doing its job of suction. Dave was amazed that such a simple object could be so vitally important to ensure the safe passage of a new born into human existence. The device was powerful but safe and within ten minutes with Cath pushing and panting for all she was worth a beautiful girl was born and the miracle of life visited all there present. Cath was exhausted but her efforts were not over just yet as she needed to expel the placenta which she did with one last groan. The gynaecologist then cut the umbilical cord before carefully checking the placenta and placing it into a tray. The nurse then took the baby away to clean her up, weigh her, and to wrap her up tightly all the while checking for any obvious faults.

Dave, still in a daze of amazement, hugged and kissed Cath before whispering in her ear

"I am so proud of you"
Cath smiled and was even more contented when the nurse placed their new born child on her breast while Dave's mind raced with joy and excitement. He pondered life with all its highs and lows, the things that make you happy and sad, the time from his own birth to this very point in time and nothing seemed to matter now because he was fulfilled as a man, fulfilled as a human being and nothing or nobody was ever going to change this. He was totally exhilarated with love and joy that ran deep within his heart, his soul, his mind, and his body, a sensation that only the experience of the birth of a child can affect upon a parent. He knew that this was surely the reason for his existence, well, one of the more important ones, and he was even more determined to make things work in his marriage to Cath despite the obvious lacking of the love he would have

wanted. Now he would compromise even to his own detriment and place his fragile dignity on the line in the knowledge that Cath would never realise, appreciate, or care less. Nonetheless he would protect his baby with his love in every way possible and now as he held her in his arms she briefly opened her eyes and snuggled into him as if she somehow knew. Then it was as if all reality passed away out of the delivery room and there he was deep within the universe where only he, his baby, and unconditional love existed. This beautiful moment was only shattered by a distant voice which amplified when Dave and his beloved baby were brought back to reality, back into the delivery room where the nurse was assertively giving instructions to her colleague to fetch Cath a cup of tea and a clean gown after she cleaned up. She, on the other hand would take baby to the nursery saying that both needed rest after their arduous journey and despite his reluctance, Dave handed over his new love to the awaiting nurse.

Cath was immediately taken away to be cleaned up and she looked radiant but contented as she took some much needed sleep. Dave kissed her on the cheek so as not to disturb and then checked their new born from the nursery window where she also slept among the others. He then telephoned everyone within his and Cath's family and friends exuding joy to anyone who would care to listen. Now by this time is was eight o'clock in the evening and he realised that he had nothing to eat all day so decided to go to a café and have a light snack knowing that with all the excitement that he would not be able for a heavy meal. He returned to the hospital at ten thirty to ensure that Cath and their new baby were well cared for in his absence and settled down for the night. The corridor was dark and silent with all the hectic activity stopped for the day and no other baby was deciding to make a new entrance which can occur at any time day or night. He gently opened the door to discover Cath was awake and weeping as her eyes were red with tears. Her sister Paula was present sitting at a distance in an armchair with face that an angel couldn't love.

"Ah honey what's wrong, are you OK?"

Cath couldn't speak but just nodded and Dave suspected that something had happened so turning to Paula said

"What's going on here?"

"Nothing!"

Paula retorted in an undignified manner.

"If I thought that you had anything to do with Cath being upset I would have your guts for garters"

"Well it's just not right" –

Dave cut her off mid-rant and very assertively said

"Enough of that auld shit, now get the fuck out of here and don't come back you old misery"

Paula left slamming the door behind and Dave sat on the bed and put his arms around Cath to comfort her. He knew rightly that Paula was seething with envy and she had to take this green eyed monster out and with venom insulted Cath cutting her to the bone with her vicious words. He just could not get his thick head around Paula's resentment or how she could callously wound a person who was after going through a traumatic time having a baby and what made this worse it being her own sister. She wanted to be the first having a baby with her husband but now Cath and Dave upset her plans and she was livid because now she could not brag to her friends. It was then that Dave realised that Paula didn't want a baby because she wanted to be a mother to express in reality the fruit of her love within her marriage but to have one as a trophy to boast about and to prove to the on looking world that she was not barren but a fully functioning woman. It was for this very reason that she did everything possible to conceive by buying instruments that would detect when she was ovulating and hassling her husband into making love at the opportune moment whether he wanted to or not. She also heard of a method with a better chance of conception by holding her legs up in the air after the act of love making ensuring that all of the sperm stayed inside. Dave felt that this was preposterous, not the fact that someone wanted to conceive but the reason thereof, but he kept this to himself. Paula in her state of spitefulness came especially up to see Cath when no one was about, not to congratulate her but to goad her with wickedness, to make her cry, never realising this didn't solve her own problems. Dave now again ensured that Cath was comfortable and settled for the night's sleep and asked the night nurse to give her something to help her relax. She told him that she had offered this earlier but she refused. Dave assured the nurse that she would gladly accept it now and what he didn't know was that the nurse had already offered Cath a gentle sleeping pill but Paula told her that she didn't need one and sent her away.

The First Angel sent from Heaven

There was a very distinct bonding between Dave and his baby for much defined reasons and not only for the fact that she was his first born but because of their living situation. The mobile home that they shared had only two rooms, a bedroom, and a living room and neither was suitable for a crib. Also when their only means of heating, a little electric fire was switched on, it caused condensation to form everywhere. This was a problem that scared both Cath and Dave but this was exacerbated by cold weather when ice would form on the walls of the mobile. So Dave decided to sleep with the baby in his arms to protect her from the damp and the cold ice on the walls and this suited everyone as Cath got a night's sleep and so did Dave and his beloved child.
They were all as cosy as a family could be and everything seemed good with the world and a true sense of happiness filled Dave and with a contentment that he could live without a doubt. He soon learned to make up formula SMA feed bottles, sterilise everything, change nappies, and dress his little mite in baby grows, vest, and complete with plastic knickers, becoming a 'dab hand' with all of this which was never a problem for him. He even got a papoose to hold her close to him while walking preferring it to the usual baby buggy, so that she faced the world with him and not beside him thus the bonding was complete. This could be the making of his life, his life with Cath if things progressed in the same sort of way where all was shared and Dave was willing and able.
The day soon arrived for the christening in the big cathedral in town and as tradition their best man and bridesmaid were to be godparents so Paula and Jack were down for the ritual. It was a beautiful ceremony and their first born was christened Molly, a name acceptable to both Cath and Dave, however in his mind he would call her his Little Angel.
But no matter what she was titled, love abounds and bonded them in an inexplicable way with their togetherness. Dave wanted to celebrate now and show his child, the fruit of his loins, to the world and to all his friends especially as two of his sisters took the time to be present for the ceremony but Cath had other ideas and preferred just to go home to their mobile. He didn't understand this for a number of reasons because Cath loved to party and never missed an opportunity especially when someone else was paying but now she

portrayed a completely different persona to everyone who all agreed with her sentiments admiring her attitude and seemingly new found responsibility, but Dave knew differently.
This was not the first time he saw her act out a situation nor would it be his last as she learned to be very psychologically astute playing the 'poor me card' with the expertise of a seasoned theatre actress. Her act was oh look at me I have responsibilities and I am not the person you see or you perceived in the past. This was a psychosomatic mind changing con but was Dave the only one to see it? He knew there was an under current, a set reason for this deceptive depiction of her attitude but just could not put his finger on it. She could see that he loved his daughter so much and was she just jealous that the limelight would be taken away for her so she decided to drop a bombshell with this false representation of her true self. This put a dampener on the day especially for Dave because he had arranged a soirée in his local bar with champagne and this would cause him the greatest of embarrassments with no one turning up and he had to make elaborate excuses! However Dave's sister offered a cup of tea in her house and Cath readily agreed so Dave went along reluctantly.

These thoughts came pouring fast and furiously back to Dave as he sat there alone in the chill of the courthouse foyer and a cold shiver seemed to envelope him affecting every atom of his being. He pondered as to why he was here in court letting a stranger decide his life and that of his family when he and Cath could have done this in an amicable agreement? But Cath would not hear tell of any arrangement that Dave came up with because she always thought she would lose out in some way. However Dave was always fair and would compromise with anything having formulated four different scenarios in writing for Cath to consider but she would not agree to any of his proposals. She was also being well schooled in these matters by the sisterhood, a fraternity of divorcees whom Cath made friends with twelve years before and it was at this time that she began to man bully using all the psychological tricks to get her way. This group detested men but used them for free drinks with the certainty of sex at the end of the night. Once when in the bar they all frequented, a friend of Dave's pointed at two of them and asked
> "Hey buddy what about those over there dancing on the floor?"

"What about them?"
"Would you, would you?"
"Would I what?"
"Would you have sex with them?"
"Well they hang about with my wife and anyway they are not really my type"
"They are not my type either but I shagged the two of them"
"Wow my God, the two together?"
"No they wouldn't agree to a threesome so I shagged them one week after the other"
"Ah you are not serious, are you?"
"Yes I am mate, they are mad for it and all you need to do is buy them a few drinks"
"Have you a date with one of them tonight?"
"Are you fecking raving? I wouldn't be seen dead with them in public and you know that I am married"
"No I didn't know that you were married but did they know?"
"Sure they did but they don't care as long as they have a good time"!

Dave was shocked with these revelations and only half believed them until a respectable gentleman that was acquainted with him confirmed the antics of the group calling them 'loose women'. So from then on Dave nick named the two Slumberland and Odearest after two types of bed mattresses stating that they had them strapped unto their backs. Another friend was cruder about the pair saying that 'they had more pricks than a second hand dart board'. Dave wondered was Cath in the same category because she hung about with them so she would be tarred with the same brush and like the old adage goes 'show me your friends and I will tell you who you are'! However, Dave put this out of his mind but he did recall Cath coming home very late on numerous occasions staggering drunk and with her clothing and hair dishevelled. She also would switch off her mobile phone and could not be contacted when she went out with these loose women if in fact this was who she was with but what was she hiding?

New House

The dreary hum in the courthouse foyer didn't help his anguish and more thoughts of life with Cath came flooding into his mind and back to the time when he took Cath on a proper honeymoon. It was ten months after they got wed and Dave was entitled to 'back money' from the Inland Revenue with income tax paid being single. This was because he went from being a single to a married person within the tax year so that allowances were very much improved. But first an event occurred which was more crucial to their lives. The cold easterly winds of spring swept the country keeping the temperature down below zero as Cath and Dave struggled to keep themselves and their baby warm in their exposed mobile home at the edge of the wide open field. The condensation still amassed on the walls which turned to ice at night and they couldn't leave the gas heater on for fear of fire or toxic fumes so the three of them huddled together in bed wrapped in a heavy duvet where Molly slept soundly in Dave's arms.

He took it on himself to approach all the town councillors to put forward a case for his new family to be allocated a council house and they agreed to do so after hearing of their living status. Then a good friend of Cath's also a councillor, approached them to say that the council's housing/health inspector would be calling out to interview them and also to view for himself their living conditions. He also schooled them as to what to say in answer to his questions which was most helpful seeing that they had no experience in this kind of situation.

It was a bright sunny day that the council's housing inspector arrived and he was a curt, no nonsense medical doctor that dealt in facts. Dave was worried about his visit because the weather had improved and this made their mobile much warmer than in the previous months. However the inspector realised these were not good conditions for a couple to reside in, never mind a new baby. The heat of the sun melted the frozen ground on the pathway up to the mobile causing it to become a muddy path and the inspector had difficulty in negotiating it, which immediately furthered their cause. He asked them would they have any problem in being allocated a house in either of the two big estates in town and they were schooled to reply that they would not like to live in these. He thanked them for their honesty and Dave said that his mother's family came from a street in the centre of town where the council were building again. The official took note of this and left immediately slipping and sliding on the path while muttering to himself. Dave smiled and said

"I think that went very well"

Being pessimistic Cath replied

"Don't get your hopes up, as you would never know what he will decide."

However Dave remained upbeat and lifted Molly and proclaimed to her 'we are going to get you a new house just for you, me and mammy'.

Then within three months they got news in the post that they indeed had been allocated a house on the street where Dave's family resided about seventy years beforehand but this was a brand spanking new house and they were overjoyed. However they had nothing to put into the house, no furniture, no major appliances so all of this had to be acquired bit by bit as they had no savings to buy them immediately. They had four bare walls but at least there was a kitchen unit already fitted and linoleum covering the ground floor with wooden floors upstairs on the first floor. They acquired Cath's old bed that she shared with her sister and a dining table and some chairs that were as old as the hills from Dave's uncle but beggars cannot be choosers as the saying goes.

Dave went out and bought a cooker, refrigerator, washing machine, microwave oven, and TV set for a fraction of the cost from a business that had gone into liquidation. He had to bargain with the guy in charge and it was all a cash sale with no credit cards or cheques accepted but he enjoyed the experience as he never had to do this before because all dealings were done by his mam in buying household stuff. He continued to work hard, doing twelve hours on most days and Cath went back to work part time in the hair salon. She also did some hairdressing in the kitchen of their new house which was not ideal or hygienic as they had to prepare, cook, and dine there also, but it needed to be done at this time. Then one night he came home late to discover Cath sweeping hair up from the floor with a small dustpan and brush after cutting a client's hair. He couldn't believe what he was seeing and couldn't understand why she hadn't bought a proper sweeping brush as they were already two months in the house. He soon learned that she was leaving everything up to him to buy all the essentials needed and also to look after all the household bills which he didn't mind doing but a simple thing like a sweeping brush he thought she should have bought herself. He broached the subject with her by saying

"What the feck are you at?"
"Oh just tiding up after work"
"Don't you have a proper brush to do that?"
"Em no"
"Do you mean to tell me that we have been here for two months and you were sweeping up all this time just using a dustpan?"
"Yes that's right"
"Oh my God" "That means the floors have never been properly swept or washed in over two months"!
"Sure they are not dirty and anyway hairs that are on the floor after I finish work I just sweep up with this dustpan"

Dave just could not believe what he was hearing and tried to figure as to why Cath would leave herself in this position. She was either too lazy to be bothered to go out and buy what she needed or didn't mind living in dirt or too miserable and tight with her own money to spend it on family business thus leaving all up to Dave. He knew she was not a dumb blond being a true red head but she acted like she was at times. But no matter what the reason the job was not being done and Dave was going to sort it out as usual. He knew also that she was of the mind that when you are married that the bread winner pays for all and the rule she was standing by was 'what's yours is mine and what's mine is my own'. However despite this Dave, the very next day, took some time out and went into a hardware shop which was less than one hundred yards from their house and bought a brush and bucket with a mop along with cloth dusters. When he arrived home he found the house empty as Cath had taken Molly out for a walk in the pram so now he set about brushing and mopping all the floors downstairs with the aroma of pine filling the air.

The months passed uneventfully with the mundane tasks of married life occupying most of their time but it was all work and no play. Dave decided to remedy this by taking Cath away for a fortnight's holiday, a sort of second honeymoon as they hadn't really enjoyed the first. He also went out and ordered a living room carpet to be fitted the following week and he was happy they he had spent the money wisely.

Cath was delighted when Dave came in and surprised her with the news and she boasted to all her friends that her husband was taking her away for two weeks sun in the Canary Islands where Playa Del Ingles was to be their base. Together they made all the arrangements to have Molly looked after while they were away but Dave was now having second thoughts about the vacation as he would be leaving his baby behind and for a whole two weeks. Nevertheless he went ahead with the plan as he knew that a hot climate would not be suitable for a five month old baby and with all the travelling sure it would make her very uncomfortable.

His sister Margaret would mind her while they were away and she welcomed this as she loved babies and had plenty of experience as she had four of her own but above all of this was the fact that she was the only one that Dave and Cath trusted with their little fragile angel.

The day soon came around for their departure and Cath had to take some relaxing pills as she was afraid of flying. Dave drove to the airport on the rather grey afternoon and would leave his car in the airport car park. Cath was relaxed and happy as they made their way to the lounge after checking in. The lounge was full of holiday makers and they wondered were any of them going on the same flight and they soon met up with a couple from the southern end of the country. They discovered that not only were they going on the same flight but also staying in the same apartment complex. The four sat, talked, and drank while waiting on their flight to be called and Dave never saw Cath so relaxed and chilled out as the pills and alcohol took good effect. She ambled down the boarding chute nonchalantly humming a tune as if she was about to board a service bus. The aircraft was a brand spanking new Airbus A340 of the Spanish National Airline Iberia fleet and Dave could tell by the crew that they were very proud of this, their flagship. He ordered champagne and when the crew realised they were on honeymoon so to speak it was given free gratis as was everything else ordered for the entire flight.

They arrived in Las Palmas after dark and their one hour sojourn to Playa Del Ingles passed without major event until they checked into their hotel when Dave discovered that he had lost the key to his suitcase. The next day he had to attire in Cath's clothing and tried to find the least feminine top and shorts but only had leather shoes at his disposal as the rest of his footwear were firmly locked away in his inaccessible case. Cath could not stop laughing when she saw him dressed in her sequinned white top and white shorts but he didn't care as he felt that nobody would know him as they walked about this paradise, this sin city in the sun.

Playa Del Ingles boasted everything to cater for all types of holidaymaker with seedy bars and strip clubs as well as cuisine from all over the world but the daylight attraction was its miles of white sandy beach with sand dunes which were ideal for the naturalist to gain their all over suntan. Cath and Dave ambled about in the blazing heat of the day looking for a locksmith as he didn't want to damage his case when he heard a familiar accent call out to him.

"Jaysus there's a Paddy if I ever saw one"

Dave looked around in an attempt to locate where the mysterious voice came from and spotted two gents laughing uncontrollably in the shade. He immediately tried to hide his sequinned tee shirt but it was twinkling more in the sunshine so he abandoned his embarrassment and walked over to join the two.

"Well lads, what's the story?"

"Why the fuck are you dressed like that? Not that it's any of my business but I am just saying!"

"I lost the keys of me suitcase and had to wear her clothes."

He explained pointing to Cath who pretended not to be there. The boys continued to laugh out loud and when they eventually stopped giggling they stammered to say

"Well we thought you were a misguided Irish crosser dresser with your white sparkly shirt and brogue shoes with black socks"

Another five minutes of laughter began but in the middle of this they managed to order a round of drinks to include Dave and Cath who was still unimpressed with the proceedings. However she eventually came around and began to enjoy the banter. The lads promised to come around to Dave's hotel and pick the lock at seven that evening much to the relief of the couple.

Cath got dressed up for the evening while Dave remained wearing her clothes until the boys came over to unlock his case. Seven o'clock came and went with no sign of them so they decided to go to the hotel bar to wait in a less obvious, more relaxing location. The evening progressed but there were hardly any customers in the bar and it was now fifteen minutes after ten. Dave began to think that this must be a rough bar and that's why they had no customers and also the reason why the boys didn't turn up for them. A band began to set up and were accompanied by an Irish lady who Dave approached to enquire what was happening and why so late into the evening.

> "Ah japers you are not at home now, sure the craic only starts here at midnight and goes on until the wee hours"

She explained in her southern Irish Cork accent.

> "Oh right"

Dave retorted more in shock than surprise as the licensing laws were strictly adhered to in Ireland and only in some bars would you get a late drink but this was open season here and he thought it to be very intriguing.

> "We have a Hawaiian Night on here tonight with all the regalia supplied to our patrons. So will you be staying?"
>
> "Yes of course as there is nowhere to go now"!

He explained his ordeal and she almost cried with laughter but also felt sorry for him and ordered free drink for him and Cath who was getting more inebriated as each moment passed. The hostess Susan was a petite lady with short blonde hair and a very bubbly personality which was very suitable in her chosen profession. The band began to play at around midnight and little by little the crowd started to build up. Susan went around distributing Hawaiian grass skirts to all who wanted to participate in the night's frivolity. Dave accepted his with pleasure but he noticed that Cath was sound asleep even though they were seated in close proximity to the stage area and the noise of the band. He did not let this mar his enjoyment for after all he was on holiday also so he donned the grass skirt around his head instead of his waist so that he could look like Bob Marley, the reggae king. He joined forces with Susan on stage much to her delight and they both sang and entertained the audience for two hours with fun and games. There were people from all over Europe present as well as Irish but they all seemed to enjoy the night. At the end of the night Dave slung Cath over his shoulder and carried her up to bed and awoke late the next morning with his head pounding with a hangover. Cath had already left and was at the swimming pool lounging in the hot sun. It was ten o'clock when Dave emerged having downed a litre of fresh orange juice and slumped down beside her, their friends from the plane trip were already there. The banter began and was a great laugh even for those in close proximity but Dave admitted he did not remember much about the proceeding of the previous night and he knew that Cath didn't either as she slept through it. Dave went to the bar and when he was away a German couple approached Cath and asked was her husband on again that night in cabaret in the hotel? Cath hadn't a clue what they were talking about and thought they must be making a mistake in identity so she just smiled and agreed. They said oh good we have told some friends and they are coming over to see him in the show as he is a fantastic entertainer. Cath had been joined by the couple they had met on the plane on the way over when Dave returned and they sunbathed for most of the day. The couple were very funny and likable but they didn't seem to mix well with others and wanted to do everything with Dave and Cath which cramped their every move. The husband came out with a hilarious expression when asked by his wife did he love her and he replied "Of course I love you aren't I riding you?"

Their time there seemed to pass all too quickly and it was on this holiday, this second honeymoon, that sex occurred for the second time and Cath discovered that she was pregnant a few weeks after returning home. Dave was delighted because they had a new three bed roomed house and one more baby wouldn't tax the household budget by that much but a new thought struck him now. He was a very monogamous, loyal person so how could he split his love in half with a new baby and his princess Molly? He absolutely adored his first born and no mistake but felt he would be sort of betraying her by loving another baby even though he or she would be a sibling.

The splattering of files and papers dropped by a legal assistant chased all these thoughts away from Dave's mind and he rushed to help her gather them up noticing that one else was willing to help the embarrassed young lady who was being venomously scowled at by her bespectacled wigged boss. He returned to his seat and wondered when his turn would come to face the judge but his thoughts drifted again.

I Name This Child

Now if the first of Dave's children Molly caused envy with Cath's sister Paula, the second one, Wally a boy, seemed to drive her over the edge and the long knives were out. This jealousy was not directed at Cath but at her husband who maintained his devil may care attitude towards life and this didn't go down well with Paula and her husband John so in an effort to appease them Dave and Cath decided to have John as Wally's godfather. He was delighted with this decision and Dave knew that they couldn't have selected a better person to sponsor their child because he would act over and above the call of duty.

John was a nice man, an only child who was reared by his widowed mother who spoiled him but in the proper way. He possessed an out going personality who could mix with the best of company but he lacked real confidence in himself so was inclined to cling to people and be really annoyed if they didn't call or he was excluded by mistake or intention from any activity in which they were involved. He would vociferously reproach any of his friends that he felt guilty of such an act and assertively put them, what he deemed, in their place. Paula, his beloved wife, added fuel to his insecure emotional fire by pointing out any transgressions of his friends and this attitude acted to have their friends avoid them at all costs. They were well suited as a couple with emotional needs that were never fulfilled to their expectations no matter how they tried or worse still endeavoured to recruit people to satisfy their desires. Together they would purchase expensive gifts for their friends but these gifts carried a huge price tag for the recipients because they bore a kind of emotional blackmail because the donor would call in their marker at the appropriate time.

Dave felt that this a ludicrous way to live life being constantly on guard and where the clock paid a big influence to their day when they would visit friends and family to keep each and every one of them sweet in a most ironic way for they would actually be trying to buy the affections and loyalties of the unsuspecting recipients. However, Dave saw through their scheme and smirked at the idiocy of such a belief because he knew that real friends do not need expensive gifts for they love you as you are or they don't; it is as simple as that but that was something that John and Paula never learned.

Dave was in a position now that he had more money than he had in any previous job and could afford all that he and his family needed with two holidays each year one abroad and one at home. It is true to say that even though there was a definite absence of love in the marriage and as much as the children compensated for this it never really made up for the romantic love he hungered for, a true love that exists between a man and a woman. He felt that if Cath even showed a little love or sentiment then everyone would be happy and she would gain even more from him but he felt that everything she did was heartless, cold, and calculating just to gain her way. He thought deeply about this and came to the conclusion that all marriages were the same and the male was not supposed to feel romance but just do his job of breadwinning and never complain. Dave worked hard to achieve this status while Cath just came along for the ride but he decided to have a holiday trip with a colleague that he nicknamed Pinky and his new wife that he nicknamed Porky, but these names emanated from their holiday. This guy Pinky was a picture of perfection where there was never a hair out of place like a part of his anatomy that never moved while Porky his wife in contrast was a short dumpy girl from the south coast of Ireland that had an accent that would have peeled the skin from one's face. He was quiet, reserved and very successful in his job that Dave didn't quite understand as they were salesmen and while he looked the part he certainly didn't sound like it! However the four got on well together despite their complete differences but there was a hidden scheme that went undetected by Dave and Cath. It all started even before they went on vacation when Dave's colleague's wife Porky, arranged to have her hair styled in their home. Cath worked for four hours on her head but when it was completed she thanked Cath and left without paying. Cath was flabbergasted by her audacity and mentioned it to Dave but he felt it was just an oversight on her behalf and perhaps her husband Pinky would pay as he was earning a fortune. However this did not happen and Cath never mentioned it to her new non-paying client but there was more drama afoot from these devious couple.

The day arrived for the holiday and Dave's boss came to the house to take them to the airport but while inside having a coffee the doorbell rang and it was Dave's colleague Pinky to ask for a loan of one hundred pounds as he had trouble getting it out of the ATM machine at his bank. Dave was astounded by this request but was interrupted before saying anything by their boss who overheard the conversation from the kitchen and offered to loan the cash to him. He was startled by seeing his boss there but he refused saying that he would be alright and Dave wondered why he asked in the first place. However the two couples made their merry way to the airport in their boss's car and boarded the three hour flight to guaranteed sunshine on the island of Ibiza off the coast of Spain.

They were having a ball where they ate and drank like kings and queens but on the evening of the fourth day the proverbial bomb was unexpectedly dropped by Dave's colleague Pinky just as they made their way out to a fancy restaurant dress in all their finery. Dave and Pinky walked ahead of their wives on the short journey to the town centre

"Dave, can you help me out as I have no money?"

"Yes sure I can give you a loan till you change a traveller's cheque in the morning"

"No you don't understand! I have no money left, I have ran out and I have no means of getting any"

"What! You come on a fourteen day holiday and you have no money after just four days. How much did you take with you in the first place?"

"I took two hundred pounds"

"Ah for fucks sake, two hundred fucking pounds for the two of you to live off for fourteen days! What were you thinking of? I know that Spain is cheap but you cannot live on fresh air here"

"Well can you help me out or not?"

"I will see what I can do, OK!"

Cath was surprised when they passed Dave's favourite restaurant and headed for a fast food joint and when she did eventually make eye contact with him he just shrugged his shoulders but she knew that something was wrong! Dave had to think of how he was going to manage to look after the four of them for the next ten days and nights so he put a plan into action. He dismissed the thought that flashed across his mind that his colleague was a scrounger, a parasite living off other people and felt that surely this could never be true. However later on in the evening after paying for all their meals and following drinks he decided to have a early night and emptied out his pockets and gave the contents to Pinky and Porky to stay on which they accepted. This was his chance to tell Cath what had happened and Pinky's revelation! Cath could not believe that a couple would come on holiday for fourteen days and only have money to last four days and no means to get more. However Dave decided to bank-roll his colleague Pinky and every time he changed a cheque he gave him half which was about sixty pounds and he changed five in total for the remainder of the holidays which meant that Pinky owed him three hundred pounds, not forgetting Porky's owed Cath twenty five pounds for her hair do!

The days rolled past slowly for Dave and Cath with their enjoyment waning with each day as their mates became more parasitic, depending on them for cash, company, in fact everything and they were not embarrassed or regretful of their situation. Their relationship became somewhat frayed as they glued themselves like leeches to their host Dave and Cath who felt trapped in a situation that was not of their making and was never expected. What was happening was Pinky would get the cash from Dave then buy expensive cologne and presents for friends and family at home but would have none left for food or entertainment thus expecting Dave to foot the bill for this also. Dave did his best for him but was sure that he would repay him when he got home.

Now there were two very distinct things happening here with one being the fact that Dave's colleague Pinky and his wife Porky came on holiday with hardly any money and expected Dave to pay for them and the second one was that Cath observed all of this and the way Dave handled the situation and discovered that Dave was a soft touch giving his money away but expecting a return.

Dave christened his colleague Pinky the Parasite because of the obvious reasons and also for a time when he came from the beach one day badly sunburned and he was a radiant glow of Lobster Red and his wife Porky the Pig said that he will get a great tan in the next day or so. Dave had to walk away and have a good laugh to himself in the confines of his room. So now Dave had Pinky, Porky, and he proceeded to name their kids as Stinky and Dinky to complete the set of poetic titles for the family.

The fourteen days rolled on and while Dave enjoyed the warm sunshine he was very upset by his colleague and with three days to go Pinky decided to get cash from home from his brother but still asked for money to tide him over till his money came. However the

brother only sent one hundred pounds and this would just about look after the cost of their food and entertainment.
They all came home with healthy suntans except for Pinky who remained lobster like and a week passed and their was no sign of him repaying the money owed to Dave so he contacted him and asked to come around and pay what he owed. Pinky arrived the next day with fifty pounds in an envelope and handed it to Dave.

"What's this?"

"That's what I owe you"

Dave produced his cheque book with all the stubs with dates and from the fourth day he split every cheque he cashed and there were five which equalled six hundred pounds and three hundred of which was owed by Pinky.

"Ah now wait a minute I didn't get that much money from you"

"Wow man you have a hard fucking neck coming in here with only fifty pounds when you got six times that amount"

"Sure where did you get the money from the fourth day when you had nor a penny to your name" My cheque book does not lie like you are doing now"

"Well I didn't get three hundred pounds from you no matter what you say"

"You are a thief, a fraudster, and your wife came in here, got her hair done and never paid so she is in on the act also. I will blacken your name everywhere I go and tell all our colleagues about you, you despicable man"

"No one will believe you and as for my wife you will need to see her about her hair do"

"Get the fuck out and never speak to me again you fucking bastard"

Pinky left Dave's house with a smirk on his face as Cath came in to ask what happened and when he told her she just stared in amazement. He never met anyone like Pinky before and never wished to meet anyone like him ever again. He bleeds him dry and then denied it as if it never happened but what could Dave do now as he had no redress and this is a fact that didn't go unnoticed by Cath. Dave and Cath had some good moments together when they worked together in Spain to avoid the company of the parasitic guests there and when they laughed in unison when Dave conjured up nicknames for the pair. This felt good for Dave as he enjoyed someone working with him for their common good and not someone working against him that left him with the feeling of isolation and abandonment. He could learn to fall in love with someone like this despite the lack of intimacy; he felt this would come with time.

However this was not to be the case because when they came home he was left to face Pinky on his own as if the problem didn't belong to Cath but like a spy who stayed hidden observing a battle between two opponents measuring their weaknesses.

Dave took Cath and Molly to Spain the very next year before an opportunity for improving all their lives arose in a most unlikely way.

God Bless America

The abandonment really struck home now as Dave sat alone in the cold courthouse for not a friend nor one member of his family were there with him to lend some support at this time when he needed it most. He looked up and saw Cath there with her sister and brother fighting for her even with her own legal team and he felt like just giving up there and then and walking away.
This happened before, unintentionally as it turned out but it did happen although Dave was free as a bird being released from a cage. This came about with an opportunity to immigrate to the USA for the whole family which brought excitement to the household. The American Government relaxed its criteria and opened its borders and its arms to Irish citizens to reside and work in their beautiful country and Dave after lengthy discussions with Cath applied to take up their generous offer. He always wanted to better himself and now with this golden opportunity he could and that of his entire family.
The process was lengthy as with all legislation and Dave needed to get Irish Police clearance, a full medical report, employer and citizen references, and a US job offer to support his application. These all came easily and the reports were so complimentary that they made him feel like the greatest Irish model citizen of all time. He also had to attend an interview with some diplomatic staff in the American embassy in the capital to finally receive the formal stamp of approval and this also came with ease.
The embassy was a hive of activity with people applying for the right of passage and Dave smiled as he waited in turn and pondered this great adventure into the unknown. The medical process consisted of an AIDS test and a chest x-ray which was placed into a large green folder and to be taken with the person through emigration for inspection by officials. Dave didn't understand this because it seemed rather silly carrying this very large green folder onto a plane but the US officials insisted and they had method in this madness. The reason being that when officials saw a person with their green folder they immediately knew that they went through the proper channels and were taken to the top of the line for processing and with a formal greeting of 'welcome to the United States of America'. The two lads in front of Dave in the embassy were being processed and had obviously been to the States residing and working there but were illegal and un-documented. The grey haired embassy

official possessed a very tight stern facial expression that if he smiled his whole face would crack and fall apart. His manner of probing questions would leave an adept attorney in his wake also.

"Now tell me sir, you went to the US five years ago on vacation, and you only came back here last month; is this correct?"

"Yes sir that's right"!

"Why did you stay so long?" "Where did you live and how did you survive?"

"Well sir it's a long story and the first thing was I lost me plane ticket and I had not got the cash to buy another one"

"So I picked up a few odd jobs but couldn't manage to raise enough to get back here to the auld sod"!

"So pray tell me where you lived"?

"Well I stayed with friends a few nights and I slept on the street when it was warm to do so"

The official knew rightly that this was a pack of lies as did the dogs in the street but due process stated that he ask these questions or maybe he just wanted to listen to comical fantasy tales but no matter what the reason he stamped his papers and granted approval. The guy was probably working on a building site in construction earning a fortune compared to the Irish work force; sending some home and then partying with the remainder.

It was Dave's turn and the official scanned his papers vigilantly.

"Now sir you have stated that you work in finance; is this correct"?

"Yes sir it is"

"But you are going to the US to be a cook"?

"Yes that's right"

The official peered down from his half-rimmed glasses wanting an explanation because Dave's job offer was with a catering company in Boston. Dave stared back at him and said the first thing that came to mind.

"I am going to cook the books"

Now with that the official raised his eyes to heaven, stamped his papers, and told him to come back at four thirty to collect his documents. This was great news and Dave wanted to jump around as if he had scored a goal in a cup final but he remained calm and restrained his emotions for another time.

However, this whole process and excitement was marred by the bombshell that Cath dropped when deciding not to go along with Dave and now he was to go alone. He could not believe her attitude towards this and it was a huge damper on the whole excitement and any enjoyment was curtailed by her decision which could have dire consequences for both of them. Dave's company decided to have a going away party and not to be outdone his family and friends decided to do likewise and he was very agreeable to this as he loved to party even though he was the host. The last night was bizarre because Paula babysat while Cath and Dave went out and had a meal together followed by a few quiet drinks and this would be their last chance to be alone in each others company. Paula's husband John decided to join them and he took a friend with him and Dave immediately felt that this had a reason although it was not obvious at the time. This friend of Paula and John's had 'knocked up', got pregnant, a married lady and was hiding out as her friends and family were going to rough him up big time so John decided that he would put him into Dave's house for safety.

"Oh by the way this is Mick and he needs somewhere to stay for the night"

John stated nonchalantly.

"Well I hope he finds somewhere and good luck to him"

Dave replied without delay.

"But I told him he could stay in your place for a few days for safety"

"Well you can just UN-tell him now"

"But he is in trouble and people are looking for him and you wouldn't see a fella stuck, now would you"?

"Well he is not staying in my house while I am away, for fuck sake what do you think I am"?

However John insisted and actually took his friend Mick down to Dave's house but Dave stood firm on his decision and Paula who was babysitting left in her night gown with her husband and their friend.

Dave packed his bags with sadness, stumbling as he went to the bus station to begin his long arduous journey into the unknown. He bade his farewells to Cath and his beloved children Molly and Wally who didn't really understand what was happening so he held back the tears of his heavy heart and he cried leaving and the children frantically waved as the bus turned the corner and out of sight. He pondered why Cath made the decision not to go with him for this great opportunity in the great land of the brave? Was it that she just had no ambition or was it something much deeper than this? In the airport he was welcomed to America by emigration officials and his eight hour flight was uneventful as he slept most of the way and awoke just in time to see New York City below as the setting autumnal sun cast an orange haze across all the buildings. So this is it 'The Big Apple' that he read so much about and saw on Television and in the movies! This was the stuff of dreams, The Hudson River with The Manhattan Bridge straddling its banks, The Twin Towers of the World Trade Centre, and The Empire State Building were all here but his dream would have to be lived out alone for now anyway.

They say that the big city can be the loneliest place in the world and Dave didn't quite understand this until now because here he was alone not knowing anyone but with hoards of people around. He paused to see would there be any friendly faces but all he saw were blank emotionless expressions of people rushing around, their only concern was to get to their destination and not noticing anything or anyone as if they didn't exist. They were all locked into the illusionary world of their mind where their reality is played out like a rerun of a TV programme, a past event, an experience, a dialogue with an encounter or planning for a future event. All of this going on within the confines of the grey matter while on the other hand their bodies behaved in robotic movements weaving their way through the masses. 'Did I turn the cooker off'? 'Did I feed the dog'? 'I can't believe that bitch would say something like that to me' 'If I take that extra job I will be able to afford that new car'! This all swirling around in their heads like a cycle in a washing machine where every thought being an item of dirty clothing and this is their reality, this is their very own unique world. There is no room for anyone else there especially a stranger who is treated with suspicion and perhaps rightly so in this concrete jungle where the unwritten rule is 'every man for himself', the survival of the fittest, get going and get there fast, there is no time for distractions especially strangers. He never saw so many people all in one place heading for the subway and they reminded him of ants going into their anthill at first light and then eight hours or so later coming out to forage. He didn't know if he would like this anthill lifestyle being a unique individual with plans and dreams that would never be achieved in this metropolis of meaningless mingling of the masses that acted like robotic machines repeating the same actions over and over again day after day. This is what they achieved in their education system to become a machine but this is not life it is a mere existence and nothing more.

Dave felt this was a sad indictment of society especially in the metropolis and he was glad to be from a small town where people are more caring, they are very much less in a hurry and they notice other people including strangers and are so willing to help if they can. But here in NYC the staid slate grey buildings match the greyness of the people rushing around frantically like ants coming and going from their ant hills. Dave now understood the loneliness of the big city and despite the many people there, it could be the most isolated place in the world for an individual. He remained there with his 'children sickness' as opposed to 'home sickness' because he didn't miss home as much as he missed his kids. That elusive well paying job evaded him although he was short listed on several occasions which acted as another reason to go back to Ireland.

He also kept a clean sheet in the loyalty stakes never once dirtying his copy book although he was tempted on more than one occasion; however he did not believe in being unfaithful even though his marriage was anything but fulfilling or satisfying. Dave just about endured his loneliness for fourteen weeks and it was that special time of year, Christmas, and one thing of which he was certain was that he could not be away from his children as he felt it would be cruel for all concerned.

He boarded a train before catching the red-eye back to the land of his birth where the shamrock was bedazzled with glitter alongside the brightly coloured Christmas trees that welcomed all festive visitors in Dublin Airport. After collecting his luggage he made his way to the bus terminal for the two hour journey home.

Cath opened the door and stood there mouth agape as she did not expect Dave's arrival so soon and as she was shocked made no attempt of a greeting. However, Molly and Wally, their two children, stood for a while behind her before running into his open arms and he thought well at least someone is glad to see me!

    "Well how are you doing?"

He asked more out of habit than inquiry but there was no answer as Cath's mind tried to come to terms with the vision she saw in front of her and when he eventually managed to haul his bags into the house she gave him a hug. He was happy with this even though it was an awkward 'Doctor Sheldon Cooper' of the TV situation comedy series The Big Bang Theory, type of embrace! She made tea and they sat down together to chat; the children would not let him out of their sight, half afraid that he would leave again and he promised to himself they he would not do so ever again. He told them about his adventures in the Big Apple and they listened attentively and with pleasure as he always made the tales exciting and funny that made them laugh out loud; but most of all he told Cath about his plan to start afresh with life and their relationship. Dave put two plans forward for her consideration with one having a life in the USA and the other to remain in Ireland and make a go of their rather odd life together but he was willing to give it another try especially for the sake of their children. Cath said that she would think about it but she felt that plan A was off the table because moving to the US would be too much of an upheaval for her and for the children.

Dave proceeded to unpack his bags in his bedroom being scrutinised by the children and they were not disappointed because he brought them toys with sweets, 'candy' as the Americans would say. He also had clothing outfits for the three most important people in his life; a bright red cord three quarter length coat that was sung and warm for Cath, trousers, shirt and waist coat for Wally, and for Molly a party dress made of red lace with gold braid embroidered into the material. They all looked fantastic in their new clothing and with Christmas on the doorstep sure they would be belles of the ball! Although Dave had a return airline ticket to New York he did not use it but as planned decided to have another try of making the marriage work and Cath complied somewhat with the plan. They actually began to do things together like cleaning the house, making the beds, and in doing this chore at the end of January they were flirting, joking, and messing which ended up in them making love together on the floor. Then in early winter of that year the stork bird flew into their house with the arrival of their third baby a beautiful girl that they named Dolly. They were now used to the routine of feeding bottles and diapers; with all the crying and cuddling involved with a new born. Dolly right from the very beginning announced her individual persona first to her parents and then to the world. Her distinct idiosyncrasies were obvious when she was uncomfortable, in need of attention, a nappy change, or to be fed she would bawl the house down in no uncertain terms. This was different than that of her other older siblings who were quieter and certainly less demanding but she received the same amount of love from Dave and Cath as well as from her sister and brother.

Life was simple and easy for the couple and their children who managed everything that living could throw at them and there was a peace and calmness in the air. Dave and Cath also managed to get on well together despite the fact of the missing romance; however a certain harmony was in existence and portrayed like in a business partnership. Dave was aware of this soulless collaboration but no matter how hard he tried he just could not fix it. So what he did was to put his energy and time into the children which was now feasible as his new job allowed. He would spend time with Molly who had just begun junior school helping her with her homework and he took Wally to the park to kick a ball about as they both loved soccer football. He also babysat Dolly and this allowed Cath to work at her hairstyling because she was now building a home based business increasing her clientele by the week.

Dave continued to be responsible for all the household bills although his salary was a mere fraction of what it was before he went to America. This left him feeling that he had all the trappings of a married man but led a singular life because Cath would not socialise with him so he would alone attend functions of weddings, celebration parties and even funerals.

His job demanded that he work especially from six to nine o'clock in the evening often travelling to other towns in his district and one night while driving he figured out what was wrong with him as he had an uneasy feeling for months. He discovered that he was lonely because he felt trapped and isolated in a dysfunctional marriage with no affection, no friendship, and no companionship whatsoever. This is not the way it is supposed to be or is it, he thought to himself? This was not anything like his dream of a home with a loving wife with all the trimmings; they were just illusions with snares and he seemed to be the only one trapped within. His ambitions were dampened and discarded by his partner who dismissed every last one of them even the thought of a new life in America. He also wanted to buy a business when he was earning a good salary and there were two bars one of which had a restaurant that came onto the market at a giveaway asking price. His plan was to buy one of these in the guise of a private limited company and employ staff with a manager that he would oversee while still retaining his secure job. However, Cath shafted the idea without even a second thought saying that it would turn him into an alcoholic just like his father before him. This cruel statement uttered by her, hurt Dave to no end and it was noticed and noted by her. Cath made up rules as she went along and they applied to everyone concerned except her and this was because she was growing in confidence having broken away from her own family and now she was breaking away from her employer who both kept her down and subservient. Dave was responsible for this because he married her and showed her that she didn't need anyone to happily live life, He allowed her to open her wings and fly freely. But the one person that she never broke free from was her dominant sister Paula who kept interfering in Cath's life and with everyone who was attached with her. Dave used to joke that some people have interfering mother-in-laws but I don't as I have your sister and he was only half joking with this but wholly in earnest.

Angel

Two years after their third child Cath found that she was pregnant again with their fourth child which amazed Dave because they rarely had sex and in the fifteen years of being with her they only engaged in the act about ten times and four of these resulted in pregnancies. He reckoned that she was very fertile and that he was very virile but this was her fifth pregnancy because before she met him, she had casual sex with a guy she just met and became pregnant and all of this while going with a steady boyfriend. She got rid of this baby by going to England for an abortion as firstly, she didn't want the child and second she did not want the shame of being classed as an unmarried mother, a person stigmatised and whom she would look down upon.

The pregnancy was nothing out of the ordinary except some strange things happened to her during it. One of these was a religious ceremony for expectant mothers and when she went to get blessed she felt a presence near to her but when she looked around there was no one there. Also she got the distinct aroma of lily flowers when she went to certain places and could not explain it as this was mid-winter when no flowers were in bloom. Dave thought this to be strange indeed but had read that expectant mothers sometimes have strange cravings and normal smells that would make them physically sick.

The months seemed to fly by and one night when Cath was asleep Dave felt the baby kick in her tummy and he began to talk to it. He prayed that it would be healthy and normal but he got a bad feeling that something was not right and this scared him as he had no reason to think this. He got some holy water and blessed Cath and the unborn child naming her in a kind of baptism rite. Cath stirred but didn't wake up and he didn't tell her how he felt or what he did because he didn't want to scare her in any way as she had only two months to go before the birth.

Daylight seeped in through the open window of Dave and Cath's bedroom to announce a bright summer's day. Dave awoke to find Cath already awake but moaning in pain and immediately recognised from her fidgety movements that she was in labour. He asked her was she OK and she replied that it was beginning. He immediately jumped out of bed, got dressed and went into the next door neighbour to look after their children while he took Cath to hospital. So after packing a bag he led Cath out and into the car for the short journey to the local hospital. The trip was surreal in the fact that there was a definite serenity surrounding them and both he and Cath were more quiet than usual. Dave put this down to the unusual circumstances of being up so early as well as Cath almost ready to deliver another baby.

The maternity unit greeted them where the nurse took Cath down to the delivery ward and this was the first time that they had gone here unexpectedly because the other three maternity trips were all pre-planned. There was hardly any staff, just a single midwife that had years of experience and who could deliver a baby blindfolded providing there were no complications. However, Dave felt uneasy because this was the first time that he was not permitted into the delivery room having being there at the birth of their three other children. It seemed like no time had passed at all when he heard a baby's cry but his smile changed to a grimace as a cold sweat broke out on his brow as the nurse in a panic stuck her head out of the delivery room and shouted down the echoing corridor

"There is no oxygen down here". "Will somebody get some immediately?"

There was a hush for seconds and Dave wanted to rush down to the labour ward despite the nurse's gesture that he remain where he was. The next moment a porter scurried past him with a tank of oxygen on a trolley and turned into the ward without stopping. There was the sound of a frantic commotion for what seemed like ages only to be replaced with eerie silence when everything stopped or went into slow motion. The birds stopped their happy morning songs and darkness fell on Dave's peripheral vision as he expected the worse but did not know for sure.

The nurse appeared from out of the labour room and approached Dave with her head bowed and as she neared him she spoke gently

"I am afraid we have lost the baby"

Dave did not speak as his grey face became even more ashen now and going into automation began walking towards the labour room. The hush was deafening when he approached Cath's bedside and she held her new born baby in her arms that only stayed a little while here on earth

"Oh Cath she is beautiful as if she is sleeping"

Dave whispered trying to check back the tears but his heart was breaking with the sight of his little baby angel as he thought of her.

She had dark hair and a sallow complexion and everything looked perfect with not one blemish to be seen. Cath could not speak as she was too upset so Dave took her in his arms and comforted her. He knew he had to be strong when taking charge of all the necessary procedures, answering questions and the job that he found most difficult of all, to inform the family. He went to collect his three other children but stopped off in the parochial house to ask a priest friend to come and conduct a baptismal ceremony in the hospital which he agreed to do and finally he went to the undertaker to make funeral arrangements. This took longer than expected as he had to buy a graveyard plot to lay his angel to rest. So after all of this he finally went home to his children who were waiting on the news of a new brother or sister for them. He tried breaking the news to them as gently as possible saying that their sister was really an angel and that God needed her for heaven instead of coming here to earth. They asked could they see her and Dave said of course and that they would be having a baptism service that afternoon. He then got them to wash and dressed them in their finest while making breakfast beforehand.

The baptism ceremony was beautiful and held in an oratory chapel in the hospital which the nurses decorated with white lily flowers that wafted their aroma throughout the entire room. They also had candles lit which added to the sense of solemnity and purity to the occasion where a beam of sunlight came in through the window that shone on the crib. Dave thought this to be so fitting with light surrounding an angel sent from heaven but only for a short visit. His children were happy with his explanation but he now struggled with the meaning of death or life and didn't understand why as he gazed upon the tiny body that would never see the light of day, the stars twinkling at night, feel the wind on her face, hear the birds singing, or smell the scent of flowers.

The nurses had dressed her in a white baby suit with her hands joined holding a pink carnation flower and they all brushed a solemn tear from their eyes for this was the reality of heartbreak personified. Dave and Cath thanked the priest for conducting a beautiful ceremony where he included all the family and after ensuring that Cath was comfortable he went back home with their children who remained more quiet than usual. That night they all slept together in the one bed as no one wanted to be alone at this sad time.

The next day began with cold wet weather of drizzling rain falling gently from foreboding grey clouds which only mirrored the sentiments of everyone around Dave's household. He dressed and got the children dressed and gave them breakfast before getting a neighbour to baby-sit. He had important things to do and Cath and he decided not to take them to the small funeral. He wept as he left his children hugging them together before he drove up to the hospital to see Cath to make sure that she was comfortable and coping. His fears were alleviated when he saw her sitting up and she smiled when she saw him. He had arranged for her friend to be with her at the time of the funeral so that she wouldn't feel alone but perhaps it was a blessing that she was in hospital as the trauma of the funeral could have been too much for anyone to cope with.
Dave was coping well with the predicament going into automation in the crisis and keeping busy so he had no time to dwell. However the time came around that he dreaded most, the funeral, when his little darling angel would be laid to rest. He tried to think of other things as he drove through the rain to the funeral home but the thoughts of death kept cloaking his mind like an evil dark shadow. He thought about Cath and his children and how would they cope with this grief which was overwhelming now as his heart was being torn inside but he tried to stay strong.
He gingerly went through the front door of the funeral home not knowing what to expect and there was the distinct aroma of lilies mixed with burning candle wax. A tiny white coffin was situated in the middle of the room and Dave approached to see his little girl and thoughts of disbelief struck him now.
'What am I doing here'?
'This shouldn't be happening, not now, not ever'!
He went on his knees and tried to pray but it was useless and kept holding her hand beside her little flower. She look beautiful with her dark hair and sallow skin glowing as she was dressed in white and still holding on to her little pink carnation. In fact the whole place seemed to be glowing in a soft white mist that emanated from her tiny body and Dave was certain now that she was indeed an angel. His thoughts now jumped to that he would never know his child, never know her personality, never see her smile or a happy look on her face that would make him delight in bliss as with his other children. Just then as if his angel was reading his thoughts, a smile

seemed to come upon her face and Dave, through his tears gave thanks.

There were some people there who were crying at the scene and the female attendant who knew Dave came over and offered her sympathies with a hug as tears streamed from both their eyes. She led him away into a side office because the undertaker needed to place the lid on the coffin and he then handed it to Dave for the drive out to the cemetery.

It was twelve noon exactly because The Angelus Bells rang out in a nearby church and in the hospital Cath and their friend prayed and certain strength came through their tears.

On the other side of town, Dave cradled the little white coffin in his lap in the front seat of the funeral car knowing that this would be the last time he would hold his baby as more tears flowed rendering him weak and speechless. The car pulled up at the graveside and the undertaker moved around to open the door for Dave. They walked very slowly to the grave with Dave's heart pounding in agony not wanting to be in this nightmare and when it was time to hand the coffin over he didn't want to let go. The priest conducted the ceremony with gentleness and everyone there was affected in grief. Dave was oblivious to everything throughout the whole thing never looking to see who was there or what was being said but he was certain that his family were present. He now just wanted to get away from there as he felt he was going to faint and fall into the grave after his baby as his grief overtook his entire body and mind.

Dave went home to collect his children and they went to the hospital to where Cath was eagerly awaiting their arrival. There, this little family huddled together where they found comfort and peace in each others embrace.

If only things would stay this way it would be more comfortable for everyone in the family but alas this would never be the case and he would constantly struggle to keep everyone happy.

In later years Cath even used the children in her twisted psychological games to wound Dave especially Dolly who became a pawn. Cath's game was to gain control of all of her children minds and to torture Dave as she pleased. One time Dolly wanted a kitten as a pet but Cath didn't like animals at all but the cat was got for her. However, one day Dave came home from work and was relaxing in the sitting room when Dolly came in crying with big sobs and tears running down her face as she asked him

> "What did you do with my kitten"?

Dave was taken aback by the question and said

> "What do you mean honey"?
>
> "My wee kitten has gone missing and mammy said that you sent it away"
>
> "Wow do you really think that I would do that on you or your kitten"?
>
> "I don't know but mammy said"

Dave took her up on his knee and comforted her and told her he would go out and look for her kitten right there and then and if he couldn't find it he would get her a new one the very next day. Dolly was satisfied with this and he did what he promised looked around the block of houses and when he could not find he went and got her a new one. He could not believe that Cath would use the children in this way but began to realise that she was capable of anything even to go as far as the destruction of the minds of her children.

Another time when Dave was off sick from work he joined a leisure centre and took Dolly with him. She was glad to go along as she was a little older now and was noticing that she was getting plump. This was because Cath stopped cooking for the children when the divorce battle began and they were sent down to the chip shop for their meals. However, this arrangement did not suit Cath whatsoever as she thought the Dave would be trying to win Dolly over but this was something that never crossed his mind. They had great fun together in the gym, swimming pool, and he was just delighted to have her along with him. Cath formulated a plan to stop this arrangement and said to Dolly

> "I would love to take you away on holiday to Spain but your Dad won't let you go"
>
> "Oh how could he stop me"?
>
> "Well we need his consent for me to take you with me but he will not give it"

So Dolly, thinking that her parents had already discussed this, went into Dave and demanded that he sign a form for a passport. He was taken aback and asked was she just getting official identification to which she reacted strongly asking

> "Are you going to sign this or not"?

"Here, what's with the attitude, I am only asking you a question"!

With that she stormed out of the room and slammed the door as she could be very thick.

Cath then came to the door and says

"Will you for God's sake sign the form; I am going to take her on holiday"

"Why couldn't she just tell me this instead of all that cloak and dagger stuff, sure it's not a secret"! "Give me the form and I know a peace commissioner close by who can witness my signature so it is all set".

Dave did as he said and gave the form back to Cath and forgot all about it but a few weeks later he got a telephone call to his mobile from the passport office asking did he have Dolly's passport?

"What would I be doing with her passport?"

"We posted it out last week and it has gone missing"

"Gone missing? But why would I have it and how did you get my number"?

"Your wife suggested that you might have it and did not hand it over to her"

"Oh I see what's going on here"

Dave replied and having to tell the official that he was going through a messy divorce with Dolly's mam and she could be holding it but not saying. That evening when she and Cath came in that evening Dolly verbally attacked Dave shouting

"Where's my fucking passport you?"

"Don't you ever talk to me like that; I haven't got your passport"!

All the time Cath stood behind her smirking with pleasure, a smirk that Dave had become to know and hate. The passport did indeed come in the post and Cath had it but actually contacted the passport office and made up the story to get Dave into trouble or so she thought but then when that didn't work she told Dolly that it came and that Dave had it. The sad thing about this episode is that Dolly went off to Spain without even saying goodbye to her dad as she was not on speaking terms because she was led to believe untruths about him by Cath. He thought it to be very sad and sinister that she would use her children like this and he just couldn't believe that she would stoop so low but he fully realised this when Dave opened a letter addressed to both of them from Dolly's school. This letter stated that she felt traumatised by the imminent divorce of her parents and would we like her to see the school psychologist. Dave telephoned the school to agree to this as he knew it would help her to cope but Cath went behind his back and told them that her child didn't need a psychologist that she would counsel her in all her needs. However in hindsight, Dave knew that Cath would lose control of her daughter's mind if a complete professional outsider were to talk to her and may discover the truth which Cath was very careful to conceal from everyone including Dolly.

Cath had now established full control of Dolly's mind with regard to Dave because all experiences that a person has, remains hidden deep within the realms of the subconscious whether they are true or false they are there and Cath was fully aware of this. So with these staged episodes of the 'kitten' and the 'passport' on her daughter Dolly, for Cath it was mission accomplished with the scenario of us against him.

Cath also endeavoured to poison the minds of their other children Molly and Wally but because they are less vociferous than Dolly it was less noticeable. However they were 'radicalised' against Dave by Cath who behaved like an evil rogue cleric determined to destroy the object of their hatred for whatever reason. She would also recruit and employ unsuspecting mercenaries who would be oblivious to their involvement or that they were being used as pawns in someone else's revenge and because of this Cath would be exonerated from all blame as she expertly used subliminal messaging to all she recruited. Thus she did not have to do anything more because others did her bidding for her while she looked on and smirked with happiness. Dave thought this to be totally evil that one person could recruit so many; including the persons closest to him and that he loved most, to try and destroy him.

These memories all came flooding back as Dave sat pensively in the staid cold foyer of the courthouse and he was alone again with not even one member of his family nor was there any friend there to support him just when he needed it most; no, all friendly faces were blatantly absent.

The Socially Excluded

Cath's sister Paula and her husband John were trying for a baby but couldn't seem to manage and this led to more jealousy because everyone close to her were having babies and more than one, even her sister Cath whom she often referred to as a clown. So she read up on the subject and discovered that the time of ovulation is the most ideal time to engage in sexual intercourse and get pregnant. She diligently monitored her menstrual cycle and taking note of her temperature which is one of the signs of ovulation and when this time would come around her husband would be summoned to perform the worthy deed and this could be day or night or at any time at all, such was her determination to conceive.

Now after the staid act of sex she would hold her legs in the air for maybe half an hour and this was done so that none of the precious sperm would dribble out of her vagina. Paula's husband was a big man weighing almost three hundred pounds and Paula was a frail woman weighing in at perhaps one hundred and twenty pounds and Cath and Dave often discussed how they managed to have sex with his big bulk and her frailty. The conventional missionary position was a non starter with three hundred pounds on top of one hundred they figured as he would flatten her and besides he never saw his penis for ages with his protruding stomach that would certainly get in the way with this method. They decided it would be doggie style or with her on top. Dave asked Cath to ask Paula straight out what way they did it, however she refused saying that they never would discuss such things, not even in private, thus it remained a complete mystery. Sure where there is a will there is a way. However Paula possessed a strange attitude towards her body, sex, and having a baby, not that she ever had the experienced but just learned from what other people revealed. She thought it was very degrading for a woman to have a baby being stripped from the waist down, her legs wide apart and strapped at the ankles into stirrups where the world could see her fanny! No that was certainly not for her at all and she believed this to be undignified especially for her. Whereas Cath, on the other hand wouldn't care less who saw what, when in the throes of labour pains, as she just wanted to get it over and done with. Eventually, with John on sex call twenty four seven and with all the crucial diligent timing of ovulation, and with holding her legs in the air after sex, Paula announced the news that she was pregnant. There was great joy with a new life coming into their household that would surely make their family more complete. The nine months seemed to fly past and Paula went to another city to have the baby so that if anyone was going to see her fanny it was going to be complete strangers and not someone she could run into at home. The Angels brought a little girl to them and they called her Emma and she was beautiful as babies are. There was great joy and Dave felt this also but like with all the other episodes in their life, he was excluded even from going to the next city to visit Paula. John came and collected Cath to go on such visits and Dave was never asked even if he wanted to go and he did. The day of the Christening came and it was a big affair with all their friends and family invited to celebrate and this also included Cath and the children but Dave was left out. Again, John collected Cath and the children from their home and took them away to the party while Dave was left at home. He felt very sad and wept as he sat alone in the empty house which echoed with every movement he made. He just couldn't understand as to why he was excluded from the gathering for he did not do anything wrong nor did he have a fight or argument with them. He began to feel anger at the audacity of Paula and John for inviting his family and leaving him out, he thought 'what kind of people are these to do such a thing without even batting an eyelid'? He knew how they felt when John was excluded from a colleague's party which he didn't know that well but he and Paula hit the roof and made it known how let down they were but now they do it on someone else. Dave felt that this was the height of hypocrisy and something that he never wanted his children to learn or experience, excluding people, and here they were seeing it in reality happening to their own father and by their mother's sister and family.

This was not the only time for Dave to be on the receiving end of their exclusion because all further celebrations, Emma's First Communion and Confirmation he was left out when Cath on her own or with the children were invited and he felt that this was very wrong. He remembered the First Communion event which was a big occasion in the life of Emma but her parents made this an opulent affair not unlike the TV Series 'My Big Fat Gypsy Wedding' showing off to their family and friends and Emma's big day was used as an excuse to pull this off. Dave recognised this and felt sorry for Emma because it was not her fault and despite her parents strange attitude she was a nice well-mannered child. So he went up town and bought her a watch with a white strap to mark the occasion and unseen and unannounced he drove down to the street where she lived and luckily she was outside alone and he was able to give her the gift without anyone knowing. She was delighted and hugged him in through the car window before he drove away.

Of course Dave often confronted Cath about him being excluded but she didn't care as Cath just does what Cath wants to do and her excuse was that she didn't want to offend Paula so he had to be the scapegoat. She often told him that she felt like a piggy in the middle between Paula and him, but he objected stating that he was her husband or was supposed to be and that he should come first; alas this was never to be the case.

After Dave came home from America he had no job to go to so he attempted to start his own business in a part time capacity while attending a 'back to education scheme' operated by the government. He was gifted academically so he found this not to be a problem but his business never really took off so he looked about for employment. The scheme lasted three years and then he was determined to secure gainful employment with some company or another and would have considered doing anything at all. However during the time of the scheme he was still looking after the family and the home, paying all the bills and providing enough for everyone to even have a holiday. Now it was not anything fancy but he would take the family including their dog Shep, camping to different scenic places in their country. They all loved this including Cath because they were getting to see their country while spending time together in the very close knit settings of the car and the tent. They would go to cafes or restaurants for their meals and just sleep in the tent which suited everyone.

Dave kept on applying for employment and was called for an interview with a semi-state body and the job was an adventure with all kinds of duties. Dave was delighted with being called and did a good interview but there were such a lot of people who applied for this position that his chances were about eighty to one. Every day for two weeks he watched for the postman but no correspondence came which left him feeling disappointed so he thought 'I suppose no news is good news' but he remained anxious as he had not been employed in almost five years. Then a letter with the company's logo came floating down from the letterbox in Dave's house and he caught it in his outstretched hand, 'wow this is a good sign' he thought. He ripped the envelope and began to read the very formal letter and yes he had been offered the position for a prescribed probationary period and he was to start the following week. He was so delighted that he fell to his knees with his arms raised clutching the letter and giving thanks to God with a single tear crawling slowly down his face. After five years of doing different government employment schemes where he felt that he was not properly employed, he had now secured a job that could last for life, well just over thirty years till retirement age and he was going to ensure that it would, doing absolutely nothing to jeopardise his position. Cath came home from her own government job-scheme that she had undertaken to become registered in government social welfare circles and with doing so she could claim welfare. Dave greeted her and immediately gave her the news; she seemed happy and had some good news herself. She told him that she was selected to go to Sweden on a two week job and different culture experience and she was going the following week.

"Oh there is a problem Cath"?

"What do you mean 'there is a problem'?

"Well I am to start my new job next week and after waiting for almost five years I don't want to miss this opportunity"!

"Oh there is no problem Dave because I am going to Sweden and why does it always have to be all about you"?

"Hold on here a minute. This is not about me but about the family you know, you, me, and the kids and this job will give us a better life so it is more important that you going on a two week trip to some place in Europe for a holiday with taxpayers money and that is exactly what it is"

"Would you ever fuck off and get a life I am going on this trip so like it or lump it"

"Who is going to look after the children while you are on holiday because I will be working"?

"Of course you will be looking after the kids like you always do and that's it"!

"You're a selfish bastard and no doubt"

Cath didn't want to hear any more so she walked away humming a tune and the more he shouted after her the louder she hummed. Now, he would have to go to the company cap in hand and tell them that he could not start on the due date and ask them could they please defer it for two weeks because his wife was going on a job experience trip to Europe. He went into the receptionist whom he had known a very long time and told her his news and she was shocked saying

    "Wow Dave, I don't know if they will be too happy with this as they are sticklers for formality"

Dave felt sad and with beginning to well up the receptionist noticed and felt sorry for him

    "Listen, leave it with me and I will try to swing it for you OK"

Dave was delighted and felt that there are some great people about and he thanked her sincerely for her efforts and kindness.

The next week came and Cath went away off on her expenses paid holiday without a care in the world leaving Dave to look after the children and missing out on his job. However Dave got a phone call from the receptionist to say that the company would defer his starting date and he was over the moon with joy. He went out and as a gesture of gratitude bought her flowers and chocolates because she deserved them without a doubt.

Some people are just parasites living off other people and this can be by their nature, their choice or by circumstances and with Cath it seemed to be by nature and by choice. She never seemed to have an ambition to do anything for herself and all her gains would be on the back of society and the backs of other people because she would never take on any responsibilities for anything. This also applied to her working life where she was employed in an unregistered business so she never paid income tax or social security always getting paid cash in hand in what is call the black market economy. However she did claim and receive state welfare that she never contributed to in any way when she was not working and felt that this was always her right and this included a paid holiday to Sweden. Cath never owned a car or a house but nonetheless drove around unlicensed thus uninsured in other people's motors and certainly lived in a house that was never her own, but her arrogance and her ego would never allow her to be embarrassed or ashamed with this status. In fact she would often boast about it to her friends. Perhaps it was her life and the way she experienced things being done and took it that this is the way to go even if it is the wrong way but how could she know if she wasn't told any different. This left her cold and cynical not only about her working conditions but also her mindset where people are concerned but she observed the unwritten rules – be nice to everyone but you can always insult them with gossip when they have left your presence! Now this make you everyone's friend like running with the fox but at the same time chasing with the hounds thus no one sees the real you and Cath was expert at this just agreeing with everyone. However everything in her life was false but she learned quickly to live with it even though deep inside she resented all and was twisted with envy. She resented being the middle child in the family that was made to go to work when just fourteen years of age while her older and younger siblings received a secondary education but never spoke out to defend her position or criticize her status remaining in silence but cringing. She resented her boss and the power she had over her and being subservient in the same way as the protagonist in Denis Decourt's French Film 'The Page Turner' but she never risked revenge like in that movie preferring to remain to be submissive both at work and socially.

She resented the way she looked: short and stubby with red hair and prominent freckles so she disguised what she could, dying her hair and using layer after layer of make-up to hide her freckles. The perfect Pandora's Box and alas for Dave he was the one who would unlock her hidden secrets of a black heart that even the devil would rate. He unleashed a demon not only unto him but also onto society but being clever as demons are, her treachery was not revealed to all, but remained hidden, and one would need to be very astute to see this. Always pleasant, smiling and everyone's friend, feigning concern but every question is loaded, seeking out information to be used and abused to meet her needs. Cath mixed truth with untruth, a trait possessed with all evil, and being well versed in psychology she used the power of suggestion in subliminal but very effective ways to achieve her objectives. Thus the person or persons would be loaded with misinformation and some times the person would be recruited unaware to them but would carry out her bidding. This would remain true to her game plan exonerating her from any blame, being everyone's friend while her recruits did all her work in destroying the reputation of the subject she wished to hurt. Dave was beginning to become aware of this trait of Cath's but in the early days often fell victim of it when for a long time she was suggesting that his family home which was equally owned by he and his sister and in which Mary still resided; that he should get his share when urging him to go and get it. This caused a terrible friction between Dave, Mary, and her long term partner, so much so that it almost came down to a physical fight. Cath just sat back and smirked while others done her bidding as usual but Dave realized this and backed off from her constant subliminal messaging to him. He thought of her as a cleverer 'Hannibal Lecter' in the movie The Silence of the Lambs, cleverer because she was never found out in general but only by the few who were clever enough to see.

Lizzy's wedding

The grey morning gave way to a light sprinkling of drizzling rain as Dave awoke and gathered his thoughts. Today he had to 'sleep with the enemy' so to speak, as Jane's daughter was getting wed and he and Cath were invited along with Paula and John so he knew sparks would be flying from Paula's tongue if things were not going her way. He dreaded the thought of even being in her company for an hour never mind for an entire day as she always behaved like a spoiled child whose candy sweets were taken away. She loved to be in control of every situation and all the people around her which left Dave on edge because his personality did not fit in with her in the slightest and he never knew what he might do or say that would cause a row. He was clever, witty and entirely honest so most times this did not suit and could upset Paula and her entourage.

Jane, of course is Cath's boss so that is why she and Dave were invited but Paula had often baby sat for her hence her invite, although Jane detested both her and John because while babysitting for her they would take full advantage of her home. He would often take showers and sleep in her bed and not for sex because Paula was a 'Frigid Brigid' just like her sister Cath. John, being a very big man of over three hundred pounds, always left evidence of where he had been because he was very hirsute and sweated profusely. Thus copious amounts of body hair would remain in Jane's shower room and in her bed which she reviled. However, not to lose face and to be her true insincere self, she invited them.

Dave dressed in his finest black suit, white shirt and blue tie, while Cath plastered her exposed body with thick make-up that always reminded him of Polly-Filler for filling in holes in concrete walls. But the sun kisses always won as her prominent reddish freckles always peeped out through the thick make-up. She could be described as after taking a suntan through a sieve but she looked more like a Dalmatian Dog who donned cling film. However despite all this she did look presentable in her new powder blue dress although her freshly tinted eyebrows from red to black made her distinctively resemble Baby Jane Hudson played by Bette Davis in a movie with a similar title.

They walked up the short distance to the church intending to collect their car later and drive out to the wedding reception to be held in a hotel two miles outside town. They hardly spoke on the way and when inside the church Cath made a bee-line to where Paula and John were seated. She went past John to sit beside Paula and Dave was left on the outside of the pew.

After all the pomp and ceremony Paula, the self appointed chief usher told Dave and Cath not to take their car as they would drive them out to the reception and this was reluctantly agreed especially on Dave's behalf. But it was a big mistake for him as now they were in control of where and when he could go.

The girls got into the back seat while the boys occupied the front and while driving out of town Paula suggested that they stop for a drink first. They all readily agreed but Dave thought this to be very unusual as his in-laws always needed to be on time and in the thick of things even thought it would be none of their business. However he put it down to them deciding to have a more relaxed lifestyle which was another error of judgement for Dave.

They stopped off at a pub restaurant on the outskirts of town where Dave bought a round of drinks followed by John. Then a short time later some of Jane's relations who were also friends of Paula, came in and Dave being the gentleman that he is, went up to buy them a drink but when he returned to the table his party including his wife had gone. At first he thought that they were playing a joke but soon realised that this was not the case for he went outside to discover that their car was gone. He was in a state of shock, of rage, and sad all in one and he just could not believe that they could do such a thing, especially his wife.

So now he was left with Paula's friends who were quite embarrassed with the situation and the actions of Cath and company but in an attempt to cover it up just joked and laughed.

Dave was in a quandary now as to what to do next so he put their despicable transgression out of his mind for then and began to relax and enjoy his drinks within their company. He then decided to accept the offer of a lift from this company to the reception hence Dave's third mistake on this day.

They arrived at the hotel which was thronged with people going into the reception and Dave was expecting to see Cath waiting for him in the car park or at the door but she was nowhere to be seen and he felt let down again. He eventually found her in the bar engaged in conversation with Paula and John. His arrival went unnoticed for the most part so he went and got himself a drink.

When the hotel staff called the guests for the meal Paula rose to her feet and ushered her friends to the table before doing likewise with her husband, Cath and Dave, ensuring that each sat where she had designed. Dave did not like this one bit but went along with her orders so as not to cause a fuss, or worse still a fight. Pleasantries were exchanged during the meal allowing Dave to forget for a moment what had just happened and with the customary boring speeches finalising the repast the hotel staff announced that they needed everyone to clear the dining area to make room for dancing. Cath and her party disappeared again and was nowhere to be found so Dave went back to the bar. He didn't feel so alone here as friendly people engaged him in conversation but when the staff began to usher the guests back into the ballroom he followed to find Cath with her sister Paula and all her friends sitting tightly in a corner with no room for him and nobody tried to make room. He was ignored by the entire company as if he was not there so he sadly went back to the bar.

Another man would have stormed out of the hotel and gone home or whatever but not Dave as he could be quite naïve in matters like this but he tried to figure out what was really happening and more importantly for him what was in Cath's mind. He could not understand any of her actions all day because they did not have a fight or a disagreement of any kind and he wanted to see this out in case she had a secret plan. She did worse than treat him like a stranger for you would not do these things and whereas he did not accept them he remained there in the hotel as if to be entrapped in some kind of masochistic trance of mental self flagellation. He, also very similar to the character, a Doctor Malcolm Crowe who was played by Bruce Willis in the movie 'The Sixth Sense' when he died but he didn't know he died or that he was invisible to the people around him thus he was ignored except for one person who could see him and talk with him.

He returned to the bar but occasionally he would peep into the ballroom as if he were a child and barred from an adult party and on one such occasion he saw 'God's gift to men' Cath and Paula, hoist up their skirts as far as they dared to tease the old men in front of them but the young were disgusted as it was like your mother intentionally showing her knickers. Dave thought it to be funny though and thought to himself 'Oh my God, a pair of asses looking

over a whitewashed wall' and remembered a time when a young lad came up to them and asked
"Are you two sisters?"
And smugly smiling and expecting a compliment, they said in unison, "Yes we are"!
But the next question was curt and emotionless from the lips of the expressionless young man when he said,
"Do you not let Cinderella out?"
Dave understood this man's sentiments as his pal used to say that when Cath and Paula were young they were so ugly that their mother use to feed them with a sling shot and tie a pork chop around their necks so that the dog would play with them!
Dave began to enjoy the evening as he struck up friendships with a few people at the bar and contentedly relaxed making the best of a bad situation. However at this point Cath approached with Paula and John in the background and almost demanded

>"Get your coat, we are going home now"
>"Well that's some greeting now! You have not spoken to me all day and now you come over and order me to leave just when I was after buying a round of drinks"
>"Well we are going, so come now if you want a lift home"?

With those final words Cath walked out the door after Paula and her partner. Dave was in shock as this event was sprung upon him unexpectedly but before he could gather his thoughts his so called wife had left him again half way through a evening adding the final insult to injury with an embarrassing move that left him speechless and alone in a strange place that he was not much enjoying in the first place. Nevertheless he finished off his drink and bade farewell to his new friends, called a taxi and went home.
The writing was vividly etched on the wall that their relationship was in deep trouble and Dave recognised this but what to do about it, well he just did not know. He had tried talking to Cath but to no avail and then when he asked her to go to marriage guidance for help she just laughed off the idea saying

>"Sure why would I need to go to marriage guidance? I am happy and you are the one with the problems so you should go if you feel you need to"!

Dave knew that she was right because she had no problems in her marriage and everything was the way she wanted. She had nothing to worry about, no responsibilities, no mortgage, and no bills whatsoever, she had a free car whenever she needed, holidays abroad that she never had to save for, and she had a free house which she never looked after except on special occasions when she would be shamed into it. In fact she wouldn't even sweep the floor except when after cutting a client's hair in the kitchen where she cooked and the family ate. Dave hated this arrangement because he knew it was unhealthy and unhygienic with the hair of strangers floating about in the air with the stench of peroxide and other chemicals involved in hair dressing. He offered to buy her the lease of a busy salon in town and redecorate it but she point blank refused as she didn't want the responsibility, preferring to work underhand in the black economy getting cash into her hand while putting her family health at risk. One of the children actually had to go to the emergency room of the hospital to have a hair removed from around her toe as it was embedded and cutting into the bone but this did not deter Cath.

She had certainly no problems in life or in her marriage.

Dave was very unhappy with the situation and was a lonely man because he lived a singular life but had all the responsibilities of being married with bills and mortgage that he solely looked after. He never thought marriage was to be like this but rather a shared experience where both spouses took on the mantle of household tasks; however he was left doing this alone.

He felt that he could not just walk away as he feared for the welfare of his three children and thought they wouldn't be properly looked after as he knew Cath had an engrained selfishness and extreme jealously that would affect any kind of relationship even with that of her children. He also knew that she resented being a mother and a housewife, detested the tasks involved and only half heartedly carried them out. There was a distinct absence of love, respect and companionship in their relationship but it was Dave who felt left out and for a long time didn't realise what was wrong. He used to get into his car and drive aimlessly, confused with his life until he discovered that he was plain and simply lonely as he had no one to talk with, no one to share his feelings. His supposedly best friend, his wife Cath, had no interest in him or cared less what he felt or thought and if he did tell her anything, she would only use it later to hurt him. She would often suggest to him sublimely that he was no good of a husband, no good of a father, and no good of a person and when someone constantly suggests this, the person begins to think that it is right.

Their whole marriage was a bogus sham, a pretence that all was perfect when in fact nothing was right, not one thing. Their sex life was non existent and in twenty years of knowing each other love making was only just into double figures. Before they got married there was only heavy petting until their holiday when they engaged in the act and Cath got pregnant and then there were three more pregnancies when they were married.

At times when Dave was feeling romantic and passionate he cuddled up to Cath in bed but she very often would push him away and turn her back to him leading him to say

"For fuck sake Cath, you will do that to me once too often"

Cath turned around and opened her legs wide and said

"Go on then get up"

Dave was horrified and disgusted by this and firmly put his foot on Cath's hip and pushed her out of bed. It was a totally act of disrespect on her behalf that scarred Dave to the core.

The day after the wedding he woke up, his head pounding with a hangover from the day before and sat on the edge of the bed pondering the events. Cath lay motionless with her mouth open snoring like the proverbial animal that gives pork and he wondered why he ever got married to such a heartless person who meted out pain and grief constantly. This day should have been a happy day as he was going on a trip to see his beloved football team Manchester in England but his joy disappeared in the dark evil mists of the events of the previous day but he half blamed himself for allowing such things to occur and putting himself into such situations. He knew quite well that he would be alone in enemy territory but he was careless not thinking that the foe would treat him with such angst and distain.

He opened the wardrobe to pack a small bag for his trip and his rage intensified as Cath snorted and snored contentedly. He pulled at a shirt that seemed determined not to come out so he yanked harder and as he did so discovered that the wire hanger was caught on Cath new dress ripping it down the seam from the back zipper. He felt good with this accident and remembered the Leonard Cohen song which had the line of 'I tortured the dress that you wore for the world to look through'. Well he did torture the dress and now you could look through it so he proceeded to do the same thing with another one of her dresses. It felt good for him at that moment for Cath echoed in harmony with the ripping sound with her snores. He went downstairs and took his three children out to the local hotel for breakfast, a routine that they were well used to and loved doing very much. When they came home Cath was already up traipsing around the kitchen, her hair standing on end with smeared mascara that highlighted her bloodshot eyes. She looked scary as she faced Dave.

"What the fuck have you done?" She enquired in a rather slurred tone.

"What are you talking about?" he retorted, not making eye contact.

"You know what! You are a bad bastard, a useless, good for nothing bastard."

"What are you on about now?" He enquired again and added "What about your antics yesterday? You didn't want me there for whatever reason and you made this very obvious treating me like a piece of dirt!"

"But you didn't take the hint, did you? Now look at my good dress it's ruined."

"That's your own fault! You will have to learn that you cannot abuse anyone like you abused me yesterday and get away with it."

"I was only going along with our Paula" Cath began to sob.

"Here, I am fed up with her and all her interfering. I am supposed to be your husband and partner and it is me you should be with and not her".

"I am so tired of the both of you and I feel like a piggy in the middle with you on one side and her on the other" Cath pleaded.

"Listen, you married me for better or for worse and it is me who should come first, I am you husband"

Cath ran up stairs crying and immediately Dave felt sorry for her and regretted what he did on her dresses. He went out for a walk to clear his mind and think about the situation while he walked along the river bank. Cath's crying did not excuse her behaviour at the wedding nor did her sister's persuading, as you can take the horse to the well but you cannot make him drink. In other words you cannot make someone do something that they don't really want to do! He felt terrible about ripping her dresses and felt there was no excuse for this action either but this was what worried him most as it was not in his nature to take revenge and he feared that Cath with all her antics was turning him into a monster. However he did realise that Paula could make life miserable for anyone who went against her wishes but why was Cath allowing her to take advantage to the detriment of her marriage and this in reality is what was happening. He was now in a quandary as to what to do next. He knew his trip to England was ruined and he could never enjoy it so he decided not to go although he had paid for it in advance. So he decided to give all his spending money to Cath to get new dresses in remorse for his actions and she took it without saying a word. He didn't know till later that she had her dresses sewn up as only the back seams were apart so she did not buy anything new but nonetheless kept the money he had given her.

More Straws Breaking

The years passed and Dave continued to make the most of what he had despite the lack of love and companionship in his marriage which he hungered for, but which Cath just could not give. He re-mortgaged the house to install oil heating while making it energy efficient by changing all the windows and doors to PVC thus excluding any draughts from outside.

He redesigned the kitchen cum dining room to make it fit for purpose while fitting a new kitchen to meet Cath's desire, with double patio doors leading into their small garden giving more light while dining. To save on money he did plenty of the work himself, fitting wall tiles and floor boards as well as painting every downstairs room.

Dave also took the family on holiday to all parts of Ireland most times camping which the children loved as well as their King Charles dog and took them to Manchester, England to see his team United play on more than one occasion. The children loved the funfairs of Blackpool with their Ferris wheels and roller coasters so he arranged a week of fun in England's premier resort Pleasure Beach but the place they loved most was the Orlando Resort in Florida USA where they experienced Disneyland, Universal Studios, Cape Canaveral, Daytona Beach on the Atlantic Coast with Clearwater and St Pete's Beach on the Gulf Coast. This place far outweighed their visits to Spain's Costa del Sol for sun holidays. However Dave felt that his efforts were never appreciated by Cath although he knew the children were having a ball of fun, experiencing places, people and things that none of their peers ever did.

On the run up to their trip to Florida, Dave was finishing off the house and purchased wood to enclose the side entrance to their home, but Cath made plans to spend the weekend away in a local hotel for a reunion conference but she did not discuss this with Dave and it came as a total surprise when she did reveal her intentions.

> "Ah Cath I have ordered the wood for to finish off the side entrance and I won't have any help if you go away."
> "Tough! I am going here whether you like it or not"
> "What the feck is this all about?"
> "It is a reunion for the people who were sent to Sweden last year paid for by The European Commission to experience

different cultures in different countries while we associate with a cross community section of people from Northern Ireland"!

"Oh yes I remember that trip when I had to plead with my new employer to defer my starting by two weeks while you gallivanted across Europe at the taxpayers' expense"!

"Ah, you're just jealous"!

Dave was raging with her attitude especially as he had gone out and bought a holiday for her and the children and he was slaving away to finish their house while she was just going to a local hotel to spend the two weekend nights with her friends. He just couldn't believe her selfish attitude and it was for him, like her sticking up her middle finger at him and saying 'fuck you'! Although he was trying to be a good husband and father, giving up alcohol and smoking because she suggested in one of their many arguments that he was an alcoholic just like his 'auld dead father' as she put it, whom she had never known or met. However she kept on drinking and smoking in front of him, even in their home.

When the Friday came for her to go away, the children were dropped off into Dave's workplace by Paula's husband John without announcement and he scampered away even before seeing Dave because he knew full well that he was doing wrong. Dave was shocked by Cath's audacity and her self-centredness to get their children dropped off into his office not knowing if they would be welcomed by the boss and staff but now he could see for sure that she just didn't care about him or their children as long as her plans were being accommodated.

A whole mixture of emotions filled Dave's mind with that of embarrassment, anger, frustration, but these were overtaken by an overwhelming sympathy for his three lovely children who were just babies and they didn't deserve to be treated like this especially by the person who is supposed to be closest to them, their mother. Now almost weeping, he knelt down beside where they were sitting in reception and hugged them not knowing what else to do. He gathered his thoughts for he knew he had to keep them happy for three hours until he finished work for the day so he took them to a nearby shop and to try to keep them amused, got colouring books which they loved and put them back in reception while he went about his chores. Then when five o'clock came and everyone left for home Dave locked up the building and took his children to a restaurant because they had not eaten a meal that day. On the way home the children had to squeeze into the car which was filled with wood but they thought it was great fun but dangerous so he drove with extra care.

They watched a movie at home and then Dave put them to bed doing the usual chores of putting their dirty clothing into the laundry and then making sure they said their prayers. They also had fun with this as Dave's would say his prayer loudly 'Holy Mary mother of God, send me down a couple of 'bob' which the kids thought was very funny.

The next day over breakfast Dave decided to take the children away to a fun place for the weekend as he didn't want them to miss out while their mother was away and he thought that if she can have fun well so can they! They all packed a little back pack with swimming gear as well as a change of clothing and headed off. This was their first time going away without their mother and all of them felt this strange including Dave. However when they reached their destination they booked into a hotel and immediately went down to a leisure centre that had a full size indoor swimming pool along with water slides and plumes and small kiddies rides on the outside. The children had a wonderful day filled with fun and after their evening meal they fell asleep quickly in their hotel room as the day's activities tired them out completely. The next day was Palm Sunday and being religious Dave took them, after a hearty breakfast, to mass, a church service where they received a small branch of a palm tree to celebrate the biblical story of Christ's entry into Jerusalem! They then drove leisurely home taking in all the great scenic sights along the way and also stopping for dinner. When they arrived home it was dark and the children were sleepy from the long journey but a shock lay in store for Dave!

Cath had arrived home from her weekend with her friends and with no one in the house called her sister and her friends saying that the children were missing and that she thought that Dave had kidnapped them! They congregated in his house sympathising with Cath who was doing a fantastic job of vilifying Dave when he was doing something good for his children. They were just about to phone the police to report a kidnapping when Dave and the kids arrived home and he saw Cath's sister and her friends rush out of the house as if it was on fire, perhaps because they realised that they would be making a false report and that Cath exaggerated the whole thing being full of alcohol and not able to think straight. In any case Dave just could not believe the audacity of Cath, controversially going away on a drunken weekend, a freebie courtesy of the taxpayer, coming home drunk as a lord and with involving her friends who were about to report her husband for kidnapping their children! This whole scenario did not go down well with Dave and another piece of his heart dissolved in loneliness and in isolation because despite the fact that he had all the responsibilities of a married person he now realised that he had no partner willing to share anything. Now there was a big dampener on their holiday to Florida which Dave had paid for and he knew that Cath would not even take spending money but would let her husband pay for everything. Dave would not care about this if he had a partner and a companion in this marriage but alas Cath didn't fit into any of these descriptions.

Sour Grapes

Cath became more dominant as time went on and did an assertive course courtesy of the tax payer. Dave felt it was a bullying course she did because she tried to show who is boss while practising her new found audacity on him as if he wasn't suffering enough by her cruel psychological methods. Her new strategy was to invite her friends around to the house for an evening, making a big fuss with expensive wine and cheese and savouries with exotic dessert that she would not buy for Dave or the children. Dave thought this to be so ironic for a person who would hardly sweep the floor always saying that she would love a maid to do her housework but she didn't do any at all. However her pretentious nights were arranged and this meant that Dave and the children had to remain upstairs as the living room and kitchen were out of bounds. These nights occurred regularly upsetting the household and Dave was tired of it never having a say as Cath would arrange them when she felt like it. Her friends were fairly much the same as her because they were artificial and although they wore Chanel, they were as common as muck. The theme was never changing gossiping for hours while backstabbing anyone who was not in earshot and this could be friends or work colleagues but it didn't matter to them as they all equally got a lashing from unrefined crude tongues. There was even one who if she decided to have tea, it had to be made in a special way and served in a China Cup which was always on hand but Dave didn't even know that they had such things as China Cups in their house. Now Cath detested these people as much as she detested Dave but jealousy was the dominant factor at work here because she wanted to be like them in all of their ostentatious ways but like The Greeks bearing gifts she befriended all that she needed. Dave hadn't noticed it before but he began to observe the way Cath operated and being everyone's friend she never fell out with anyone but got others to fall out with each other by backstabbing. But although she was caught out on a few occasions she got away with it with more deceit. At this stage Dave was sick and tired of this whole pretentious rabble coming to his house, confining him and the children to the upstairs while feasting on food and drink that would not be offered to him. It got so bad that he decided to get revenge but he didn't know quite what to do. He watched a documentary on television where couples split up where one took revenge on their former partner and this planted a few ideas in his head. In one case the woman having access to her ex's apartment and knowing he was away for a month, sprinkled seeds on his luxury carpet, and then drenched it with water, this would result in a green growth covering his living space. Another woman ripped all the guys clothing at the seams which left a lot of sewing to be done. Dave thought these to be so funny and whereas they were a pain in the arse they were relatively harmless pranks so he wanted to do something on the same lines and sort of sabotage one of Cath opulent nights. There was one coming up soon so he had to act fast.

Dave was out doing shopping in the local store when an old friend happened to come along and noticing that he was looking sad says

> "Hi buddy, what happening with you? You look as if someone has rained on your parade"!
>
> "Ah well mate, it is just life and especially married life"
>
> "Oh do I sense all is not right in the home house"?
>
> "Yes you could say that OK"

Dave explained what was going on and why he was fed up being a prisoner in his own house and his friend gave him some advice

> "Don't take life so seriously especially married life because it is the worst scenario that humans ever conjured up"

Dave looked at his friend with amazement and wondered what he was going to say next?

> "You see they invented marriage where they expect two people to live in an institution together for the rest of their lives, sure this is a recipe for disaster and who in their right mind would want to live in an institution? These two people that come together don't really know each and when they get to learn this sure they might not even like one another never mind love. So my advice to you is not to take it so seriously because we, men and women, are from two different planets and the worse thing God did in this respect was to give us thinking minds!"

Dave protested his status and wanted to assert himself in his marriage but also wanted to have fun in doing so. So his friend suggested he watch the movie 'The War of the Roses' starring Michael Douglas, Kathleen Turner, and Danny De Vito to learn how he could get revenge on his wife but he also gave him a word of warning that this could be the starting point of a no return situation. He also didn't recommend pissing on her fish dinner, as happened in the movie, especially with her witnessing the event. This set Dave thinking and he immediately went and rented out the DVD of the movie. He watched it alone and laughed most of the way through it, thinking it was one of the funniest but classic movies ever. Now with Cath's night imminent he had to do something fast but what to do was the question for him?

He went to the kitchen to make coffee and when opening the refrigerator to get some milk he spotted six bottles of expensive white wine Cath had placed there for chilling. She had used a whole shelf laying the bottles down horizontally with Pavlova Dessert taking up the next one down and a mixture of cheeses on the next. He noticed that she hadn't bought a single item for him or the kids which made him sad and then angry and determined to take revenge. He got an idea and removed the wine taking them to the bathroom and taking a sharp knife, carefully removed the tin foil at the top. He then carefully removed the cork from each bottle and emptied a quarter of the wine down the sink. He filled a jug that was in the bathroom for the purpose of rinsing hair, with his fresh steaming urine and carefully poured it into the wine bottles making sure that each was filled to the exact same level before replacing the corks and the foil. He found this a difficult task as some of the corks just didn't want to go back into the bottles. Checking his work he was pleased with its accuracy and thinking that no one will ever notice. Just as he was taking the 'new flavoured' wine back down the stairs to the fridge he heard Cath fumbling at the front door to gain entry. A cold sweat enveloped him causing his face to turn ashen and his heart beat to amplify in his ears as he froze half way down the stairs. What would he do now? What excuse could he invent with his arms full of her bottles?

Just then he heard someone call to her and she stopped and went outside away from the door to talk to them and he sighed with relief before scurrying to the fridge to return the bottles just in the nick of time. She opened the door with ease this time and walked down the short hallway and into the kitchen without even taking notice of Dave who now sat reading a newspaper. Cath immediately opened the fridge door and felt the wine as if by some quirk of intuition knowing that they were tampered with and the flush on Dave's cheeks soon disappeared but she turned and said to him

"This fridge is not working right because I put this wine in ages ago and it is still warm! I am going to turn it up."

Dave was so relieved and nonchalantly replied
> "Please yourself"

He noticed that she had her hair styled differently; a new dress and thick make-up covered her face.
> "Gee you are all spruced up and what is the occasion? Are you going out on a date?"
>
> "Ah don't be silly, I have my girls' night tonight; did you forget"?
>
> "Oh right; another night for me and the kids to be prisoners upstairs"
>
> "Ah will you stop moaning and like it or lump it; it's happening.

Cath held these 'girls' nights without consultation and the only reason that Dave would know were the tell tale signs of sweeping and washing the floor from the kitchen to the hallway, a task that she always complained about so never did it! But now everything was clean and tidy for the girls coming over and not like its usual unruly messy state. This was another pretence that Dave had gotten used to over the years. There was no dinner made in the house that evening so with the arrival of Cath's girl friends, Dave took the kids out swimming and then for a meal treat. Cath entertained her guests with Wine, Edam, Brie and crumbly Cheddar, while Pavlova and ice-cream were served for dessert and all scoffed down by her friends Paula, two Jane's and Bernie who complimented the host on her choice of wine and cheese. Jane was the first to express
> "Oh Cath this wine is delicious crisp with a hint of fruit"

Paula agreed adding
> "None of your cheap plonk here, this is fit for any discerning palate and so fruity"

They then gossiped for hours about everyone who was not present, assassinating character, defaming good names, sure anything goes for entertainment in this secret coven.

At about nine thirty Dave arrived home with the children who ran in to tell their mother Cath about their evening but Cath didn't want them in with her friends who were quite amused by this intrusion but still continued their discussion. Cath called out to Dave
> Dave. "Dave, can you come in here and take the children up to their beds?"

Dave when he was finished locking the car, walked into the hallway and peeped in through the door

"Come on kids; leave your mother alone with her friends. They are on the 'Piss' again.
They were not amused by Dave's comment and Paula asked
"What did he say"?
While Jane uttered
"The cheek of him"!
The children ran out and up the stairs followed by Dave who had a smile of satisfaction on his face. Because he knew quite well that these people who took up space in his house were all pretending to be something that they were not and the proof of this was in their conversations that were like empty vessels making the most noise. He also knew that being so pretentious that they would not know Chardonnay from Shite or indeed Perignon from Piss as with the present case of wine scoffed down and enjoyed by all present.

The Final Straw

Dave has a beautiful niece Shell, who is not unlike him in many ways including sentiments and she hails from a very close knit family that are in a word 'fantastic'. Dave is very close to them even though they live in the next city but he would occasionally visit them more so than any other member of their family.
Shell lived Dave's dream in the fact that she was ambitious and lived and worked overseas in a good job, the opportunity arose and she took it gratefully. Dave attempted this move on several occasions in his youth but they were all unplanned, never researched thus always leading to failure, however Shell succeeded and was the living proof that your dreams can come true. She was there several years and settled in her new country when she met Harry, a military man in the US Army, and a whirlwind romance began. They were the opposite in the fact that Shell was stable and reliable whereas Harry was like the Sirocco Wind, you didn't know from where it came and you couldn't know to where it was going. This was unusual for a military man who had to strictly obey orders but when the uniform was discarded, the other man Harry would emerge. He was a very likeable guy, full of fun and absolutely wild and this is why he became a close friend to Dave who on occasion had the same attitude. Harry was from South America so his first language was Spanish and his family were a mixture of Inca, Chinese, and Spanish, and with these genes he looked incredibly handsome. He insisted that his 'Stag Party' was to be held in Dave's city and he felt greatly honoured by this as he had only met him once before but must have made a great impression. Dave and Cath hosted the overnight stay in their home without fuss and the children loved to have visitors stay.
The wedding was a great day full of pomp and ceremony but also great fun with Shell and Harry displaying their prowess in Salsa dancing which was spectacular in all respects. They both returned to their respective jobs after their honeymoon and it was about a year later that Dave had the next contact with Harry and Shell. They were home on a visit and came down to see Dave especially and Harry wanted to talk to Dave
"I hear that you love Hawaii"
Harry said in a non-provoking way.

"Hawaii, wow that is heaven on earth but I only saw it in the movies and in photography"

Dave replied excitedly thinking of his paradise so far away on the other side of the planet. Harry interrupted his thoughts

"Well what if I told you that you have three years to make up your mind and get there because I was transferred to be stationed on the island of Oahu near to Honolulu with Waikiki Beach, Pearl Harbour and you are welcome to come and stay with me; so all you would need is the price of the trip and spending money"

Dave was in shock with his mouth agape but speechless and he could have been knocked over with a feather.

"Oh fuck, you are inviting me to Hawaii? I don't believe it!"

"Well you may believe it as it is true"

"Oh fuck, oh fuck, oh fuck"

Just then Shell and Cath came up to them and Shell asked Harry

"Well did you tell him"?

"Yep"

"And what did he say"

"He said – oh fuck, oh fuck, oh fuck"

They both exploded in a fit of laughter at Dave's shocked expression that remained on his face when Cath inquired

"Tell him what"?

Shell said

"Oh I am sorry Cath, Harry was transferred to Hawaii and we are going to be stationed there for three years and we are inviting you to come and visit us there within those years"

This time is was Cath's turn to be shocked as she stared into space with a nervous excited expression on her face for she like Dave could not believe what she was hearing. They saw it in the old Elvis movie 'Blue Hawaii' and always dreamed of visiting but never thought that the opportunity would ever arise.

Dave began to save from the very next week after hearing the great invitation of a vacation in Hawaii from Harry and Shell and he asked Cath to do likewise because it is an excellent opportunity not to be missed but he couldn't manage to raise the fare for both of them because of his low salary. She agreed to do her best to save even for her spending money and arrange to get the children minded while they were abroad. Cath's boss offered which left them feeling content as they knew they were in good hands.

The day arrived for their fantastic journey and Dave felt that he was in a surreal dream as they were flying like jet-setters first into London to catch a flight to Los Angeles and then another flight to their final destination Honolulu Hawaii in the middle of the Pacific Ocean. The trip to Heathrow was just an hour's flying time and it was mainly business people travelling who didn't match the enthusiasm of the two intrepid travellers brimming with expectation. They boarded the non-stop flight to LA and here we had some more people that were on vacation and the excited expression showed on their faces that lasted even though it was a twelve hour flight. The 777 Boeing jet navigated north across Scotland and on to Iceland which seemed like a giant Christmas Cake with sparkling white icing as the winter snow still covered everything below while Dave viewed the spectacle from his lofty position of thirty five thousand feet. They then crossed Greenland and Canada until they came to the Rocky Mountain Range on the western seaboard of the American continent before turning due south down to the 'City of Angels'. Dave marvelled at the engineering feats of man to create a flying machine of huge tonnage capable of navigating half way around the world carrying over three hundred people in comfort and with such ease at five hundred miles an hour and at six miles high.

Dave and Cath were greeted at Honolulu airport by Shell who had lei garlands as with Hawaiian tradition and these were made from beautiful fresh flowers of purple, red, and white. An aura of joy descended upon the visitors as Shell embraced each of them in turn

"You are very welcome here uncle Dave and Cath"

Shell always gave Dave his full title and he was very happy with this because he felt it verified his importance to her and it also made him feel good. They drove to Shell and Harry's home on the army base in the north of the island which took about an hour. Harry was on duty and as it was late evening they retired to their bedroom for much needed sleep. Their room was bright and airy and had a double and a single bed. Dave jumped into the double bed expecting Cath to join him but she didn't and opted to sleep in the single. He was unsure if this was because she just wanted a night's sleep without any interruptions or was it something else but in any case he did not mind at all because he had a great big double bed all for himself.

The heat of the early morning sunlight blasted into their room awakening Dave with its pleasant warmth and this was a pleasant surprise for it rarely happened at home. Hawaii was theirs for a full month to explore these beautiful islands and to discover what their relationship was all about with all its turmoil, twists and turns. This was a chance to rediscover themselves and each other being away from everyone, away from the places and people they were familiar with because it was them and them alone for a majority of the time. This was because Harry and Shell naturally had to work during the day so Dave and Cath could get to know each other all over again without any interruptions or calls of duty so to speak.

The camp where they stayed was nothing like Dave had imagined because it was like a small town in the US and had all the facilities imaginable and they explored it using pedal bicycles belonging to their hosts. However, their conversation was just courteous and polite even over meals and it was then that it struck Dave that they were complete and utter strangers with absolutely nothing in common except for their lovely children. He let her cycle in front of him as he pondered all of this observing her body as it motioned from side to side with her shorts and clinging t-shirt but there was not even a single spark of physical attraction left in him for her. 'Feck, he thought to himself, this is serious because if I am to live with this stranger who is now in front of me, for the rest of my life with not even an eye attraction never mind an arousal in my groin region sure I may as well be dead'. This very though made him shudder in fear of the future and as a forty something year old man and that was a lot of time to spend in misery. He felt that Cath felt the same way because she remained in the single bed and neither of them even suggested that they should sleep together. He would give it till the end of the holiday and if it was still the same he would need to make other plans for his future because he felt he was not getting any younger and he didn't want to spend the rest of his life in loneliness while craving romance, passion and companionship.

Hawaii was everything that Dave thought it would be and then some. Their hosts Shell and Harry took them absolutely everywhere of interest on this island of paradise with its azure blue waters gently falling onto Waikiki Beach in Honolulu City, the state capital. Dave though this to be fantastic to have a beach right on the edge of a city where you have bikini clad ladies mingling with business suits along the promenade. However in the north of the island is the surfer's realm where thirty foot waves can be caught by the not so faint hearted who can defy gravity and peril of sea and shark to ride nature's rollercoaster in the deep swells of the Pacific Ocean. These places are where holiday makers came and stayed so a two week vacation turned into a lifetime of pleasure. Dave ventured into this foamy brine on a 'boogie board' and enjoyed going just ten yards out and the 'belly surfing' back to the beach and he felt safe with Harry beside him covering his every move because even this close to the beach the sea has no mercy.

The much storied deep water port of Pearl Harbour is also here in Honolulu and it is a busy naval ship yard with all of the US naval trappings. But it is also the sea grave of the Arizona Ship and its crew, that was sunk in the infamous air attack by the Japanese. The ship remains underwater in the harbour and it is the resting place for some of its crew who did not make it out of the sinking vessel. The United States Government along with the navy erected a solemn memorial in the form of a platform across its bows where people can come via naval launch to pay their respects. Harry and Shell took Dave and Cath here and on the way over on the naval boat, a member of the crew in his brilliant white uniform reminded the visitors that where they were going was a grave and to have respect for the gallant departed seamen killed on this dreadful morning. The four visited in silence as they viewed the large wall with the list of the sailors who lost their lives. Dave went outside to where there was a rail looking out into the harbour and he could see a round funnel shaped piece of metal jutting out of the water, a fragment of the ship and he wondered what it was actually like then when the skies darkened with enemy planes, unexpected in so many ways because no declaration of war existed between the two countries. It was early morning and almost everyone was below decks sleeping deep within the hulls of all the US ships in dock taking them by total surprise. The noise must have been deafening as the pilots from Nippon dropped their deadly cargo of bombs, some of them torpedoes. Dave tried to imagine the panic, being awakened by explosion after explosion and trying to clamber out of the bunk beds wondering what was going on with the stench of sulphur mixed with burning oil and melting metal, a cold shiver ran through him. He said a silent prayer for all the sailors who lay here with their ship. Now, because Dave was so interested in history Harry and Shell took them up to the beautiful mountainous region in the north of the island. They stopped at a viewing point high up on the narrow winding road and from here they could take in the whole landscape and look down the valley right to the sea. This ravine is what the Japanese used as a navigation source by dropping down into the valley and flying low to decrease any chance of radar detection while they fly straight into Pearl Harbour. Dave was amazed by the astuteness of the pilots and could only imagine the darkened skies with hundreds of planes massing in this beautiful valley to carry out their evil deeds. This was one of the many places of beauty and interest that their hosts took them to see on this island of paradise. Then at the end of the third week Dave wanted to view an active volcano for which the islands are famous but he had to travel to the 'Big Island' as the locals call it and the proper title is the island of Hawaii. This was confusing for the intrepid travellers who thought they were in Hawaii but it is a cluster of islands in the mid-Pacific Ocean, each with its own individual name. Dave and Cath went along to a travel agent recommended by Harry and Shell and they got an excellent deal for a weekend away on the big island with a hired car in the deal. The cost was just five hundred dollars for their flight, three nights in a five star hotel with a nice auto thrown in for good measure but they would need the car to go exploring the island. The hotel was luxury Hawaiian style and they had just missed from the week before, movie star Nicholas Cage on his honeymoon, after his marriage to Lisa Marie Presley daughter of Elvis. Of course Dave was afforded this trip because it didn't cost him a cent to stay with his niece. When they sat down for dinner they were treated in five star luxury and entertained by Hawaiian Music and Hula Dancing by beautiful local girls dressed in grass skirts who went down to the tables to dance for the diners. The men wore flowery coloured shirts and played the musical sounds unique to these islands and it was exotic and the most romantic sounds ever, whereas the girls dance was telling a story just like ballet does. Dave and Cath enjoyed the experience but alas there was no spark of romance ignited between them and Dave was disappointed by this. He felt that any that ever existed between them was truly gone, never to return and perhaps this was caused by the attitudes and sentiments which were poles apart between them.

They visited beautiful waterfalls one of which was called 'Rainbow Falls' because of the rainbow created by its mist as the water splashed down from high above. They also travelled to isolated towns that sprung up to cater for the ranchers of the district and they would not look out of place in an old Western Cowboy Movie with its raised wooden sidewalk and its quaint inhabitants. This was 'the big island' of Hawaii but it had a sparse population within its bleak black and grey volcanic mountainous landscape but sure that is why tourists visit and Dave and Cath were no different. The island also boasted very lush tropical rain forest as well as lush farmland, because land created by volcanoes contains all the minerals and nutrients necessary for this purpose.

They visited Kilauea Volcano which is the worlds most active and it is creation at work because it is making more land as its constant lava flow into the ocean solidifies, thus new land is created. It is the belief of the natives that the ancient Polynesian Goddess 'Pele' rules this mountain of fire and creation so it is the opposite of what westerners believe that fire is only a destructive concept. Dave and Cath were captivated by this awesome sight and stopped at one of the many portals into the earth's core where plumes of steam rose up into the air by the force of nature. These plumes of steam had the distinctive stench of sulphur that only added to the deep mystery of the universe and of creation because it came from the earth's core. The pair of travellers from the other side of the planet marvelled at this and thought themselves so privileged to experience such a glorious sight and sound of the hissing steam. They travelled down a road and were stopped by park police/rangers who advised that the road was impassable due to lava flow which crossed the road ahead; so 'Pele' didn't want them down here!

Their three day trip ended uneventfully as they flew back to the island of Oahu and Honolulu Airport where Shell and Harry excitedly awaited their arrival. They wanted to know everything about their trip because they had not been to the big island yet but were intending to visit. Dave reported everything in graphic detail from the posh hotel to the smoking mountain and was excited to do so to his most willing listeners; Cath on the other hand stayed silent and everyone wondered if she enjoyed it or was she uncomfortable with the whole experience.

Dave had plenty to think about and this short sabbatical to another place when totally alone only served to confirm that he and Cath were strangers with a familiarity of contempt that was just about tolerated. This holiday of a lifetime turn out to be a testing ritual for a husband and wife of fifteen years who like every couple sail through the rough waters of life and marriage and this voyage of hope docked in the port of separate ways. They endured everything that life threw at them with aplomb but this process moved them so far away from each other that they were unrecognisable so much so that one did not know the other. There was little or no conversation, nothing physical even the slightest of touch seemed out of bounds, and one did not know what the other liked or loathed. Dave wondered how they arrived at this stage unaware in the trouble and turmoil of life but accepting that this was how it should be, with both of them unhappy with their lot. Cath seemed happy to live like this but Dave could not and it was at this time he decided to change things for the saving of his mind, his heart, his soul and his body.

The Reds

Cath and Dave's middle child, Wally, took a liking for soccer football and displayed some signs of skill from an early age and Dave noticed this when he took him to the park for a kick around. He talked football to him and the boy listened intently, taking all in without saying much. He was a quiet boy who seemed to breeze through life without any hassle; whereas he would be present where the action was but didn't get involved unless called upon to do so and this was very much like his mum.
Dave took his to see the 'red devils' at a very young age, to the theatre of dreams when they took a flight for the weekend to England. While he didn't only see a match, he also got a special guided tour of the stadium and met some of the players. This was because Dave had a big association with the club and a friend was a pal of the club's secretary so they had the best seats in the house with all the extras thrown in for good measure.
The very next day they went shopping in the big city and Dave bought some footballing stuff for Wally and some girly stuff for his two little ladies Molly and Dolly at home but he also bought a leather coat for Cath. Then, when they went around a corner and into another street, he saw a jacket in a shop window that he knew Cath would love because it was so unusual, but expensive, he, nevertheless went in and bought that also.
However, Cath never returned the compliment, never ever buying any presents for her husband, not for birthdays, not for Christmas, and not for anniversaries; they just went by with Cath receiving but giving nothing and Dave was always left empty handed.
Dave had a great love for football and when he saw that his son also had an interest he proceeded to do coaching badges from his country's football association and acquired all but two away from a professional. But in the meanwhile he got him coached by some of the greatest professionals in the game and when you are in the know in football these things fall into your lap easily as contacts abound. So with all this knowledge he set about putting his new skills in action with the junior aspiring football players in his town, including his son, first in local leagues and then in international tournaments. These drew all the talent scouts from professional clubs in Britain and Dave felt that this was good to have the players in the shop window so to speak. However his sentiments were not agreed with

in many quarters including his own local league so Dave stood alone against the administration that he felt were holding back any advancement in football for the kids and he was only there for them. This difference of opinion created friction between him and the power that were there in charge.

The team travelled to their first tournament in the north of the country and were just beaten on a penalty shoot-out in the play-offs by a junior team from a professional club from England. This alerted the talent scouts who approached Dave in their hotel afterwards about some of his players but his hands were tied up with the administration and he could not do anything except refer them to his league's committee. However, this tournament served him good and he learned plenty which advanced his coaching techniques and the team improved with every game played.

The next year they travelled to mainland Britain and beat all comers except one and Dave thought that they should have won it outright but he took his eye of the ball. He went to view the opposition in the other semi-final taking notes while his assistant was picking the team in his absence and doing so under the instruction of the administrators. Dave could not believe this betrayal because he got on reasonably well with his assistant who got access to the official team sheet and had filled it in without his knowledge. This left his great side sort of rudderless because going onto the pitch they had no instruction, no strategy and no knowledge of who was good on the other side as his assistant just took over. Now whereas Dave's assistant was a great coach knowing all the drills, he fell rather short in handling people never mind kids and in Dave's opinion listened to and acted on the instructions of the wrong people especially now at this crucial time. Dave was aggrieved by this coup and the ultimate betrayal from his coaching colleague but decided not to have a confrontation in front of the kids and this decision was very much to the detriment of all involved but especially the kids.

They were hammered by six goals to nil and whereas the team were from a professional club, they were beatable and Dave knew how, as he watched them play in their semi-final taking notes on who was to be marked tightly and who on his team was to do so. But his assistant decided not to watch the opposition but rather do things by intuition, a bad mistake as it turned out. He had the audacity to turn to Dave on the sideline after twenty minutes when the team were five nil down

"What are we going to do?"

"Here, what's this 'we' business? You picked the team and sent them out without any instructions. What were you even thinking by not going to the opposition's game to see who is good; and by the way who gave you the authority to do this on me and on the kids"?

"The league did."

"When to fuck are you going to wake up? This is our team, our kids that we have got to know over a two year period and you listen to some fucking arsehole that hasn't a clue about them."

"But he has qualified with all the coaching badges ever!"

"Yes you are right but what success has he ever achieved? I will tell you, NONE ever! So they may as well have given him Blue Peter Badges for all they are worth but you listened to him not trusting in you or in me and now look what's happening? What's more you don't know how to fix it!"

Dave took charge but this was like bolting the door after the horse was truly gone and it was such a pity.

When they got home Dave submitted a full report to the league administration and he was promptly removed from the team as was his assistant but he was later reinstated while Dave was assigned as assistant to another side. Again the league made a grave error by interfering with the team by changing the manager and the head coach as although they had differences of opinion, they worked fantastically together if they were just left alone with one doing the coaching while the other took up the reins of manager. This formula worked and it was proven because they were the first Irish team to contest a final in this tournament beating all comers. They had good players that they made better and constructed a great footballing team but now the kids were 'up shit creek without a paddle' and more importantly without a rudder.

Dave's son continued with his team but was left out on many occasions, also being played out of position and it was felt that this was just petty tactics to get back at Dave. But the main cruel fact was that Wally was unhappy and seeing this, Dave wondered if he could do anything to remedy the situation. He also saw that some other players were being left out so he sat down and began to formulate a plan to put his own team together for an alternative tournament which didn't go down at all well with the administrators.

They made things difficult and even went as far as to threaten players that if they played for Dave's team they would never be selected for any tournaments ever again. Nevertheless he proceeded with the plan, getting sponsorship for the team kit as well as for the players travelling expenses so he was self sufficient in all departments. They did well despite losing a key player with a bad injury and were beaten in the semi finals by the eventual winners. Dave was happy to risk his neck for his son and the other marginal players who didn't get a look in, but sure good deeds never go unpunished. Wally had no team in his home town now so Dave arranged trials with a professional club in the capital with which he was successful. But because now the marriage was in shreds, there was little or no communication between his parents so Dave missed most of his games because he didn't know and he had no car as it was 'written off' after a crash. Wally's uncle John sometimes took Cath but Dave was left out on all of these occasions. So now the league administrators didn't want Dave involved in any of their teams in any tournaments and ensured that he would not because they offered him only subservient roles which he would never accept. Everything he did was all for his son's happiness and his future in football so he didn't mind one bit.

It was only much later when Wally was an adult but still in his teens that Cath got involved in her son's football even though she never ever went to see him play in his own home town league. Dave took a back seat so his experienced advice was never heard as Wally preferred to speak to his mother. He eventually signed for his home town professional club but made only a rare appearance as substitute. Cath, along with her sister, went to every game to watch her son on the sideline because this was her 'prized bull' and she was going to be there to take the credit, the plaudits, and any prize but she was left disappointed because it never happened for him and his breakthrough never came. Despite this Dave felt that he had the skill and talent to play professionally but he backed the wrong horse and whereas a mother can give support, although with ulterior motives in this case, she doesn't know what it is like to be a football player and never will.

Solace

Dave was tired of all the petty arguments, the disagreements and 'tit for tat' things that they both engaged in; he wanted out to get some peace of mind but Cath made things very difficult after he stated that he wanted out of the marriage. She only half believed him and continued on with her self centred ways as her arrogance dismissed any thought of Dave leaving; anyway she just wouldn't let him leave. He wondered how he would tell the children but one day he decided he would so he gathered them together in the living room for the big reveal but he was only testing the water with them.

> "Well guys, I want you to think about something very important but I don't want you answer straight away, I want you to really think about it, OK"?
> "What is it?"

Dave looked at them intensely for a moment and wondered if he was doing the right thing to drop a bombshell into the lives of the three teen angels he loved but was sure they had to notice and be aware that things were just not right between Cath and him. So he continued hesitantly

> "What would you think of me living in another place away from here? As you know me and your mam are not getting on and fighting all the time so for peace would you think it is a good idea? Like I said, don't answer now but go away and think about it and take as long as you like OK?"
> "OK Dad"!

A week passed and his girls both came to him with a question

> "Dad, if you go and live somewhere else could we come and visit you and maybe stay over?"
> "Well of course you can and any time at all, no problem"
> "OK then we don't mind if you go"

Dave hugged them both and his heart was breaking with the realisation that this could actually happen and with their loving selfless response. However another week passed and his son had not come to him so he approached him and asked

> "Well son, did you think about what I asked you. Now I am not rushing you but just want to know if you thought about it"?
> "Yeh I thought about it"
> "And?"

"I wouldn't like it at all"

So that was it, for Dave's plan was truly scuppered now with this reaction from his son that really surprised him as he thought that it would be the girls that objected and not him. Now he had to rethink his whole strategy but one thing was for sure, he couldn't go on living the life he had with Cath. It was unbearable with no love, no friendship, and whereas he had all the trappings, the responsibilities of a married man he led the life of a single guy with Cath not wanting to go anywhere with him. He had to attend weddings, funerals, twenty first parties, wedding anniversaries, and even a night out alone and this made him feel terrible. Of course Cath had her nights out with the girls and attended their parties alone also but Dave was never invited and when he was she just carried on as if he was not there. He was sick and tired of this life he had or hadn't got. He was lonely and stood alone against Cath, against her sister Paula, and against her friends who all seemed to hold precedence in Cath's life, above him and above the children. Their marriage was a sham like many of the things in Cath's life but it was now defunct and Dave knew he could not act out a happy family deception any longer.

It was the fall and nine months after their make or break holiday in Hawaii when an old friend came to work in Dave's office and immediately they struck up and renewed their old relationship with having breaks together. They talked about everything under the sun including their intimate romantic relationships and this lady went through the mill with her former partner who was an alcoholic. But thankfully she left all that behind in the past and had a new partner and was very happy. They kept on talking, about her neighbour Sharon who was in a similar situation to Dave so he sympathised and empathised with her status in life. Dave enquired

"Who is this person Sharon that you keep on talking about?"
"Ah she is a lovely woman who has it difficult"
"But who is she? Would I know her"?
"Sharon Dawson, she lived beside me all her married life"
"Wow I know her and used to work with her years ago"!
"You know I had a big crush on her but she was even married then; so she must have got wed at a very young age"!?

"Ah I must tell her that news and yes she was young getting married but they are at loggerheads nearly every day and she left him many times before but always came back"
"Tell me about it"!

Dave had forgotten all about their conversation and just carried on with his work but the next day the new employee came in and at their tea break says

"Dave, I was telling Sharon that you had a crush on her and she said she remembers you and also had a crush on you"!
"Sharon, Sharon who"?
"Ah you dopy fecker Sharon Dawson who we were talking about yesterday"
"Ah get away to fuck, I don't believe it, Sharon Dawson, well that's a blast from the past"
"Well why don't you give her a ring, here is her number"?
"What me"? "Sure what would I say to her"?
"Ask her out silly"
"Ah no, I don't want to complicate things with her or me for that matter"
"Well you have nothing to lose"!

Dave put the scrap of paper with Sharon's number into his pocket but forgot all about their conversation and he wouldn't dare to ring her as he would be too embarrassed to do so. However life remained awful for him and he felt trapped in a marriage that he could see no way of ending without a massive fight and he wasn't prepared for that in any sense. One evening after going home from work Cath picked an argument with Dave and he stormed off in a rage; driving seemed to help cool him down as it kept his mind occupied and concentrated. A phone call from the security company came to say that an alarm had been activated and could he come at once. He drove to his work place and after turning off the alarm, did a search of the entire building but nothing was out of place so he let the security go and decided to lock up the building alone. He sat down at the reception area thinking about the evening and wondered how long would he have to endure this traumatic life with Cath? He was just about to leave, when taking the keys from his pocket, a piece of paper floated to the ground and picking it up he saw that it was Sharon's number. He picked it on and went back to reception staring at it and wondering if he would dare to ring? He decided he would and his heart pounded more with every number he pushed on his mobile phone and he was half hoping that she would not answer. It began to ring but there was no answer, then all of a sudden her voice, from her answering service and he listened intently 'Hello this is Sharon, I am sorry I missed your call but if you leave your name and number I will get back to you'. The beep sounded for him to leave a message and he fidgeted and stuttered before coming out with "Hello this is Dave; gee you are very snobby on the phone. Give me a call please?!" He hung up and he was sweating and sort of regretting it, thinking 'sure I only gave her the name Dave ah she will never know who it is; ya big eejit!' What if her neighbour was just playing a joke on him, oh feck, this was all he could think as his mind swirled in a mass of confused thought.

Early the next morning he went to work and received a phone call

"Hello this is Sharon"

"Yes Sharon, --- Sharon who"?

"Here how many Sharon's do you know? It's Sharon Dawson"!

Dave had genuinely forgotten that he had called her the previous evening and was never expecting her to return his call, never in a million years. This was because his pride, dignity and self-confidence were all stripped away little by little, by Cath who subliminally told him that he was a useless man, no good for anyone and he couldn't do anything right, that he was a useless husband and father that only thought of himself. So packed up with all this garbage that was so cleverly placed deep in his mind he thought 'sure who would want me'?

"Ach Sharon, sorry I was taken aback by your call and by the way, I know thousands of Sharon's. Sure there is even an island somewhere in the Med where everyone is called Sharon, even the men"

Sharon laughed and laughed before saying

"You are mad"

"No I am not mad, my mother had me tested"!

There was more laughter and Dave plucked up the courage to ask

"Well would you…em, would you.....would you like to meet?"

"Yes I would like that very much"!

They arranged to meet that very evening at seven thirty and decided to go for a drive, not to anywhere in particular. Dave was anxious and excited all in one but never really thought about having a liaison with another human being as it was well over twenty years since he had a date with someone new. So it was a surreal situation for him and he could not believe that Sharon would be interested in him. He drove down the road to where they arranged to meet and coming from opposite directions met exactly in the middle. Sharon looked beautiful, petite with long straight dark hair and sad blue eyes in the way they slanted that were highlighted in her sallow skin. She wore dark trousers with a white shirt and seemed to float as she ambled alone the roadway, smiled an angelic smile as she recognised Dave at the wheel of his car. She got in and began to talk as if they had been together for ever and even the silent periods were not uncomfortable. They drove and ended up in a lovely lakeside village that had a beautiful walkway around its shores and the autumnal sun would keep them warm as they walked and talked.

Dave stopped at the almost empty car park and as Sharon struggled to open her seat belt Dave leaned over to help and what seemed to be the most natural thing in the world their eyes met in that loving way, a way that neither of them experienced in a very long time, and they kissed passionately without thinking. It seemed to last for ages and it felt so good and so right. They walked slowly hand in hand around the lake and talked for ages about everything and as the sun began to set they decided to drive back to the life that they both detested or more, being with a partner that worked against them instead of supporting them. They didn't want this evening of pleasant simplicity to end as it was an escape away from the drudgery of life under the cosh of a dominant spouse. This was not a paramour, an illicit love affair in any sense of the term because their marriages were over, dysfunctional and broken down completely, and they were just acting out a sham of living like happy families which neither of them was comfortable with. There was no romance or sex in their marriages either because Sharon slept in a spare room while Dave slept on the couch in the living room. They would counsel each other with love and compassion especially after their perspective exes gave them a hard time over some trivial meaningless ineptitude highlighted on their behalf.

There was no doubt that there was a big physical attraction between Dave and Sharon and for him she was everything that Cath was not. She was womanly, gentle, petite with dark hair and had clear sallow skin as opposed to red hair and freckles a combination that Dave just did not find attractive at all. But most of all she was into him big time and expressed her love in her own unique gentle way by buying him presents with cards just out of the blue and the first time she did this it made him cry.

"Ah Dave what's wrong? Don't you like what I bought?"
"No it's not that. They are beautiful."
"Then what is it"?
"I have known my ex for almost twenty five years and she never did anything like this for me"
"What she never bought you presents?"
"No"!
"Not even for your birthday or Christmas"
"No"
"Oh my God, that is terrible"

Sharon found it hard to believe that anyone could be so selfish but unfortunately Dave was telling the truth. She bought him a Silver Cross Pen because she knew he worked in an office and was writing plenty of notes and Dave felt assured that Sharon would support him in whatever he decided to do as long as they would be together.
They parted briefly for two weeks as she went with her family on holiday and so that he wouldn't miss her she wrote a love note for each day she was away, only to be opened as the days went by. This piece of romantic thought was well before the best selling book 'P.S. I love You' by Cecelia Ahern and Dave thought this to be the most romantic thing that ever happened to him. He began to fall deeply in love with her but they were both still living with their respective ex partners. It was at this time that he decided that a definite plan of action needed to be taken for him to leave Cath once and for all.
He tried to imagine what it would be like to wake up every morning beside the person who is in love with you, the person who is there for you, the person who will be your friend and lover for ever, it made him feel good and warm inside. He wondered could this dream become a reality, could he ever achieve this.
Sharon came home from holiday and had presents for Dave that melted his heart and their friendship became a true romance because one evening while parked on a deserted beach they made love for the first time. They were talking for hours when all of a sudden Sharon leapt on Dave, straddling his lap and kissing him passionately her hair draping over the side of his face and neck. They removed each others clothing and he was amazed with Sharon because this was the first time in a long time that a woman had taken

the initiative for making love and every move she made got him more excited within his being. Her pallid skin was a feature of her entire hour glass body and everything was perfect for Dave with small pert breasts that rose and fell with her heavy breathing. They explored each others bodies in a gentle sensitive fashion, she loved every part of him, and he loved every part of her. When he touched her vagina she was swimming with love juice and when Dave mentioned it to her she says 'ah that's the way you make me feel Dave'. He took her hand and directed it to his now erect throbbing penis and said 'and this is the way you make me feel'.

"You are so beautiful and everything that I ever desired in a woman but most of all I love your company and want to be with you all the time"

"You know Dave that is exactly the same way that I feel about you and you have my heart, so be gentle with it"

"I will never do anything to hurt you; we both had too much heartbreak in our lives already and now it's our time to experience true love and happiness"

"Yes I agree and I am so happy that you came into my life" - Dave interrupted her by kissing her passionately and then they made love, slow and sensitive with every deliberate move causing their bodies to writhe in ecstasy. The intensity was so great they could have exploded into the cosmos and she spoke throughout as she manoeuvred slowly on top whispering 'I can feel your hardness inside of me' and he responded with 'not only our bodies are connected but our entire beings' and that's the way they both felt. Their squirming body movements accelerated, her whispers became louder and louder reaching a crescendo with a scream as they both climaxed in unison, together as one. Dave also screamed with joy as his penis erupted like a volcano inside her and kept on doing so as it throbbed relentlessly. Sharon collapsed in a joyous heap onto Dave's chest and went to dismount but he held her in position not wanting the moment to pass as their bodily fluid flowed and mingled in delight. They lay there in silence holding each other gently. Dave pulled the soft car rug up around Sharon to keep her silken body warm before making love two more times within an hour and each time was more intense than the other. This reminded them both of the loving making scene from James Cameron's Movie 'Titanic' when Jack (Leonardo DiCaprio) made love to Rose (Kate Winslet) in the back seat of a nineteen twelve Rolls Royce in the cargo hold of the ship. Dave and Sharon were not on the Titanic but their love for each other grew huge and greater than the big ship as they lay breathless in the back of Dave's steamed up car. But would their relationship hit an iceberg along the way and sink just like the storied ship?

It was just going past midnight and as they lay there breathless for a while, Dave came up with an idea

"Here is something mad, are you up for it"?
"Yes but what is it"?
"What if we go skinny dipping"?
"Ah you're joking, right"?
"No let's go"!

And as these words came out of his mouth Dave opened the door and paused to wait for Sharon who hesitantly emerged. They both ran hand in hand naked for the twenty metres to the water's edge and splashed in the cool water lapping around their already goose bumped bodies. The water was cold to begin but they soon warmed up as they immersed into the brine and embraced each other.

"Well Dave, you certainly take me and my life to new heights"!
"What don't you like doing mad things"?
"Oh I certainly do with you but I would never dream of doing them otherwise"

They looked into each other's eyes and after a brief pause Sharon whispered

"I love you"
"I love you too honey"

They embraced and kissed each other passionately again for ages and neither of them even felt the cold water, being taken to realms of ecstasy.

They were so suited to each other with both liking the same sort of things, doing thing together, being in each other's company and there was also a great physical attraction both clothed as well as naked. They could and did tell each other their most intimate secrets without fear and without holding anything back. They both had a wild side even though Sharon gave the impression to the onlooker that she was a shy retiring kind of person but as they say 'the quiet ones are always the worst' but in Dave's mind she was his ideal woman both mentally and physically and he tried to imagine what life would be like if they had got together years before! One thing is for certain he would have rode her senseless because with her he felt that he could ride for Ireland in the world riding championships. He viewed her creamy body now with droplets of salt water covering most of her skin so neat and petite and everything was just the way he liked. She didn't mow the entire lawn but rather clipped around the side, wore the latest trendy underwear with thongs and matching tops and he loved all of this but the best thing was that he found her and that she loved him greatly for who he was and just as he was.

Meanwhile, what Dave didn't know was that Cath had also met up with somebody that she was interested in as a prospective partner. Billy was a 'well off' hillbilly from a rural background and she had met him in a bar that she frequented with her girl friends. He was having an affair with one of them but all new men that came into this promiscuous company seemed to do the rounds with them and they would share, compare notes and then take him or kick him to the kerb when his usefulness had run out. He was a married man and had a family of his own but it was a broken marriage although they still lived together just like so many do, however this would not cause Cath to dismiss him even though he was passed around like a new toy by her friends.
Dave suspicions about his lack of feelings were confirmed. Although he didn't know about Cath's secret liaisons, he did see her coming home in the early hours of the morning, drunk as a monkey with her clothing and hair very dishevelled. He wondered did she have sex after twenty or so years of not wanting to since they met. But he just laughed at her stumbling and her slurring nonsense talk and once she even accused him of locking her out when she couldn't find the keyhole in the door. She would even switch off her phone so that no one could contact her, not even in an emergency. An emergency did occur when her son Wally was assaulted and robbed late one evening and Dave had to comfort and console him alone while the police investigated but when they tried to contact Cath her mobile was switched off and this was her attempt of hiding from exposure of the truth. However Dave couldn't care less what she did as long as it did not interfere with him or the children. But she engaged in crass double standards because what she did, she always tried to justified to herself, to the children, and to others and it was quite OK for her to go out all night with the girls or guys, get stoned drunk and arrive home in an incoherent condition; whereas if Dave

did this she would castigate him to everyone but especially to their children. He heard her doing so on many occasions; poisoning their minds against him, a trait that she was expert at.

So 'Hillbilly' Billy was ideal for Cath because he was well off and was into country music that she also liked, for before she met Dave she frequented all the hoedown country and western clubs that had a clientele of yahoos and farmers that Cath pursued and Billy fitted the bill perfectly. Then after luring him firmly into her treacherous tangled web he could replace Dave in her game of life while lavishing her with all she wanted in holidays, jewellery, cars, and even money; sure it is the same as prostitution but on a greater grander scale.

The sinister part of Cath's plan was to make her paramour acceptable to the children, to make Billy acceptable to them even though he was still legally married as was she but meanwhile at the same time promoting as unfair and evil anything or anyone that Dave did or met in the romantic context. She succeeded in this because she kept hidden the fact that she was having an affair with Billy and only revealed him when she learned about Dave's. She saw her opportunity after demonising Dave to the children by saying that he was destroying their lives by cheating on them and will abandon them because he doesn't care about them.

One evening when Dave was alone in the house his eldest daughter came in, looked in the living room where he was seated, said nothing and just went upstairs. He thought this was strange so he followed her

    "What's wrong honey?"
    "Nothing"
    "But why are you treating me like a stranger, like I wasn't there at all"?
    "You were never there for me and never will be. You never did anything for me".
    "Ah is that what you think"?
    "Yes it is"
    "If you only knew the truth"

She did not look at him while saying these cold words which travelled like poisoned arrows into Dave's heart and soul. He withdrew and slowly walked back downstairs and closed the door. His heart was breaking and he wept for a long time, her words echoing in his ears disturbing his mind with traumatic effect. He pondered hard on what to do but he knew for certain that these were not her words but the words of her mother Cath who constantly drummed this indelible lie into her mind and perhaps into the minds the rest of the children. He wrote a verse from his heart

I was never there for You

No I was there for you

When I joined as one to create you
And watched you grow in a cocoon
Nor when I observed you come into this life
No frills and no silver spoon

No I was never there for you

When I stayed in a loveless union
That battered hurt and abused me
But I took it all 'cause I love you
But you're duped and still cannot see

No I was never there for you

When I saw you take your first breath
And cradled you close in my arms
To protect you from ice on the walls
And steer you away from all harm

No I was never there for you

When I worked all those long hours
To put a roof over your head
And make sure you were not cold or hungry
But safe and dry in a bed

No I was never there for you

When I saw you take your first steps
Where you toddled right into my way
You smiled as I stopped you from falling

Like I'm trying to do to this day

No I was never there for you

So you think I was never there for you
Well I have tried to answer you see
But a question I have for you now
Where you ever there for me?

No I was never there for you

My love it has no pre-conditions
And no matter what you do or say
I will love you forever in heaven
And for here till my dying day

Please read this carefully and know the truth.
Dad

He printed out three copies and left one for each of his children on their bed in the hope that they would understand and know the truth. Dave was always there for them and they were the only reason he stayed with Cath for they were the only good thing in his otherwise unpleasant life but it was a life he chose for the sake of his children. He felt that Cath would not look after them properly in any way and would set them against each other as she did with others for her own amusement or for a more sinister plan that she had hatched. He knew the way she operated: divide and conquer was her motto and she had the ability to instigate an argument between two people by saying something to one out of earshot of the other and then walk away smirking while the two belted into each other. She had the knack of putting the proverbial 'cat among the pigeons' and she used it on everyone she knew with precision leaving her masked of all blame with the recipients oblivious to what had happened to them. Cath did this on Dave so many times and he was caught unaware on several occasions as she liked to be in total control of a person which gave her satisfaction. She began on Dave with not going to the places he frequented before they were married and all his friends were the scum of the earth; of course Dave never believed this for one moment. The first opportunity that he got when he broke off their engagement he reunited with his old buddies and promptly went to his old haunting ground. Then she had to go there to meet up with him again despite her detestation of the place and his friends.

Counselling Lies and Mediation

Dave was a great football fan and at the start of the season he looked up the fixture list for his team Manchester and picked a game versus West Ham United as he wanted to see the special player Paulo Di Canio who played with them. The fixture was due in January of the next year so he booked his passage for a car and two people: him and his son.

Christmas came and went but there was no sign of peace and joy for Dave as the bickering and arguments continued with Cath without any truce over the festive season with the war of the Kelly's continuing just like in the movie 'The War of the Roses'. However he tried to bring some sort of normality for his kids and as usual bought presents, make-up and perfumes for the girls, aftershaves and sports items for his son. He even gave a light admonishment gift for Cath in the book by Kim Woodburn and Aggie McKenzie 'How Clean is Your House'. This was a truthful rebuke of her lack of cleanliness with regard to her normal household chores even to sweeping dirt off the floor. She returned the compliment with the video tape 'Give up your aul Sins'

In January the proposed game was cancelled because of TV rights and the game was refixed for another date however he still intended to go, if for a break if nothing else. Cath however took exception to this and started a big argument in front of the children which annoyed Dave greatly but she continued like a hot chilli being rubbed on an open ulcer. She accused him of going away with Sharon whom she referred to as 'that auld slut'. She assumed this because she had searched his bag and found the ferry ticket which stated for two persons D and W Kelly. However she didn't look at the initials and just took it for granted that he was going away with Sharon. This was not the case but she didn't know and immediately jumped to the wrong conclusions.

He just could not take any more insults so he pulled the ticket out of Cath's hand and got his already packed bag and left but his time he had somewhere to go. He immediately went to Sharon's rented house as she had legally separated months before and was living alone. Dave did intend to join her but only when he too got legally separated to keep everything right. Cath whether by mistake or by design actually drove Dave into the arms of Sharon but it was something that she would abhor because of jealousy and because she would hate to think that Dave could have a life and be happy. Sharon was delighted to see Dave and he told her what happened and she comforted him. Then after making sweet passionate love they lay in bed together talking all night until daylight became apparent through the thick curtains. He sat up and said

> "Here would you like to do something mad?"
> "Well what is it"?
> "Now come on Sharon, are you on for it or not"?
> "Ah Dave I want to know what it is this time before I agree to it because the last time you asked me that I was running into the sea naked with you. I don't think that the neighbours would appreciate two naked bodies running down the road at any time never mind this early in the morning"

They both laughed out loud before he said

> "How about coming to England with me now?"
> "What now, now at this very moment"?
> "Yes why not"?
> "But I am not prepared, not ready to go"
> "Listen just fling a few pairs of clean knickers in a bag and come on and anyway if I have my way you will not be wearing them too often"
> "Ah trust you to think of that"

They both laughed again as she scrambled to get ready to go to England for a romantic time together. Now because it was a last minute plan they missed the sailing so they had to remain in the city until the next one due that evening. They did some window shopping and visited the national art gallery taking in with amazement the Caravaggio masterpiece that featured there. They had so much in common liking almost all of the same things in art, in music and in movies.

The sailing was on the largest ferry ship in Europe if not the entire world and they slept in each other's arms dreaming of a new better life together.

They travelled north to the Lake District and settled for a small village on the shores of the beautiful Lake Windermere to stay in. It was breath taking with all of its buildings constructed from local natural stone and the architecture and planning was perfect. This very spiritual couple, Dave and Sharon, were home at last as they strolled hand in hand around the motherland of William

Woodsworth and Beatrix Potter. Their other world seemed like a distant land as they marvelled in this new world of ideals. Meanwhile back in Ireland Cath was fuming in a rage and contacted a friend that worked in a travel agent's to ask about her husband's travel arrangements. The friend told she could not divulge that information because it is illegal and breaking the client confidentiality rule. However, Cath told some lies and insisted that she must know but the friend told her she could not do anything and told her she would ring her later for a friendly chat. She did telephone Cath that evening and illegally gave her the information she requested but all she could tell her that his car and two people D and W Kelly were booked for the morning sailing and returning two days later. This was enough for Cath to go seeking Sharon's ex-husband in his home and knocked on his door

"Where is your wife"?

"What"?

"Do you know where you wife is"?

"Ah we are separated and do not live together"

This revelation shocked Cath into a crying tantrum and seeing how upset she was asked her in

"What's this all about pet"?

"Well your wife is away in England with my husband and I just wanted to see did you know anything about it?"

"No, to be honest we are separated and have been for nearly six months so we don't really talk that much. But I didn't know anything about this."

"I found out that he was planning to go away with her and this surely confirms it with them cheating on us both and our children, disgracing them as they swan about in his big fancy car"

"Ah that would suit Sharon alright sitting in the front seat waving like the queen. Do you know that she is a very vain person always wanting to improve herself when she has, or should I say had, everything here. I gave her all that she ever wanted but it was never good enough because she wanted more. I just can't make her out at all with her constant dieting and a mouse would eat more than her in a week."

"What are we going to do about it"?

"Ah pet there is not much we can do and I am so sorry for you."

This was enough information that Cath could use as ammunition to fire at Dave on the first opportunity and she would bide her time until that exact moment came around.

Sharon and Dave arrived home into her new rented house and they were planning their new life together and they were relatively happy with their set up. Cath text Dave a few times but he did not answer, preferring not to have an argument just at that time although he kept on paying all the bills associated with his defunct marriage. He was able to do this because of the extra delivery job he picked up at the weekends. However, he was worried about his children, and were they being properly being cared for because Cath had a tendency to take her woes out on others. He secretly went to see them and gave them the housekeeping money for Cath. He also worried about Sharon and could she handle Cath's onslaught of insults as well as making thing difficult for her which was certainly going to happen. But what he didn't know that Sharon was a strong woman who lived all her life on rough estates and could handle anything that was thrown at her so the impression that Dave had of her as a shy timid unimposing woman was far from the reality. He found this out later the hard way when after driving all day, he came home to her and just before going to bed Sharon went to the bathroom while Dave fell asleep. He was woken by shouting and screaming from Sharon and it was so out of character that he just could not believe it. She was dressed in her sexy silk outfit, a black bodice with suspenders holding black stockings but she was like a woman possessed and there was no talking to her even to find out what was the problem. She fired the mobile phone that he bought for her so he in a rage told her to fuck off and calm down. What happened with her was that she was going to surprise him by wearing the sexy gear which he loved so much but when she came into the bedroom he was asleep and she got into a rage with seeing Dave asleep. She felt that this was a rejection and the old feelings from her lost marriage welled up inside her and just exploded out. Dave did not know she planned on dressing up as she had not said and being so tired fell asleep but he would have remained awake if he had known because he loved riding Sharon any way at all because it was not just riding, it was love making with the woman he was in love.

Sharon noticed Dave's uneasiness and thought that he was having second thoughts about them living together and she asked him so. He answered honestly and told her he didn't have second thoughts but he told her his worries about her and his children. She understood that but still had a nagging doubt and after two weeks of her saying this he felt that she didn't want him there with her so both of them thought the exact same thing that one didn't want to be with the other. This was a strange predicament for Dave because he knew full well he wanted to be with Sharon and his worries were if she could handle all the confrontations that Cath would surely impose on her along with the lies and insults and these were his only fears. There existed a communication breakdown between them, not that they were not talking but what was said was being totally misconstrued and misunderstood by both of them.

Dave asked Sharon if she wanted him to leave and she said that maybe it is for the best as I think that you miss your kids too much. This confirmed to him his negative beliefs about what Sharon thought and he couldn't believe what was happening because he had made the break and was willing to see it through no matter what. He was not looking forward to going back to the person who made his life hell and would now surely do her utmost to make it even worse when he returned. He though 'am I mad in the head, leaving the woman that I love and that loves me, to go back where I am despised, mistreated, and abused'?

Dave got his phone and answered one of Cath's text messages and they agreed to meet on neutral ground to discuss what was going to happen and how they would decide on an amiable outcome to the ending of their dysfunctional marriage. He hated the thoughts of seeing and hearing Cath again but maybe they would come to some quick arrangement.

Dave looked over at Sharon as she sat on the bed and there were tears in her eyes and she looked so beautiful, just like a porcelain doll. He went over and they embraced in a gentle loving way that only two people in love can do. Both of their hearts were breaking as tears flowed from both their eyes. She didn't want him to leave and he didn't want to leave but neither of them knew!

The Return

Dave met up with Cath at a local hotel to discuss their future or lack of, in this case and he wanted to make an amiable agreement, an agreement in which they were both happy. However Cath would not agree to anything he suggested so he asked her to formulate something but of course she would not hear of it. He suggested mediation in passing and she agreed to go to counselling; that not only surprised but shocked him because years before when he suggested that they go, she had refused point blank saying that she had no problems in her marriage.

What Dave didn't know was that Cath agreed to attend marriage guidance counselling, run by laity from the Catholic Church, not to rescue her marriage but to experience counselling in reality. This was because she was doing a counselling course to become a therapeutic counsellor and this experience would be really beneficial to her. She displayed her expertise by fooling the counsellor in her actions and acting out the whole 'poor me victim' scenario while agreeing to things suggested by this amateur counsellor. Nonetheless she dismissed everything immediately when she came outside and would always state this to Dave's face.

> "Don't think that I am going to be a fool for you; cooking a meal for Valentine's Day, oh the very thought of it makes me sick"!
>
> "Why the fuck didn't you say this inside to the counsellor you two faced lying fucker?"

This went on for almost eight sessions and Dave could not take anymore and went to see the counsellor alone to explain his case. He had also kept a diary of his interactions with Cath but the counsellor didn't want to know any of this and dismissed him out of hand. Cath had acted and lied throughout every one of the sessions and the counsellor believed every bit of her sham antics and he just couldn't believe that she would take sides.

They moved onto the next level of separation and this was obtained by attending a 'mediating service' for intending divorcee couples. This service is more clinical where the assets of each are revealed by consent and a mutual agreement is endeavoured to be reached. Cath again lied about everything and didn't even flinch when she told the mediator that her children's allowance benefit was only half of what she was receiving. Sure the lady was able to look up a welfare book to reveal the truth and Dave knew quite well that he was not going to get a fair agreement from Cath in any sense of the word.

After one session while walking together Cath began to rebuke Dave aggressively and at the same time castigating his entire family and just by chance Mary, Dave's sister was able to hear the whole conversation. This was because Dave had his phone switched off but when leaving the session switched it back on and by mistake hit the redial button that called Mary, the last person he called. She couldn't believe it was Cath talking because it was not like the person she knew her to be and being so rude, so crude, and so aggressive, it was just like a different person. But this was the real Cath hidden perfectly in fake smiles and false friendliness.

Cath knew for certain that she had lost Dave when one evening she came in drunk and even though she engaged in a horrible war with him, she wanted sex. She attempted to use all her womanly sexual charms by standing half naked in front of him rubbing her bare breasts and lifting up her skirt to reveal her knickerless vagina but Dave was having none of it and dismissed her with scorn. He was now too clever as fall into another of her traps and anyway her antics disgusted him so much that he almost got sick. He wasn't quite sure what her plan was but he did know she was quite capable of anything like crying 'rape' or it could have been just an attempt to boost her ego to boast that she still had attraction and could get a man aroused even though she didn't particularly like sex. But no matter what her plan was, it didn't work and she left the room rejected and Dave thought about that old cliché 'hell hath no fury like a woman scorned'.

Dave was immune to her ways and he knew her life game and from the beginning she set out to take control, firstly by isolating Dave from his family and friends saying that they were no good and if she succeeded in getting him to believe this he would depend on her, making him like putty in her hands. Cath also condemned the places that he went to, in chipping away at everything until there was nothing left in his emotional locker and he told her so. But she persisted and when this didn't work she stooped to the lowest by radicalising and brainwashing his beautiful young children against him just like a despicable rogue cleric.

The Couch

Life became more fragile for Dave and for six long years he resided in the living room of their house while sleeping on the couch. He had to be self sufficient so everything he needed had to be kept within this room and it was not good for anyone concerned as he need to keep the room locked to protect his privacy in the height of his battle with Cath. He bought televisions and music centres for his children's rooms so that they wouldn't miss out on any entertainment but he knew this was not right and that it was no way for them to live a home life which was supposed to be a happy place. He blamed Cath for this while Cath blamed him and there existed an impasse leaving a situation where everyone lost! Dave wanted to move out and be with Sharon but he thought that she didn't want him in his present situation and he was also told by friends that went through a divorce to not leave the family home. Cath wanted him out but she did nothing to ensure that this would happen by non agreement to any proposal from him or from the independent mediating service.

These times Dave considered the dark nights of the soul, his soul which was being affected big time with subliminal psychological attacks from Cath. He turned to alcohol to relieve the torment even if only for a few hours but this created more misery for him and for all. Cath would often lead him into a false sense of security pretending to be friendly and suggest that she would concur with some arrangement but then change her tune in a mind game and demoralise Dave with a knife cutting psychological wound.

He felt abandonment by all his family, his friends, his children, and even by himself as he languished in the mire of depression and despair. This caused Sharon to once say that Dave was too good for his own good as he tried to please and make everyone happy but didn't please anyone, not even himself.

Now life seemed useless for Dave and he had come this far always trying to make everyone happy, everyone that is except himself! He felt that he didn't make anyone happy and his sham slip shod of a life did not work because he got married for the wrong reasons so it was always destined to doom. His children were estranged to him now even though they lived under the same roof but Cath made sure they were on her side against him and most contact and conversations had to be approved by her in advance. But they were duped by her into thinking that he was a bad person, a bad father, and a bad husband who went out on the town embarrassing them drinking and going with bad women. She also conjured and set into their minds that he was never there for them, did nothing for them nor did he take them anywhere because he was a selfish man, period. This made Dave's heart ache for his children to have their impressionable minds poisoned against the person that loved them most but what could he do about it as she was firmly on the horse's back holding the reins and galloping into hell. It is a true saying that 'hell hath no fury like a woman scorned' and this woman with the black heart was well and truly scorned.

He had lost everything that was dear to him, his children, and the woman with whom he was in love but most of all he lost the essence of life, dignity, pride, self esteem and hope. He went into the darkest place for a human being to experience: despair, a tapering blackness that most time has no escape and he was firmly sliding deeper into its depths.

It was Saturday night and his town was buzzing with an air of excitement and of happy people enjoying the night life, couples were hand in hand and in love but for Dave it was like looking into the past when he spent many hours and nights here without a care in the world. He drove on aimlessly, away from the bright lights and into the darkened night, his body numb but his mind concentrated and fixed on the job on hand. He though how unhappy that he made everyone even the ones he loved and that they would be better off without him so if he went out of their lives forever they would be better off.

He found himself on the darkened docks that were closed for the night and with the only bar there also closed as the last revellers had gone a few hours before. This was the night he would make everyone in his life happy, even himself. He got out of the car and went over to the edge; the dark water looked blacker than ever even though the yellow lights flickered on the swirling motion of its incoming tide. He chose the deepest section and he knew where it was because he came here often to see the ships docking with the largest ships docked at this point. He returned to his car and swinging it around to get a longer faster drive that would take him away from the edge for less chance of detection until the next day. He revved the car and sank his foot on the accelerator; there was no expression on his face except for his eyes half closed like slits of determination. The car screeched into motion and two seconds later screeched again as Dave applied the brake but the car kept on going forward skidding towards the blackness and the cold icy water of the now full tide, the loose grain from an unloaded ship, giving momentum to the braking car. It kept on going when at the last moment suddenly came to a halt with its front wheels on the outside edge of the next world.

After a moment or two Dave got out of the car and immediately fell to his knees and bowing his head rested his forehead on the ground just inches from the water. He wept and gave thanks to God that just at the last moment he came to his senses because everything mattered to him in his life and that all these difficulties were lessons to be learned. He knew for sure that his children would dearly miss him so instead of dying for them he would remain living for them. He looked around and saw that a thick anchor rope had prevented the car from going into the deep river but he did not see it when he was behind the wheel as it rose and fell with the motion of the incoming tide. He thought that nature had a definite hand in preventing him from doing a cowardly act when he is a fighter, who before this would never give up no matter what the odds were against him. So from that moment on he vowed to fight Cath tooth and nail with everything at his disposal.

Fight Is On

Dave was very aware of the old cliché of 'my wife does not understand me' as a ploy used by a married man when chatting up and hitting on a prospective female to engage in an affair. But it was more than this for him, as Cath not only didn't understand him but never tried nor cared as to what way he was, except as to how she could use him. She never communicated with him save for to highlight his faults and what he was not doing like sharing in the household chores. But he was confused as she didn't engage in any chores except to brush the floor after she cut a clients hair although she would sometimes cook for the family in the same space as she did her hairdressing work.

Cath resented and despised being a wife and a mother with all that it entailed but now she wanted Dave to take on the mantle of both father and mother while she did her work in their kitchen despite the hygienic health dangers to everyone who entered especially her family. Cath often stated that she would love a maid just like her old boss Jane, whom she envied to no end, to do her chores but this could never happen as their finances would not permit it and as she had no ambition to put this in place. Dave thought it to be a ridiculous idea as they had only a kitchen - dining room downstairs and three bedrooms and bathroom on the first floor. He helped out with the three children doing schoolwork and taking them places for hobbies of karate, swimming, athletics and football. He also did the weekly shopping and felt he just could not do anything more but Cath was never satisfied and wanted to be free from all chores associated with being a mother and a wife but at the same time having no ambition to better her station and status in life.

On the other hand Dave had ambition and was always on the look out for opportunities to improve things for him and his family however Cath smothered and stifled all of these with negativity and subliminally stating that he was useless at everything like being a bad husband, being a bad father, and generally being a bad useless person. Now when someone that you live with and sleep with constantly tells you this, you begin to believe it as it is etched within your mind and this was firmly placed there by Cath. However, his ambitions were big and in that time of recession, businesses were coming on stream to the market at a give away price and Dave could afford them as he had a good job with great earning potential. There were two bars that came on the market for sale freehold and having done thorough research, he knew that they were feasible propositions that would work.

Dave was now trapped in his own circumstances, a creation of his own making because he married a woman who didn't love him and who would never give her heart or share anything with him. He needed love but never received it from Cath whose selfishness was nothing he ever experienced before and he didn't know how to deal with it. He wanted out but felt that he couldn't just walk away from his beautiful children whom he loved with all his heart because he knew full well that she would punish them in her own unique, psychologically inimitable way like she did on him. This process was already beginning when Cath decided not to function as a mother in one task and that was not to cook for the children. She got take-away fast food for them which they naturally loved with sugary soft drinks but they were receiving no nutrition or roughage but just grease and because of this they gained weight especially the girls who didn't partake in any sporting activity whatsoever. Dave tried to alleviate some of this culinary retribution of Cath's by taking them out for lunch, especially on Sundays when she would be in bed with a massive hangover or out with her friends having lunch herself. He didn't know how to correct this to provide food for his children although he thought long and hard about this dreadful situation. The cash he was providing for food, she was saving and he knew this because the money he was leaving was building up and not being used at all. He discovered that she was now planning another foreign holiday that she took three times a year without shame while her children were suffering from her non functioning motherhood with not shopping or cooking for them. She, with her friends, visited Morocco, Italy, Spain, Portugal, and even Germany on a supposed Christmas shopping trip, living the affluent lifestyle, out partying every weekend with her friends while denying her children their basic rights of cooking and feeding. She would also switch off her phone when out, creating a situation where she could not be contacted which left a suspicion that she was having an affair and this was revealed when a major crisis arose at home when Wally got mugged on his first night out at a disco.
Dave then decided to get shopping vouchers in their local supermarket that could not be redeemed for cash so that she had to

shop for food for her children in order to use the vouchers. Perhaps this was a very extreme measure but he could not think of any other way to provide for his children to feed them properly as he had to work every day and sometimes even on Sundays which only served to exasperate the children's ordeal and add to his dilemma. He had to learn to be self-sufficient, doing all his own shopping, cooking, and washing while he continued paying all the household bills, including the mortgage which Cath never shared although she was earning plenty of money from her own business of hairdressing in the kitchen of their home.

This was a very strange situation for all concerned with Cath using their kitchen as a hairdressing shop and Dave living in their sitting room so both places were off limits to the children because the kitchen was occupied by strangers while Cath was working and had clients there and the sitting room was locked when Dave was not there. He was forced to lock the sitting room door because Cath would go in to snoop into Dave's personal stuff and once she threw out the couch he had bought to sleep on but she brought in an old couch that stank to high hell which she purchased off Travellers going around selling door to door. So with all this happening he had to buy a couch that he could sleep on and a wardrobe because she was destroying his clothes.

Cross Swords

Dave's legal team of solicitor Tom and barrister Justin rushed over to him stating nonchalantly 'we are up next' and a sick feeling jabbed into his stomach before enveloping his whole body. Tremors of nervousness began causing him to stammer out
> "Oh I don't want to do this as I have a bad feeling about the whole thing!"
> "You will be fine and nothing bad is going to happen to you. We have a good case"

Dave was reassured by his legal team.
They walked into the courtroom together, with Dave experiencing jelly legs as he felt weak and took a place at the back of the room with his team underneath the bench. Cath and her legal team took up a place near the entrance door and she had her head bowed as if to gain sympathy from all present but Dave's legal team knew all the intimate details of their marriage and they had a good case for a legal separation. They knew the marriage had broken down, if it ever started, and that no love was ever shared between the parties. Dave acted like a responsible married man ensuring that his family were comfortably housed with every modern convenience where he paid all the household bills including the groceries. He took them on holidays every year visiting Disneyland in Florida, Europe for beach holidays, Britain and at home in Ireland. He engaged fully as a husband and as a father in every respect, taking on all the necessary responsibilities but did this alone as his wife never shared anything like living costs, even though she had her own business which she operated from their family home. This left Dave paying for her business in energy costs of heating water and hairdryers which were constantly working. Despite all of this he lived the life of a single man because Cath would not go anywhere which involved his family or friends so he had to go alone to weddings, special parties, funerals and functions that a normal couple would go to. He felt lonely, isolated and on his own within this hellhole of a marriage which completely ruined his confidence and dented his pride and dignity, for Cath engaged in the most covert psychological operation constantly telling him he was no good of a husband, no good of a father, and no good of a person but this was all done sublimely under the radar and she was expert at this. She learned which buttons to press to make him angry in front of other people because if out

together for a night when she didn't want to be there, she would say some bad things about him when they were away from their table and when they came back, all the others would see is Dave's anger displayed, while she would cower down like a little lamb. She learned how to make him sad by bringing up past events in his life that she had only been told of: like him missing his father and never knowing him as he had abandoned him and his mother which he was heartbroken about. Also missed ambitions where he wanted to be somebody but never got the opportunity of education because of poverty. Cath would often say to him even in front of the children

"You're just like your auld father, a good for nothing alcoholic and you will never be happy with anything"

She would then smirk with satisfaction while he sobbed, knowing that she was half right. She forced him to re-live the agony of his shattered dreams and expectations while the children looked on but she was cold hearted in her teasing and mocking.

There were no normal sexual relations in the marriage and in their twenty five years knowing each other they made love about fifteen times and four of these resulted in pregnancies. Each one of these four conceptions Dave could name the time and the place as sex didn't happen often so it was obvious to him when and where it occurred. He often wondered if she was a homosexual in reality because she objected to sex so much and one time he literally pushed her out of bed for degrading him as a dog, degrading the act of love making within a marriage as an uneventful casual thing, and degrading herself as a prostitute. This was because one night in bed together he was romantic but Cath turned her back to him and when he told her that she would do that once too often she turned onto her back, opened her legs, and said

"Go on then get up"

He knew she had scant regard for ethics or morals except when other people were looking or listening but this despicable act he felt, was one too far, even for her.

Presents were another thing she just didn't bother with in their twenty married years so he never received a Christmas, Birthday, Anniversary, or any other kind of present from her during that time and when he did mention it to her during their final days, she brusquely stated

"Ah you are too hard to buy for"

So she never did although she got presents for all occasions with flowers, chocolate, and clothing but the compliment was never returned.

He finally accepted that this was the way she was and could never change and any other man would have left her years before if even getting hooked up with her in the first place. Cath took everything and gave nothing in return except abuse and insults and she knew quite well that this was totally wrong because she would never let anyone else see her true colours and hid them with expertise. She would act completely differently in front of other people whether in groups or singularly and everyone though she was a wonderful, nice and good person but a black heart hid underneath that false veneer of her expression.

Cath had amassed a small fortune of thirty five thousand pounds during their marriage, hiding it in two Credit Union accounts and two bank accounts. There were also savings in government prize bonds and a government saving scheme which doubled what was paid in over five years. Dave was flabbergasted when he discovered this and he was unsure if it was because she was miserly and would not spend money or she had another wretched plan up her sleeve to throw Dave out of her life when she had enough saved. She often would say in an argument that things would change when the children got older and her time would come!

Dave didn't know, bother, or care what she had before but when they went to mediation to resolve their marriage in an amicable fashion she blatantly lied to the mediator about her income. He knew this when she lied about her government children's allowance stating that she only received seventy pounds per week when she got well over one hundred pounds per week. She was not even embarrassed when the mediator took out an allowance rate book and pointed this out and if she had the nerve to lie about this she would lie about everything else.

Cath claimed that her total weekly income was two hundred pounds per week, one hundred and thirty from her business and the seventy pounds that Dave left for food but Dave knew full well that she had over one hundred clients; fifteen clients on Fridays alone at an average of twenty euro per head would make three hundred euro. So when the battle was truly on and the legal eagles were involved he mentioned this to his legal team but was told that it was just his word against hers, thus he needed evidence. She was careless on a number of occasions when leaving account statements lying around and Dave photocopied them and gave to his legal team to be used as evidence to support his case.

Dave was also friendly with a guy in the security business and was telling him of his plight and the guy suggested installing a hidden security camera.

"Wow, would that not get noticed in my house?"

"No way if you place it in the right position"

The next week they met up and when Dave saw the device he just couldn't believe it as it was smaller than a LED bulb with a foot long wire attached. The guy demonstrated it with a monitor and the pictures were clearer than a TV set, so he decided to use it. He felt bad having to go to all this trouble but he was fighting for his life, his dignity, and the truth to be revealed. He also felt like James Bond in the espionage world of the secret service with a high-tech surveillance gadget. When the house was empty he installed the camera and when tested it worked perfectly with sound as well as vision and for the next three weeks he recorded on video tape all that was happening within his house with visitors being the main purpose. This proved he was correct and it was not just an assumption or his word against anyone's but it was there in full colour and sound and a proven fact. He gave the tape to his legal team so they had all the evidence.

Dave felt his case was watertight now that his legal team had all the proof they needed to counter her dishonesty and surely she would not have the nerve to lie under oath in a court of law?

"All rise"

The announcement was exclaimed from a court official and that sickening gut feeling returned to Dave that had earlier caused him to shiver. A bespectacled grey haired judge called McMichael walked into the room from a back door behind and to the side of his bench. Everyone rose and sat down again when the judge did so.

Dave's barrister Justin opened the proceedings, stating the case of Dave versus Cath where Dave wanted a legal separation on the grounds of irreconcilable differences and called Cath to the stand. She took the oath swearing to Almighty God to tell the truth and the whole truth.

After establishing who she was, the barrister began

"Mrs Kelly in your affidavit of means you say that your income is two hundred pounds and yet it says you spend five hundred! The maths just doesn't add up here so please explain"?

"Well your honour, my family help me out with bills and that is why I can spend so much"!

"Ok you are stating that you only have two hundred pounds coming in and your family give you three hundred to pay your bills"?

"Yes that's correct"!

"A very generous family indeed"!

"Now moving on to your next statement that you have several foreign holiday per year and yet you state that you family have to help you out with weekly bills to the tune of three hundred pounds. You state that you visited Morocco, Italy, Germany, Spain and Portugal. How can you afford to do this Mrs Kelly? Please explain."

"I have a friend that comes to me to get her hair styled and I do not charge her so in return she takes me away on holiday a few times in the year and gives me spending money"

Dave was in a state of shock listening to Cath's bare faced lies after swearing on the bible and he felt sure that nobody could believe this yarn of fantasy being uttered in a court of law. She actually stated that her family gave her three hundred per week and her friend takes her away to foreign lands and gives her spending money several times a year! Sure who in their right mind could believe this, Dave thought to himself? Dave's barrister felt that he had established enough untruths at this point and let Cath go which disappointed him greatly as he did not question her about her having over one hundred clients and about having the sum of thirty five thousand pounds stashed away. However Dave trusted that he knew what he was doing.

Dave was then called to the stand and after swearing in, was questioned by Cath's barrister, who was a round man, small in stature with a grey face and silver hair. Dave felt that he would make a great Santa!

"Now Mr Kelly you have established that you have three hundred pounds per week net, so tell the court how you spend this money"?

"I pay the mortgage on our home and the electric, heating, groceries and loans that I have out for home improvement"
"OK! Now let us concentrate on the groceries for a moment, how do you pay for them?"
"I leave seventy euro every week for this."
"I didn't ask you that, I asked you how you pay."
"Sorry I don't understand what you mean. I leave seventy pounds for the groceries every week"
"Is this in cash"?
"Ah well, I was leaving cash but it was not being used and was building up week after week so I decided to get vouchers from the local supermarket so that they could only be spent on food for the family"!
"VOUCHERS Mr Kelly, Vouchers! Do you think that Mrs Kelly, your wife, the mother of your children is an irresponsible child to treat her in this despicable way?"
"Well but -----

Cath's barrister interrupted Dave and would not let him state why he was doing this and continued

"I put it to you that this is the reason as to why Mrs Kelly has to borrow three hundred pounds from her family every week just to look after her children"

Dave glared at Cath straight in the face; she smirked and then bowed her head knowing that she had achieved her mission to deceive everyone including her legal team with all her fantasy stories that were very far from the truth. She had fooled her family especially her good brother Noel who believed her as he offered to bank roll her to buy Dave out of the marriage but the greatest deception was her lies in this court that no one would hear as the family court sittings are held in camera, in private. Not one person is allowed in, except the legal team and their respective clients, thus there were no jurors, no press, and no public and Cath knew this was to her advantage because even her family would be shocked by the extent of her lies and her unseen audacity.

There was no cross examination, no right to reply in Dave's case and he returned to his seat seething after being lashed on the witness stand and now they waited for the judge to make his decision, his ruling based on what he had read and heard. But Dave did notice that when he sat down on his bench he began to write and didn't seem to be paying much attention to the proceedings as he never made an utterance.

> "I grant this legal separation for the reason as stated: there are irreconcilable differences in the marriage. I further make the order that Mr Kelly will vacate his dwelling within thirty days from this day. I also make the order that he will continue to pay the mortgage and pay Mrs Kelly one hundred and fifty pounds per week for her maintenance and that of her children until the last child reaches school leaving age. Then when this occurs the dwelling may be sold or Mrs Kelly may buy Mr Kelly's interest out for the sum of ninety thousand pounds".

The judge banged his gavel and arose from his large chair; Dave was in a state of shock as Cath was being congratulated by her legal team. His barrister rose to his feet and called after the judge for a stay on his orders which were unceremoniously denied but he did grant leave to appeal.

Dave sat motionless and did not notice the activity happening around him as his world seem to shatter in so many fragments and a decision loomed whether to lie down and take all this or fight back against the injustices of the whole scenario. He rose to his feet and the courtroom had emptied save for his legal team who approached him in a fluster

> "We have to appeal this straight away"

Dave didn't speak but followed them out of the court room and into an office in the foyer where they all sat around a table. The solicitor and barrister began to speak to each other about the judge's ruling and his orders. Dave hammered on the table with his fist to interrupt their debate and to gain their immediate attention and they stopped in their tracks knowing from his expression that he meant business.

> "What kind of a legal system is this?"

Solicitor Tom shrugged his shoulders in bewilderment but more so in the knowing that Dave was going to tell him in no uncertain terms!

> "I have been put through a grinding mill with it and you two may be legally credible but are incredible in the fact that you can support and abide by it when it is completely lop-sided, unfair and categorically unjust"! "I innocently trusted and threw myself down at the mercy of the law to gain justice but did I receive any?"

"Well you both know the answer to that"!

"Deceit and lies ruled the day and truth was brandished as a whore in the room"

His solicitor Tom went to speak but was stopped in his tracks as Dave continued

"Listen Tom, you assured me that this would not happen to me; being made homeless without a penny in my pocket"!

"Who on earth puts a man or anyone out of his home and away from his children just ten days before Christmas Day which is what has been done to me today?"

"Who could believe the fantasy stories of the now former Mrs Kelly that her family give her three hundred pounds per week and that her friend takes her on a foreign holiday three times a year with spending money?"

They both stared speechless, their mouths agape as he continued, turning his gaze towards barrister Justin

"Why didn't you tease out and ridicule these lies?"

"Why didn't you question her about her many clients or the fact that she has thirty five thousand amassed in savings"?

"She has succeeded in fooling everyone including her family, her legal team, the judge, and the legal system that she seems to know more about than you two put together because she knows that nobody will ever know the extent of her lies as this court is held in camera, in secret, just like a 'Kangaroo Court' and she will remain unchallenged while the public remain oblivious"!

"She has succeeded in claiming and receiving free legal aid when she is earning twice the amount that I can earn but because she runs an illegal, black economy unregistered business she gets away with it"

"The now former Mrs Kelly is a criminal according to the so called laws of this land when she claims welfare of the state while running an illegal business so why couldn't you point this out to discredit her entire testimony which is a complete testimony of lies"?

"Justice me arse"!

Dave's barrister and solicitor went to speak at the same time but Tom got in first

"We will appeal this, we will appeal"

"There should not be any reason for an appeal but you took your eye off the ball"!

"You didn't need to make a discovery order for her means because I presented the evidence to you and if it was inadmissible why wasn't an order put in place? I did everything possible to support my case but feel let down by you my legal representatives. Do your job but pay more attention this time."

Dave walked out of the room and into the cool air of the darkening winter's evening. He felt numb of all physical feeling as he ambled aimlessly but was thoroughly sickened by the travesty of justice that had just happened and because of this he lost all faith in the legal system and his faith in humanity; where one person could bestow such cruelty upon another with the words of 'man's inhumanity to man' resonated in his troubled mind. He would now have to gather himself together and build a life starting anew but this was never a problem for him and Cath knew this only too well. She thought she had taken the best of him as she had used and abused him for twenty five years; a quarter of a century but his saving grace was his children. She could try to turn them against him by deceit and by pointing out his faults but she couldn't take away his love for them, something that she just could never understand.

Dave pondered the question: is it alright and perfectly fine to live a life filled with deception and lies as Cath lives? It may not have started out like this but she soon learned that it worked perfectly for her to live a charmed existence. The first thing was to become anonymous and remain so until it served its purpose and this was achieved by getting a job in an unregistered business so no income tax or social welfare payments were ever made. She may have been subservient but she was used to this so it was no great annoyance because this was normal and it suited the cause to be hidden under the radar, so to speak. This changed when she got pregnant for the second time when she was engaged to Dave, the first was aborted in another cloak of deception as it was not suitable for her to have a baby at that time. But now she had Dave who would marry her and soon she discovered that she would receive no payment from the government while being off having a baby. Cath then decided to become registered by the state after twenty years of working in the 'black market economy' as it suited to do so and she received a payment for her trouble which began a time of taking all the free things she could get but giving absolutely nothing back.

This applied to every single part of her life, including her marriage of convenience to Dave where again she took everything but gave nothing back and felt it was alright to do this as if she was owed. Then she started her own business from the house she shared with Dave and of course it was unregistered so that now she was receiving a government welfare payment as well as the money she earned from her one hundred or so clients in her business which is in reality a crime of fraud.

Cath however, ran the gauntlet because the state did not know or seemed not to care but reacted differently when dealing with her farcical defunct marriage and with Dave's request for divorce. The family law courts believed her outrageous lies that her family donated three hundred euro per week to run the household and that her 'friend' took her away on three foreign holidays per year while also supplying her spending money. Sure who wouldn't want a family and friend such as Cath described, Dave thought to himself and could not stop the truth knowing smile that broke out on his otherwise serious face. But the judge, who was representing the law of the land, believed her tale of fantasy that defied logic and reality in the proper terms.

Cath was now in a new position of power with the realisation that she could hoodwink and deceive everyone, her family, her friends and the entire nation where she resided when she swore in front of a judge, her legal team, Dave's legal team, and in front of God that the evidence she gave was the truth, the whole truth, and nothing but the truth and be believed no matter how contemptible her lies. Cath knew quite well that her stories within this court could not be revealed outside because it was held 'in camera' where there are no persons allowed except for those concerned with the case and it is illegal to discuss or reveal the procedure that occurred therein. This suited her plan to no end and Dave felt violated and a victim of a gross miscarriage of justice that he could not make known because not only were Cath stories believed but also on top of the judgement of orders made against him. He was ordered to vacate the family home but still pay the mortgage and give half of his gross weekly wage to Cath. This in effect criminalised him because he could not physically carry out these orders because of his low income with having to rent accommodation for himself.

Dave was flabbergasted by the whole process where he told the truth openly, having legitimate documented evidence about all of his dealings for the case in which he laid himself firmly down to the law expecting justice but he felt that justice was far from what he received. On the other hand Cath had no documented evidence and her evidence was far-fetched by any stretch of the imagination but her word alone stood above legitimate documented evidence.

Dave contemplated this whole family law system with the court held in camera because this ruling was formulated to protect the innocent but in his case he felt that the innocent was victimised and violated by a gross miscarriage of justice. He also contemplated the judgement orders against him which criminalised him from the moment they were read out by the judge without a stay of their execution because he could not fulfil them.

He contemplated his legal team whom he would be paying dearly for their services but who did not question Cath more vigorously on her testimony evidence in the witness box on merely her word. He wondered why they did not proceed to obtain an order of discovery about her financial holdings when he had documented evidence that Cath had amassed thousands of euros in different accounts which he supplied to them. Everything that Cath declared or did not declare, Dave could produce evidence that she was lying but none of these were used in court, as if they didn't exist.

Dave even had video evidence of Cath's hairdressing clientele; because it was difficult to prove that she had so many, he installed a video camera that showed the numbers of different customers, them paying, and also her counting the money she earned. Alas this was deemed inadmissible as evidence in this court but yet fantasy was believed. The saddest thing was for Dave to listen to and to view his sister, Mary talking about him to Cath and not in a good way as if they were buddies in alliance against him.

Dave felt he sustained sixteen years of purgatory and five years of hell betrayed by everyone, beginning with Cath to whom he was good, his children because they believed the lies she told them about him and they sided with her. He also felt betrayed by the legal system in his country because he was criminalised as he could not fulfil the orders of the judge who was definitely one sided, unfair, and served an injustice upon him. He felt he was also betrayed by his own family as he was made homeless ten days before Christmas Day and not one of them offered to help in any way whatsoever, even though the family home was his and his sister Mary's property. He could have come to live there and this was all in his legal right to do so as the owner but he went it alone. Mary even attempted to cheat him out of his heritage by almost demanding that he sign over the house to her, stating that their other two sisters agreed with this but they had no say, no rights to the property as it was bought by Margaret, Dave and Mary as if they were one person. This meant that Mary didn't own a third but owned the whole property and the same went for Dave and his mother. But Mary wanted Dave to sign it completely over to her so that she could leave it to her son and this he felt was a selfish deed as he had three children also. He had to buy his own house and was paying a mortgage while she was living mortgage and rent free in his and her house and when the three of them bought the house originally they made an agreement that if one got married they would move out and Dave complied with this. However Mary, to get around this situation, shrewdly took in a partner to live with her but didn't get married so she would not have to move out but could still be in a married set up. She was so miserly that she didn't want to buy Dave out or to sell the house and split the proceeds fairly so they both could have an equal start.

Then when Dave's chips were well and truly down she craftily approached him saying how sorry she was and that she would help him by borrowing ten thousand euro to give to him if he signed the house over to her. He rejected this outright because he knew in his heart that she was not doing this out of any sympathy for him but being selfish and cold hearted again as she knew quite well that he was going to be made homeless with no savings or assets thus her opportunity to tempt him with cash that was only five percent of the then value of the property.

Both of Dave's sisters went to his house for Cath to style their hair at below average price but when the marriage battle began in serious Margaret stopped going but Mary shamelessly continued going and this upset Dave. She made the excuse that she would find out any information from her that could be useful to him in his war but he didn't like this at all and Cath was not a stupid woman to give any information to his sister above all people. But Mary remained there for her own selfish reasons, a cheap hairdo! This saddened him to no ends because the thought that her hairdo could mean more to her than he did was sickening. However, she kept on going there even when the fight was at its height and her own brother Dave was suffering both physically and psychologically and contemplating ending it all because with all the hassle he was in a very dark place, in the deepest depths of despair. He was taken into hospital for a week because of a severe pain in his tummy that came and went but when it was bad it doubled him over and he lay on the ground in agony. He underwent all the tests, ultrasound scans, blood tests but eventually the surgeon discovered by way of an endoscope that is inserted down the throat and into the digestive system that he had ulcers caused by stress.

Dave loves his sister Mary and all of his sisters because they shared the same parentage and have a long history together. He knows quite well that nobody is perfect but feels really betrayed and let down by Mary and her disloyalty, all because of a cheap hairdo. This whole scenario reminded him of Brutus with Julius Caesar or Judas Iscariot with Jesus Christ and their great pain which they felt when those closest betrayed them for illusionary gain of money! Et tu Brute!

I Fought the Law!

Dave threw himself down at the mercy of the law of the land in the guise of the Family Law Courts. He expected justice and fairness to everyone concerned as per the moral and civil rights of every citizen in the jurisdiction but alas this was not to be.

Cath had mislead the legal profession with yarns of woe, fantasy tales that even the dogs in the street knew to be untrue, yet the law believed her and this is what Dave found so hard to believe. After all he was the Applicant who applied to the courts to have the marriage dissolved in a fair manner with justice for all concerned. He was honest and candid with all his financial dealings and status in life, addressing all issues. However on the other hand Cath bluffed, lied, and made a mockery of Dave, made a mockery of her family, and made a mockery of the whole legal system but they were hoodwinked into believing her. She was ably abetted by her skilful legal team even though her story was incredible to say the least.

Dave could not believe the audacity of the woman who stood before him in the court, swore on the Bible to tell the truth, the whole truth and nothing but the truth, but lied straight faced without fear of any repercussions.

First her financial affidavit was that she had two hundred euro income per week yet she claimed to be spending over five hundred euro and when questioned about this she calmly claimed that her family help her out!

Second was that she admitted having three continental holidays per year and when questioned about this she again calmly stated that a friend comes to get her hair done and she doesn't charge her so the friend takes her on holiday and gives her spending money!

Third was that she didn't disclose any of her savings and she had much within two banks, a building society, two credit union accounts, SSIA saving account and prize bonds. The total of which came to over thirty thousand euro!

Dave found this so inconceivable that the law or anyone else could believe these fantastic tales of claiming that her family give her over three hundred euro per week and her friend takes her on three continental holidays per year and gives her spending money. Dave thought to himself, wouldn't everyone love a family and friend like this?

Women are just like hurricanes, for when they come into your life they are wild and wet and blow you right over. But then when they are leaving they take everything with them including your fucking house.

In an attempt to find justice he contacted everyone that he could, including government ministers, clergy, and anyone he thought could possibly assist in getting justice but there were no volunteers. They all knew that the system was a travesty but none wanted to get involved in any way, shape or form; but surely if something is wrong it is their public duty to put it right! But Dave got no satisfaction whatsoever, even though he wrote to a government member.

> *To Whom It May Concern:*
> *My name is Dave Kelly and I was part of a delegation who gave a presentation to your all party committee on Parenting, Equality and Family Law Reform in the summer of last year. I stated that I was going through a legal marriage separation and that I was very afraid of what would happen in court. I asked you all there present to assure me that the deck was not stacked in favour of women in these events. But no one answered and I wondered why but recently I found out why.*
> *You all knew this but didn't say.*
> *This is what happened to me as follows………*
> *It is sorry times that we live in when a man (judge) can decide to make one of his fellow citizens (me) homeless through no fault of my own. To add insult to injury he also decided to make me pay for the privilege by ordering that I pay for the house that he put me out of and to keep on paying for it. Also he ordered me into a financial position that is way beyond my means. What did I do wrong? What crime did I commit?*
> *I was the plaintiff in this case but I was made feel like a criminal and treated as one by the judiciary.*
> *In my naivety I trusted in the laws of this country and threw myself down at the mercy of the court system which has failed me miserably. All I wanted was fairness and justice but do you think that I received either? What astounds and saddens me most is that nothing can be done to right an*

obvious wrong. Even you, as a member of the higher echelons of society and as a leading member of the legislative ruling body of this country, namely, The Government, are helpless to do anything. If this happened in any other country and was known there would be high protest and rightly so. I also think that if the general public of this country knew what happened here and in many other cases like this, there would major public outcry for fairness, for justice and for basic human civil rights. The general public cannot openly know because of the "in camera" ruling but who is this rule designed to protect; the victims or the open knowledge of what judiciary execute behind the cover of closed doors.

I know you are a good man, a man that champions the causes of the righteous, the poor, and the weak. You are a man that strives for justice and equality not only in this country but in all countries and you're a man who is not afraid to stand up and be counted for what is right and good. Well, there is something radically wrong with the "Family Law Legal System" here when a judge has the power to rule and order as stated above without redress and without the means to appeal. (An appeal would cost a fortune in the high court) Surely to God my basic, civil, human rights have been violated and taken away from me in this instance. Surely I have the right <u>not</u> to be made homeless. - Surely I have the right <u>not</u> to be ordered (and to be placed) into a financial position that is way beyond my means. - Surely I have the right <u>not</u> to be punished when I did not commit a crime. - Surely I have the right <u>not</u> to have my self worth and dignity stripped away from me without cause or crime.

In your esteemed position of "Government Member" you can highlight the inadequacies pertaining to the "Family Law Legal System" that are biased and prejudiced against males when each and every one (males, females and children) should be <u>equally</u> protected by law and as a civil, basic human right.

As an upstanding citizen and as a member of your electoral public, please do not disconnect from me on this one. I need all the friends, assistance and advice that I can get. Please do your best to rectify an awful situation for me, for my

children and my family. Please don't let them take away my dignity or my self worth. Please don't let them criminalise me for I am not a criminal.
I don't want to be in a homeless shelter or indeed in prison for Christmas for something that is not my fault, please don't let this happen to me.

However all fell upon deaf ears and Dave was not even afforded the courtesy of a reply.

Year New Dawn

Dave spent Christmas and New Year alone in his new rented house but worried ceaselessly about his circumstances and about the future. More tragedy struck when the company he worked for went into receivership and he lost his job but this was a blessing in disguise as he could inform his legal team to bolster his appeal in the high court.

The bright spring day announced itself with a solace that engulfed Dave, for he was at rock bottom now so anything that the judiciary threw at him he felt he could handle with ease. The court house foyer didn't seem so intimidating now although another session of changing people's lives was truly on the way with all the clientele therein ashen faced expecting the worse. Dave's legal team got to work in negotiating a deal with Cath's team and there were plenty of coming and going between to the parties. But again Cath was holding out and not agreeing with anything until at the last moment a compromise was reached that released Dave from the ridiculously high expenditure imposed on him by the judge of the lesser court. He could now move on with his life such as it was because he was starting from scratch with nothing to his name while retaining the bills from the marriage. However he did not have to pay the mortgage as Cath agreed to buy him out but at a much reduced going rate which was half of what it should have been. But Dave didn't care as long as he was free from her clutches even though the money she offered only covered half of his bills.

The only thing left to do now was to go into the high court to get the presiding judge to put it into law and this was done easily without any great fuss. Cath delayed the payment to Dave for nine months which caused him to go further into debt and he was not quite sure if this was a deliberate move on her behalf but when it came it was a total relief for him. She re-mortgaged the house, gave Dave his minimal share and proceeded to completely redecorate the entire structure and this was proof that everything he told his legal team was true from the beginning, that she had amassed large sums of money and that her clientele and earnings were much greater than she said. Cath was making a new start also and she had Wally smash up Dave's wardrobe in the back garden using it for firewood and everything else that was associated with Dave. She even had the family dog that he got for the children put down.

Dave, being unemployed, re-educated himself and was awarded a diploma and college degree but he did not see the last of Cath as he had hoped. She interfered with his life, castigating him to all who would listen and she even went up to his friend to say that he should choose his company better. Dave just could not understand her attitude because they were now parted for good and he thought that maybe she felt that she didn't torture him enough or that she lost out in some way. However she proved this not to be the case because one evening she arrived at Dave's new house in her boyfriend's car to admonish him for having a girlfriend.

> "You should be ashamed of yourself traipsing around town with that tart shaming your children"
>
> "What the feck are you on about? Are you out to give me some counselling advice like you did to that woman up in Donegal?

Cath was stunned by what Dave said because she thought that no one would even know about this especially Dave. He had been told that Cath and some of her friends went away for a weekend where they acted like whores on holiday, getting men to buy their drinks and then sleeping with these strangers. In the middle of all this Cath attempted to give a lady, who was in their company for the first and last time, advice on using men for free drinks and even for sex but the lady in question was having none of it and was disgusted with her attitude. She later met Dave by chance and again by chance relayed the story.

> "What I do is none of your business. Now get off my property"
>
> "No I will not"
>
> "Get off my property or I will phone the police and have you removed"
>
> "No I will not"

Cath stood there with her hands on hips defying Dave as he took out his phone but he stopped short of dialling and asked

> "Here, who owns that car you're driving?"
>
> "It belongs to a friend of mine, a good man and much better than you. He gave your children money going on holiday and you didn't".
>
> "Ah so that's what this is all about. Money! Well you know what they say about that?"
>
> "No. What do they say?"

"Getting money, getting presents, getting holidays and getting the use of a fancy car from a 'Man Friend' – It is prostitution! So you are a prostitute, now get out of my house"

Cath stormed back to her man friend's car and was about to enter when Dave shouted to her

"Oh by the way; how much do you charge for a ride?"

Then with those last parting words Cath sped off and didn't come back again but she would continue to interfere in Dave's life in the future.

Dave's Dream

Dave slept uneasily, tossing and turning all night when he had a dream and in this dream he saw blackness and he was back on his knees at the water's edge of the docks in his town. Then out of the blackness he saw a vision of Cath standing on a grey cloud just above the water level.

She was veiled in red voile exposing her black heart with jagged edges like the teeth of a saw. Upon her head were six black crowns within each a serpent extending upwards and each one had a name - Cruelty, Corruption, Callousness, Deceit, Fraud, and Lies. All the serpents were red in colour with red eyes and a red forked tongue and from the opened mouth of each came another serpent that was blue with steel blue eyes and a blue forked tongue. Then from the opened mouth of each blue serpent came a third green serpent with green eyes and a green forked tongue. The red represented danger, rage, and anger; the blue represented the coldness of heart in frigid tundra; and the green represented jealousy and envy.

The black crowns spun furiously in unison with the jagged edged black heart and all of the snakes spat and hissed, directing their fury towards Dave who lay motionless as if paralysed by their power in front of him.

Cath smirked as she held Dave's heart in her outstretched hand squeezing it forcefully and with each drop of blood came a name - Love, Peace, Truth, Hope, Joy, and Virtue, and as they fell upon the grey cloud she trampled on them with hate. They lay motionless affected by the same black power that paralysed Dave and just as their situation seemed hopeless a speck of white light came from above and it got bigger as it neared before splitting into three white orbs. Within these orbs were three angels – Michael, Gabrielle, and Auriel who were there to protect him from all harm even from himself. The angels took up positions each side of Dave with one right in front and he could now see a shield surrounding him although it was transparent like a kind of glass wall that nothing except light could penetrate.

He relaxed somewhat because he knew that he did not give away his heart to Cath but she took it and abused it by trying to squeeze all the goodness out. However, what she did not know is that there is an endless supply therein. He was told that the whole scenario was reflective of life itself and society as created by man because it is all

an illusion filled with snares and traps for the unsuspecting.
Nonetheless it is all false and as Cath was representative of society, Dave's heart represented the good that society is trying to banish from mankind leaving it with no hope and no soul.

The light and the angels represented hope and protection from all the evils, the illusions of life that can kill a person's soul and this almost happened to Dave but with a little intervention causing a change of heart his life remained.

Dave awoke with a startle jumping up in bed but lay back down again as he realised it was only a dream. He smiled as the sun crept into his darkened bedroom to heat and brighten everything in its path and he knew for certain that as it rose in the east it would surely set in the west and life would go on and on renewing itself every day.

He was now a free person, free from Cath and all her snares and derisions so now he could live his life in peace and tranquility every day just the way he always wanted.

Yes, this was a new dawn, a new day, and a new life for Dave who could walk in the sunshine without any shackles, free to find a new life and perhaps a new love.

But that is another story!

The End

The Author

John J Lennon Cohen is an almost fifty something year old sophisticate and a nerd to some degree but he has a marvellous sense of humour that comes out in all of his writings so it could be said without fear of contradiction that comedy is his forte. He is highly educated having studied in England's Halton College in Sports, in Dublin's National College in Humanities, and in an Institute of Technology achieving a degree in Movie Production. Resident between New York, London, and Ireland but there is nothing he likes better than to travel to far flung exotic places and has visited all the continents; however his bucket list is far from completed.
He is a divorcee with three adult children.
John Lennon Cohen's influences are from the two writers that inspired his life in the writing world with John Lennon of the Beatles fame and Leonard Cohen. There is no coincidence that he selected these famous two because along with writing prose he also writes lyrics and verse and has a book published on the very subject 'Nothing Rhymes' available on all Amazon Networks; also his first novel 'Growing Up' is available on Amazon.
John has composed over one hundred lyrics in verse form and he has written many short films and screen plays in his time at college and beyond. Having successfully obtained a degree in Movie/TV/Radio Production he has turned his attention to writing a zany comedy script for TV and with a six part pilot run in the latter stages of composing he is at the moment waiting for the sometimes elusive acceptance nod from a good production company.
There is plenty more to come from this professional prolific writer so keep a watchful eye out whether it is on the Hollywood big screen, TV, or in the printed media it will be certainly worth a view.

Printed in Great Britain
by Amazon